W9-BFI-756

The Slingshot's Secret

BENJAMIN CONLON

Copyright © 2017 Benjamin Conlon

All rights reserved.

ISBN: 1979466548
ISBN-13: 978-1979466547

TO MY MOM

…but above all for the spirit of adventure, to keep alive the soul of man.

George Mallory, on climbing Everest

1

A sliver the size of a sewing needle was lodged securely between Sam Torwey's thumb and forefinger. Across his palm, a deep gash was black with dirt and grime. His shorts were torn, his arms sweaty and sunburned. On his neck, a mosquito swelled with blood.

None of it concerned him.

For three painful hours, he'd been carving a slingshot and finally, it was complete. The handle was lopsided, the surface was pitted with gouges and one arm was shorter than the other, but it wasn't bad. Certainly, it was better than his earlier attempts. Maybe he'd have something to show for the summer after all.

Sam fit a stone into the cradle of elastic and searched for a target. Across the yard, a soda can stood forgotten on a table. Sweat dripped from his neck as he raised the slingshot and brought the can into his sights. Slowly, he pulled back the stone. "Three…two…one…"

CRACK

The slingshot's brittle arms snapped under pressure, sending shards of wood and elastic into his face.

"DARN IT!" he screamed, his voice echoing down the vacant street. "DARN IT!" He trudged back to the house and slammed the slingshot into a pile of others that lay broken in the dirt. He sat down on the steps and felt his throbbing forehead. A welt was already beginning to rise.

Across the street, he saw his friend Roger reclining lazily inside his air-conditioned house. An enormous television flickered on the wall. Sam sighed. Roger had been staring at that screen, or his new phone, for the entire summer. They had barely seen each other since June. Now, summer was over. The next day would mark the beginning of sixth grade at a new school, with new teachers and new classmates. Sam didn't like to think about it.

Down the road, a green garbage truck marked *SUMMER BRUSH CLEAN UP* moved slowly in his direction. It stopped a few houses away and two men in coveralls climbed down and hauled a pair of brown bags to the truck. Sam glanced at the cans he had wheeled to the curb that morning. They overflowed with wet grass from the backyard.

When the truck arrived, one of the men grabbed the can nearest Sam and dumped it into the huge compactor. His partner flipped the second barrel, but nothing came out. He swore loudly and shook the container. The contents plopped out in a heap, knocking a pile of brush from the truck bed.

"Leave it," the driver barked. "We're running behind. Spent too much time at the school. It'll blow away." Both men hopped onto the side of the truck, and it rumbled off.

Sam walked over to the debris that had fallen to the road. Brush and a few pine cones. He frowned. The pile made him think of school again and the fall season that was coming. As he turned to go, something in the pile caught his eye.

He knelt down and brushed away the leaves. Beneath them, he discovered a piece of strangely shaped wood. Dark, smooth, and marked all over with intricate carvings, one end was forked in a nearly perfect V, while the other extended straight down.

It was, without question, a slingshot.

2

Sam stared at the object in amazement, his heart beating faster. He looked around. The street was still empty. He picked up the stick, tucked it under his shirt and walked back across the driveway and into the house.

His mother glanced up from her laptop. "What's going on?"

"Huh? Me?" Sam blurted. "Oh nothing." He felt to make sure the slingshot was covered.

She eyed him suspiciously then nodded to a nearby window. "Who's that? Did Roger's dad get a new car?"

Sam looked outside. A black Mercedes had turned onto the street. He'd never seen it before. The windows were dark. The car rolled past Roger's driveway and continued on.

"Guess not." His mother looked back at the computer. "Dinner's in half an hour. Make sure you wash up."

"Yeah, I know." He headed upstairs to his bedroom.

Inside, a bunk bed stood against the far wall. The lower bunk had been removed and a curtain of tattered sheets hung in its place. Sam brushed them aside and ducked underneath. He sat down at a wooden desk and took out the strange stick.

Its perfection was most peculiar. Tiny ripples covered the wood where the bark had been removed one section at a time. Deep lines ran between the ripples, spiraling up the handle to the forked end. Every one of the engravings was flawless.

He opened a drawer and sifted through the pile of clutter inside, hoping to uncover an elastic. Finding nothing, he spun around and pushed aside some books on a nearby shelf to reveal a small, metal safe. Sam dialed in the combination and swung open the door. He studied the polished stick one more time before putting it inside. Then he replaced the books and went downstairs.

Inside the safe, the slingshot lay motionless, still warm from the boy's hand. The metal walls blocked light from entering and hid the mysterious object in complete darkness. Hidden were the swirling lines running up the handle, the notches at the top and the three small initials carved into the base, as yet unnoticed by Sam.

A few blocks away, the garbage truck was stopped at the side of the road. The doors hung open but no one was in sight. The black Mercedes with the tinted windows was just disappearing into the distance.

3

By nightfall, Sam had forgotten the slingshot and whatever mysteries it might hold. The darkness marked an official end to summer and visions of the approaching school day swirled in his head. He was nervous about the bus ride and the unfamiliar building. He was anxious about his new classmates. Most of all, he was worried about sharing the school with seventh and eighth graders.

At dinner, his mother looked up from her laptop. "You're not eating."

He shrugged. "I'm not hungry."

"He's just sad to see the summer go," Sam's father murmured, eyes fixed on a new cell phone. "Was it a good one?"

"I don't know," Sam muttered. "It could have been better."

"Hmm? What?" Mr. Torwey hadn't been listening. "Oh, glad to hear it."

After dinner, Sam sat in his bedroom staring blankly at a comic book, unable to concentrate. He finally gave up, climbed into his bunk and turned off the lights. It was a long time before he drifted off to sleep, wishing for June.

The first day of school dawned hot and humid. Sam awoke to the sound of his father pounding on the door. "You up yet?"

Sam rolled over.

Another knock.

"Yeah, yeah. I'm coming." There was no avoiding it. He groaned and heaved himself over the edge of the bunk.

He got dressed and glanced in the mirror. A slender boy with sandy hair and blue eyes looked back. Ordinary, he thought. He picked up a battered flip phone from the desk and slipped it into his pocket. His dad had given it to him in fourth grade "just for emergencies". Both his parents had jobs requiring a lot of online work. They spent a good deal of time on computers and phones. Sam didn't care for either.

"Excited for the big day?" his mother asked as he walked into the kitchen.

"You'll be fine," his father remarked. "I had a great time in sixth grade. The only thing you need to remember…and this is really important—" His phone vibrated on the table. He looked down. "Excuse me, I have to take this."

Sam walked to a closet near the door and took a blue backpack off the same hook he'd hung it on in June. He turned it over and dumped a mound of reports and tests into the garbage can. A folded card landed on top. It was a note from his fifth grade teacher. *Dear Sam, It was a pleasure having you in class. Enjoy your summer. I'm sure it will be fantastic! –Mrs. W.*

"It's getting late," his mother said from the table. "You'd better get going. Have a great day."

"See you later," he said, with a halfhearted smile.

He headed out the door with the empty backpack slung over one shoulder. Roger was already waiting for the bus across the street. Sam waved and Roger nodded back. He wore black nylon shorts that hung down past his knees and high white socks. A mesh hat was tipped sideways on his dark, crew cut hair. Across his t-shirt *#wuddup* was scrawled in golden letters. Roger had been adopting a new style over the summer months.

"Sup," Roger said, fingers racing over a shiny iPhone.

"Not much," Sam replied. "Who are you texting?"

"Dude," Roger said. "Don't even worry about it."

He'd been saying that a lot too. *Dude, don't even worry about it.*

"Seems early to be texting."

"Whatever," Roger muttered. "Don't you have your own phone?"

"Sure, I have a phone. But I don't text so early."

"You don't text at all."

"Sometimes I do," Sam lied.

Roger eyed him. "You still got that piece of junk from your dad?"

"It's not a piece of junk."

Roger raised his eyebrows. "I wouldn't be caught dead with that thing. Honestly, if I were about to die and that phone was in my hand, I would try to stay alive so no one would see it."

"Wouldn't you try to stay alive anyway?" Sam asked.

Roger ignored him and resumed texting.

"Think we'll be in the same class?"

Roger shrugged. "The school's huge."

Before Sam could say anything else, the roar of an engine drifted through the air and a yellow school bus turned onto the street. It rumbled toward them and stopped a few feet away.

Sam had taken the bus every day for the past six years. Mrs. Hyde, the driver, was always ready with a smile. Sam was looking forward to seeing her familiar face. When the bus door opened, he was shocked to see a man sitting behind the wheel. He was short and wide with stringy brown hair and a patchy neck beard. His once white t-shirt had yellowed and dark stains marked the armpits. "Mrs. Hyde?" Sam whispered.

The driver glared down with beady eyes and growled. "You getting on or what?"

Sam gulped. "I…well…" Before he could finish, Roger brushed him aside and bounded up the steps. Sam followed reluctantly. Students of all shapes and sizes filled the seats. There were only a few familiar faces. Most of the passengers looked much older and bigger than Sam.

A group of boys, presumably eighth graders, sat perched on seat backs at the rear of the bus surveying the crowd. A few wore backwards hats and one had headphones around his neck. Another, sitting in the very last seat, held a brand new phone with a golden case. His jet-black hair was spiked with gel. In front of the boys, a pack of girls sat with phones out, fingers darting over the screens.

Roger walked down the aisle looking for a seat. Sam followed. Dozens of eyes stared up as he passed. He glanced from left to right, trying hard to look friendly. It seemed everyone else was trying to look mean. Suddenly, Sam realized Roger was gone. He stopped and scanned the crowd anxiously. Roger was a few yards away, sitting with a boy in a basketball jersey. He thought they'd sit together, like they always had.

Roger looked up. "Only seat left."

"Where am I going to sit?" Sam blurted nervously.

Roger didn't answer. He'd already resumed his conversation with the stranger.

Sam ignored the betrayal and kept walking down the aisle. The giggling and chatter coming from the back of the bus got quieter with each step, then stopped entirely. Sam glanced up and was horrified to discover the eighth graders staring at him.

The one with the spiked hair spoke. "Where do you think you're going, big guy?"

Sam froze, unsure what to say. Seconds passed. "Err…" he finally stammered, "there aren't any other seats."

"What?" the eighth grader said. "No other seats? That's sad. *Really* sad. Are you gonna cry?" There was snickering and stifled laughter.

"Maybe he wants to sit with you, Max?" a boy with bleached-blond hair suggested.

"Yeah, Trent. I think you're right." More snickering. "Don't worry, big guy. Look, you can sit here." Max reached down and slid his graffiti-covered backpack over, making room for Sam. "Have a seat."

Sam didn't know what to do. The offer seemed too good to be true, but what other choice was there? "O-okay," he murmured and inched forward. He turned to sit down, but as he did, the bag was shoved back in place.

He slid awkwardly to the floor.

"OOPS!" Max yelled. The eighth graders erupted in laughter. Sam spun around and hurried away, face reddening.

"Get out of here, loser!" Trent shouted. The laughter followed him all the way to the front of the bus. Not knowing where else to go and wanting desperately to escape from view, he approached the driver.

"Ex-excuse me," he mumbled, "there aren't any more seats." No response. The bus driver had put in a pair of earbuds. "Excuse me," Sam said in a louder voice, "I went all the way—"

"Listen, kid," the man snapped. "I just drive the bus. That's all. You got a problem with anything that goes on behind me, you deal with it."

Sam was dumbstruck. Beside him, a gangly boy with glasses and perfectly combed hair sat alone reading an enormous book. Overhearing the exchange, he looked up. "You can sit here if you want." The boy slid over to make room.

Sam sighed with relief and plopped down onto the brown bench. "Thanks."

"Of course," the boy said. "Always happy to help a man in need. What were you doing in the back of the bus anyway? Are you crazy or something? That's where the eighth graders sit."

"Yeah. I know."

"I wouldn't try that again. You might get killed. I'm Henry by the way."

"Err…I'm Sam."

"It's a pleasure to make your acquaintance. Sixth grade, I presume?"

"Uh, yeah," Sam said. "You?"

Henry nodded. "The same. I'm looking forward to it. Promises to be very exciting. Algebra. Biology. History of the Middle Ages. At least that's what I've read. Do you read much, Sam?"

"Uhh...yeah," he said, glancing back to check on the eighth graders. "Well, sometimes."

"Read anything good this summer?"

Sam had read quite a few books during the dismal summer, but doubted his seatmate would care much for

Holes or *Harry Potter*. The volume he held looked like it had been written for college students. Sam tried to think of the longest book he'd ever read.

"Err…*The Sword in the Stone*? That was pretty good."

"Ah, yes!" Henry cried. "Wonderful story, a bit dense for me, I much prefer something a bit lighter like say, *Holes*, but really a wonderful story."

Sam was shocked.

"You know," Henry said, lowering his voice, "some people think there really was a sword in the stone. It's never been found…"

Sam nodded. "That's what I've heard."

"And that's not the only treasure that's missing…there are… others…" Sam leaned in with interest, but Henry didn't elaborate.

The conversation turned instead to the approaching year. As it happened, Henry lived just a few streets away, but had attended a different elementary school. He had a strange way of talking, formal and old-fashioned. It almost sounded like he was acting. But he wasn't. Sam liked him immediately.

The boys lived in Perkinsville, Connecticut, a town of about 40,000 people. Founded in the 1600's, much of the land had since been developed. The bus moved through residential neighborhoods, past shopping centers, industrial parks and other drab scenery, until the landscape abruptly changed. On the left side of the bus, trees replaced the buildings. Sam found this surprising because he had never seen forest anywhere in Perkinsville.

"I didn't know about these woods," Henry said. "Did you?"

Sam shook his head. "I had no idea."

They slowed and turned onto a driveway leading into

the forest. Sam and Henry gazed out the window as the bus rolled along the now winding road. The woods opened into an expansive clearing. On either side of the bus, a lawn spread out like a lake of green, its smooth surface interrupted at intervals by the tangled roots of ancient-looking trees.

Sam glanced out the front window and was shocked to discover an enormous building coming into view. It stood four stories tall and was built entirely of stone. In the center, a large white dome protruded from the slate roof. The building looked cold and appeared to be in a state of disrepair. His stomach churned with apprehension. "Kind of run down, isn't it?"

"A bit dilapidated," Henry agreed. "But you can't judge a book by its cover." He reconsidered. "Well… sometimes you can. Hey, what's that?"

In front of the building, a bronze statue of a bearded man towered over the buses. The figure stood on an immense block of polished granite. Stuck to the base of the stone was a glaring red sign that seemed oddly out of place. Scrolled across it in yellow letters were four words: *Perkinsville Middle School Public.* Sam glanced at Henry, whose anxious expression mirrored his own.

The bus came to a stop and the two boys exited before the eighth graders could catch up. They were swallowed by a wave of students advancing toward the building, and it took all of Sam's effort to keep from stumbling. He never bothered to look up at the statue as he passed beneath it. It would be a long time before he'd realize its significance.

4

The mass moved toward the school taking Sam and Henry with it. They shuffled up the stairs, passed through one of the wrought-iron doors and found themselves in an enormous tiled lobby.

"Get out of my way!" someone shouted. "You're in my way!" A man with pale skin and greasy black hair waded through the students. A jagged scar zigzagged down the side of his face.

Sam turned to Henry. "Where do we go?"

"Directly back to the bus if that fellow's our teacher," Henry replied with a shudder. "Let's just follow the crowd."

At the end of the hall, a stout woman with a flat face and dark, curly hair held a clipboard. Her gray eyes scanned the crowd through a pair of black glasses. She was smiling, but Sam got the impression she wasn't really happy.

"Sixth graders to the auditorium," she said, to no one in particular. She gestured down another hallway.

A boy approached her. "Excuse me?"

The woman looked down at him, head tilted, the smile still in place. "Sixth graders to the auditorium."

"No, I just wondered where the bath—"

"Sixth graders to the auditorium," she said again, and looked away.

The auditorium was halfway down the second hallway and larger than any Sam had seen before. Row upon row of wooden seats spread over the carpeted floor, sloping gently down to a stage. There, several adults sat in folding chairs. A tattered curtain of deep lavender hung gloomily from the rafters behind them.

Sam filed into one of the rows and sat down beside a girl with neon braces. Henry settled in on his right. Roger sat a few rows away, talking with a group of boys Sam didn't recognize.

It was difficult to see much further than that. The lights hanging from the ceiling were strangely dim and there were no windows. Sam turned his attention to the stage. The adults had stopped talking and an elderly man in a lumpy, brown suit shuffled slowly toward a podium. He was slight in stature, with pink skin and wispy white hair. A pair of thick glasses rested on his nose.

He cleared his throat and gazed out at the audience. "Good morning, scholars," he exclaimed with shrill enthusiasm, "and welcome to Perkinsville Middle School Public! I'm Mr. Fiddlesbee, your principal."

"Did he say Fiddlesbee?" Henry whispered.

"I think so," Sam replied.

"That can't be right."

"This year," the principal continued, "marks the start of a new and exciting chapter in your lives! You'll be learning new subjects, meeting new teachers and making new friends! You hail from four different elementary schools, but here you are, together as one class!" He paused and smiled at the audience.

"A group of dedicated faculty members stands ready to help you on your way. I'd like to introduce just a few of them now." The old man turned enthusiastically to the adults at his left. "The first, is our new vice principal. Joining us all the way from California, Mr. Throxon!"

The vice principal had been standing in the shadows. When he stepped into the light, Sam was shocked at his size. He was at least a foot taller than everyone else on stage and twice as broad. A pale yellow shirt fit tightly on his chest and a pink tie dangled between bulging pectorals. He had a mustache and dark curly hair. He reminded Sam of an over sized teddy bear. The vice principal smiled broadly and winked at the audience.

"What's that he's holding?" Henry asked. Something spun between the vice principal's fingers.

"I don't know," Sam said. "I can't see."

"Looks like those stone balls people spin for relaxation. My great-aunt had some."

"Do they work?" Sam asked.

"I don't think so," Henry answered. "She went insane."

"Thank you, Mr. Throxon," the principal continued. "Looking forward to working with you this year! And now, for your teachers! There will be five sixth grade sections this year. Each one *unique*. Each one *special*. The first will be taught by Mr. Dean."

"That's the guy from the lobby," Sam said, "the one telling everybody to get out of his way."

Dean wore a black shirt, a silver suit and a purple tie. His skin looked waxy and even paler under the stage lights. The scar on his face seemed to glow. Though seated, he appeared to be breathing heavily, almost wheezing. Sam shivered.

"Doesn't look much like a scholar," Henry remarked. "I wonder where he got that scar?"

After Dean, Fiddlesbee read the names of three additional teachers. All women. To Sam, they looked the same. Middle aged. Brown haired. Unsmiling. "Not the most pleasant looking bunch," he whispered.

"Finally," the principal continued, "it is my distinct pleasure to introduce the head of our sixth grade team, Ms. Bethany Snell!" Mr. Fiddlesbee began to clap. Mr. Throxon joined him. "I'd like to thank her, yet again, for volunteering to take on the responsibilities of this important position."

The woman who'd been directing students to the auditorium rose and beamed at the principal, the same smile on her face.

Mr. Fiddlesbee said a few more words about the importance of working hard, then directed the students to the lobby for tours of the school. Sam and Henry shuffled out of the auditorium and back to the front of the building. A dozen or so tables had been erected along the walls of the entrance hall and a girl was shouting something above the noise of the crowd. Sam and Henry stopped to listen.

"Find the table with your last name and stay there!" she barked.

"What's your last name?" Sam asked Henry.

"Delmont."

"Mine's Torwey. I guess I'll see you after the tour."

Henry nodded.

Sam made his way through the crowd to a table labeled *Massey through Tynes* and waited awkwardly for further instructions. A few feet away, a boy he'd never seen before leaned against the paneled wall. He had short, crew cut hair and watery green eyes. Sam was surprised at his tattered clothing. Dark stains covered his t-shirt and his faded shorts were fraying at the seams. His backpack looked to be a hundred years old. Most striking was his size. He was shorter than anyone else in the room and couldn't have weighed more than sixty pounds. He caught Sam staring and looked away nervously.

A lanky eighth grader sauntered through the crowd and waved an arm. "I'm your tour guide. Let's go down this hallway." He gestured to his left. "So you can hear me."

At the end of the corridor, the guide turned to the sixth graders. "What's up? I'm Josh Basserman. Lotta people call me J-Bass. I'm in eighth grade." He glanced down at a silver cell phone, punched the screen a few times, smiled, and deposited it into his pocket.

"Sorry about that," he said. "You're lucky. I didn't read the email they sent to the tour guides, so you're going to get the unofficial tour. All the stuff you need and nothing you don't. Let's go."

It seemed to Sam that Josh was trying hard to impress the group. He rocked back and forth when he walked and kept running a hand through his hair. He looked at his phone a lot and laughed at whatever was on the screen. Sam suspected he was pretending.

"School's really big," Basserman declared. "It'll take you a while to find your way around. Old too. Not much power, or electric outlets or whatever. No air conditioning or anything. Barely any cell service, which we all hate. I miss a *ton* of texts. The internet only works from the new school computers. The teachers are terrible, so most of us play games on our phones. That can be pretty sweet."

Sam thought about his dad's old phone. He didn't

think there was much to play on it.

Josh showed them a handful of unused classrooms, the gymnasium, and the cafeteria. He pointed out some bathrooms, but advised they "hold it if possible," without explanation.

The tour concluded in the library. Like everything else in the school, it was colossal and ancient. Row upon row of books lined the walls, and a network of brass ladders, stairs and platforms crisscrossed the chamber from floor to ceiling, allowing access to the highest shelves. There were desks tucked between the stacks, each with a small, green-shaded lamp. Most of the lamps were missing bulbs. The books themselves were dark and dusty. There were no computers.

Sam noticed the tiny boy with the tattered clothing wander away from the group. He stopped a few yards away and slowly ran a hand over one of the shelves. He leaned in and studied the pattern that had been carved into the wood. Sam watched him curiously, until someone asked where the librarian was.

"Librarian? There's no librarian," Basserman replied with a laugh. "No one comes in here. It's way easier to just find what you need online." Several heads nodded in agreement.

"Alright," he continued. "You'll see everything else later. I gotta go hang with some people before class. This sheet has your homeroom numbers on it. I'll leave it here and you can figure out where to go." He tossed a piece of crumpled paper onto a nearby desk and strolled out of the library.

Sam crowded around the table with the others and spotted *Torwey-220C* halfway down the page. He looked to see if anyone else from the tour group was in his class, but saw no other *220C*s on the list. With a sigh, he turned from the desk and walked out of the library to search for his new classroom alone.

5

The school's tiled hallways spread out like a maze. It took Sam ten minutes to find the C wing and several more to locate his classroom. The door was already shut. He looked back hoping to spot another straggler. Seeing no one, he swung the door open and peered inside.

The classroom was bigger than any he was used to. Large windows provided a panoramic view of the lawn behind the school. A long counter wrapped around the perimeter of the room. On it, twenty or so computers glowed blue. Dividers sectioned the counter into individual terminals.

In the center of the room stood five rows of desks, with a student sitting at each. Sam scanned the faces. In the last row, to his great relief, was Henry, who hadn't yet taken his backpack off. Apparently, he had also arrived late. Sam gave him a nod, but did not receive one in return. Henry flicked his head just slightly, as if to indicate something at the other end of the room. There stood Ms. Snell, the teacher who had been introduced at the assembly. She wore the same odd smile.

"Another late arrival," she said.

"Sorry," Sam said. "I couldn't find—"

"Take a seat please." Sam sat down at the nearest empty desk. The teacher looked at Sam, then Henry. "The other members of the class have already introduced themselves. Why don't you each tell us your name?"

"Sure," Henry started. "I'm Henry Delmont and that's Sam…err….what's your last name again?"

Sam started to reply, but the teacher cut him off. "I'm sure he can introduce himself." She was still smiling.

"Right," Henry said sheepishly. "Okay, Sam, you go ahead and tell them your name."

"I'm Sam."

"Thank you." The teacher turned to the class, "As I was saying, my name is Ms. Snell, and I've been educating students at Perkinsville Middle School Public for the last seven years."

"Sixth grade marks an exciting and important turning point in your lives. You aren't children anymore, and I won't treat you like children. This," she said, extending both arms, "is room 220C, our home base. Here we will learn together, laugh together, maybe even cry together, on a journey into young adulthood."

Sam felt uneasy.

"The world is changing," she continued. "You need to be ready for it. I am here to prepare you. We live in a digital age, an age of… *information.* Ideas travel at the speed of light, and we are all connected. I want you to remember that. We are always *connected.*"

Sam shot a look at Henry. He appeared just as anxious.

"Everything you do affects those around you. What you *think* affects those around you. Therefore, you must think and act, *together.*"

The teacher nodded toward the glowing terminals. "Perkinsville Middle School Public is in the midst of a transformation. It's a transformation I am *personally* responsible for, me and some of my more forward thinking colleagues. The digital world has finally arrived at this school." She paused, still smiling, to let the words sink in. "The computer is our most valuable tool, our link to each other and the world!"

Sam gulped.

"Before we go any further as a class, you will need to establish yourselves as digital members of the school community."

The teacher nodded vigorously. "Many lessons…many assignments, many experiences we have, will be shared, collectively, online. I invite you all to find a terminal and begin the login process. Once you've logged in, you can start to create an online persona…a presence…a personality." Her enthusiasm continued to grow as she gestured grandly to the terminals. "At this time, I'd like each one of you to select a digital workspace!"

Sam followed Henry to the back of the room. They sat down at adjacent computers.

"Do you know what she's talking about?" Henry whispered. "Have you ever made an online persona?"

"No," Sam replied. "You?"

Henry shook his head.

Sam moved the mouse. The computer lit up. *Student Portal* blinked at the top of the page. Below this, *Enter a Username.*

He typed: Sam

This username is taken.

He typed: Sam1

This username is taken.

He typed: Sam2.

This username is taken.

He typed: Sam4532876

Enter a password.

He typed password.

Your password must contain a number.

He typed password1.

Your password must contain a capital letter.

Password1

Your password must NOT contain easily identifiable words.

"What the heck? Henry did you get a password yet?"

Henry shook his head. "I'm still working on the username. If this is going to be as important as Ms. Snell says, I want to make it perfect."

"What do you have so far?"

"Henry-the-scholar-and-lover-of-danger-and-adventure."

"Seems a little long."

"Really? I already shortened it quite a bit."

After about 30 minutes, all the students had logged in and the teacher spoke. "It is now time to begin getting to know your classmates. I encourage you to communicate with everyone. Remember, we only discuss respectful topics. Go ahead."

"Excellent," Henry said. "Tell me more about your summer, Sam."

"Excuse me, boys." Sam and Henry looked up at Ms. Snell. "This is not a time for talking."

"But I thought—" Sam started to respond.

"Use the portal, Samuel. You'll see a chat icon at the top left. Ninety percent of communication will soon be digital. We need to practice."

"Oh," he said. "Okay."

Sam turned back to his screen and clicked the *Chat* icon. He already had a message.

Henry-the-scholar-and-lover-of-danger-and-adventure would like to chat with you. Would you like to accept the invitation? Y/N. Sam clicked *Y*.

Henry-the-scholar-and-lover-of-danger-and-adventure: Hi

Sam typed *hi* back and pushed enter.

Henry-the-scholar-and-lover-of-danger-and-adventure: It's Henry

Sam4532876: I know.

Henry-the-scholar-and-lover-of-danger-and-adventure: How are you?

"Don't forget, you can save time by using one letter or symbol to represent a whole word. Communication must be done quickly," the teacher said.

Henry-the-scholar-and-lover-of-danger-and-adventure: How r u?

Sam4532876: Okay

Henry-the-scholar-and-lover-of-danger-and-adventure: I think u mean 'ok'

Sam4532876: yes

Henry-the-scholar-and-lover-of-danger-and-adventure: this is silly

Sam4532876: yes

"Time to meet another classmate!" Ms. Snell announced. "Click the *Class Manifest* tab to see a list of usernames. You need to connect with every member of the class."

Sam followed the instructions. Over the next twenty minutes, he had conversations with Jared435, Matt76 and Mike234, without any idea who he was actually talking to. He raised his hand.

"Yes, Samuel?"

"Ms. Snell, I don't know who's who."

"What do you mean?"

"Well, I know I just talked to Mike234, but I don't know who Mike is. He could be any of the boys in class."

Henry interjected. "Maybe if everyone could say his or her name again? We kind of missed it because we were late."

"Henry," Ms. Snell said in a measured tone. "This matter does not concern you."

"Well, it kind of does. I mean I'm talking to Matt76 and—"

"Excuse me," she said more firmly. Henry stopped talking. The smile returned to the teacher's face. "Samuel, one of the most wonderful parts of the internet, is that it allows us to remain anonymous. This allows the free flow of ideas. It allows us to reinvent ourselves in the way we want to be seen. Therefore we do not need to know, and should not know, the identities of the people we talk to. We should judge them on the basis of their ideas."

"Uh…okay," Sam said.

He looked back at his screen.

You have a chat request from Missy15. Would you like to accept the invitation? Y/N

Sam was nervous about talking to a girl, but then he remembered that Ms. Snell had said they'd be connecting with everyone. He reluctantly hit *Y*.

Missy15: Hi

Sam4532876 Hi. How's it going?

Missy15: Gr8! Our teacher is awesome ☺

Sam looked away from the screen and tried to determine which one of his classmates was Missy15. It was impossible.

Sam4532876: Yeah. She seems okay.

Missy15: ok? She's fantastic!

Sam wasn't sure he agreed. He decided to change subjects.

Sam4532876: How was your summer?

Missy15: It was AWESOME!!!

Sam4532876: Cool.

Missy15: What did u do?

Sam stared at the question. He still didn't know who he was talking to and he didn't want to come off as uncool. The summer had been a disaster. Nothing had happened.

He let his mind wander over the whole thing. There had been the day he'd cleaned out the garage. The day he'd watched Roger play video games. The day he'd gone to the dentist. The other day he'd watched Roger play video games, and the day he helped his father weed the garden. That was it. Those were the top five days.

Suddenly, he remembered the slingshot.

Sam4532876: Nothing too much. I did find a really cool slingshot though.

Missy15: Like a real slingshot?

Sam4532876: Yeah

No response.

Sam4532876: I mean. I think it's real.

Missy15: Did you tell the police?

Sam4532876: Uh…no?

Missy15: So where is it now?

Sam4532876: In my room. Why?

No response.

At the other side of the room, a girl with a single, long braid stood up and walked to the teacher's desk. She said something to Ms. Snell. The teacher's smile disappeared, and she followed the girl back to her computer and studied the screen.

"What's the matter?" Henry asked. "You're not typing."

"I don't know," Sam said. "I think I've been talking to that girl with the braid."

"She doesn't seem very happy."

Ms. Snell looked across the room to Sam. "My desk please."

"What'd you do?" Henry asked.

"No idea." Sam got up and walked to the teacher's desk.

"I have just received some unfortunate information," she said.

"About what?" Sam was astonished.

"A conversation you recently had online."

"Huh? With who?"

"It's come to my attention that you were discussing something called a 'slingshot' with another member of the community. That student reported the conversation to me."

"But I just said—"

"I'm not concerned with what you said. A slingshot is a dangerous device that no young person should be discussing online, much less possessing."

Sam was dumbstruck. "I found—"

The teacher raised a hand to silence him. "What that means, I'm afraid, is that you'll need to have a conversation with the vice principal about appropriate online conduct."

"What?! When?!"

"Right now," she said. The smile was back. Her eyes were unblinking. "It's important we resolve this issue immediately. Only then, can we welcome you back into the classroom community."

6

Sam plodded slowly down the deserted corridor outside room 220C in search of the vice principal's office. In one hand he held a typed note from Ms. Snell, in the other, a printout of the conversation about the slingshot.

Just off the lobby, he found a door with a cracked window. The word *Office* was stenciled across the clouded glass. He took a deep breath and pushed it open. He was surprised to discover a cozy waiting room inside. Potted plants sat on stands of varying heights and a radio played softly. Paintings of the ocean covered the walls. A woman with short, silver hair and blue earrings sat behind a desk at the center of the room. There were doors on either side of her. One had a golden placard bearing the words *Mr. Fiddlesbee- Principal.* The other had a cardboard sign with *Vice Principal* written in black marker.

The woman at the desk was sifting through a stack of cards and looked up at the sound of the door. "Hi there. Can I help you?" She had a kind face.

"Err…yeah…" Sam said quietly. "I…was wondering… I mean I need to talk to the vice principal."

"Oh," she said with an understanding smile. "Okay. Well, Mr. Throxon's not here at the moment. He'll be back soon. Why don't you have a seat?" She gestured to a wooden chair against one of the walls.

"Okay," Sam said.

"I'm going to mark down that you got here." She turned to a computer. "What's your name?"

"Sam Torwey."

"Hi, Sam. I'm Miss Partridge. It's nice to meet you. Whose class are you in?"

"Um…Ms. Snell's," Sam replied, closely studying the secretary's reaction.

"Oh," she said, her eyebrows rising as she recorded his information. "Is everything going okay?"

Sam shrugged.

Miss Partridge looked up and smiled knowingly. "The first day at a new school is hard. Things will get better. It's Mr. Throxon's first day too. He's new this year."

Sam tried to smile back.

"Sam, I'd love to chat, but I've got 250 files to make for the sixth graders - names, birthdays, parents - that kind of thing. I should probably be entering it all into the online database, but I like the old system better. Don't tell anyone." She winked at him. "You just make yourself at home."

Sam sat in the chair and tried to make sense of the morning. So much had already gone wrong. Ms. Snell's reaction seemed completely over the top. He hoped Mr. Throxon would understand. The minutes ticked slowly by. Finally, a silhouette appeared outside the office. The knob turned and the door swung open.

Sam gulped. The vice principal was even bigger up close.

"Mr. Throxon," Miss Partridge chirped, "this is Sam

Torwey. He's here to see you."

The vice principal looked down. He was smiling. "Hi there, Sam. How can I help you?"

Sam let out a sigh of relief. "Ms. Snell told me I needed to come see you."

The vice principal nodded and ran a hand through his curls. "I see. Well, come on into my office and we'll talk it out." He turned and walked through the door with the cardboard sign.

Mr. Throxon had not finished unpacking. Boxes were scattered everywhere. An old diagram of the school grounds hung by a window. Aside from that, the walls were bare. There was a desk with a computer screen and phone. Between two shabby looking chairs, a pile of books stood twenty high. Sam realized they all had the same title: *Building a Better Digital You!*

"Sit down, Sam Torwey," the vice principal said.

Sam sunk into one of the tattered chairs. The vice principal took a seat behind the desk. Before saying anything else, he reached into a pocket and removed the two shining silver spheres he'd been spinning on stage.

"I like to start each meeting with some relaxation exercises," he said. "It helps me do my best thinking." He closed his eyes, reclined slightly and began to emit low humming sounds. "Owwwwmmm….Owwwwmmm…."

Sam's mouth fell open.

"Owwwwwwmmm….Owwwmmm…." Mr. Throxon continued, the silver balls spinning rapidly in his hand.

Sam considered running from the office, but the vice principal opened his eyes a second later. "Much better," he said. "It's so important to stay balanced. Especially today, when the world moves with such speed. You might consider getting some serenity spheres like these." He held up the silver balls. "They do wonders…Now, what seems to be the problem?"

Still in shock and unsure what to say, Sam passed the note and printed conversation across the desk. The vice principal read them, then leaned back in his chair.

"Sam, Ms. Snell headed the committee that hired me. Did you know that?"

"Uhhh…no. I didn't know."

"It's true. Do you know why they hired me?"

Sam shook his head.

"Because I'm an expert on all things digital. I understand the power of computers, the power of social networking, and I have the skills to bring digital education into this school!"

Sam didn't understand.

"Mr. Fiddlesbee has been here for forty-five years. Forty-five *years*. Imagine that? Nice enough guy, but let's face it, he isn't going to bring this school into the 21st century. But I will… and that's why I'm here. I've even written a book on the subject."

Sam shot a glance at the pile of books on the floor. Just below *Building a Better Digital You!* was the name *Daniel Throxon.*

The vice principal followed his gaze. "That's the one. Those are just hard copies of course. That's why I have so many. The eBook is what really sells."

Sam nodded.

"We have a problem here, Sam. Seems like your digital self is not shaping up the way it should."

"I just mentioned a slingshot I found. I didn't mean to offend. That's the truth."

"It's not about what you meant, Sam. It's not about the truth. It's what people believe."

"But…I…"

"Listen. Here's what I need you to do…I want you to

take a copy of my book. I want you to read it. Then I want you to read it again. I want you to think about being a good digital citizen, and I want to you encourage your friends to do the same."

"But, the slingshot, it just kind of appeared. I'm real sorry."

"Don't worry about the slingshot, Sam. And don't worry about paying me for the book. It's just a paper copy."

"Pay you? I—"

"What you *can* do is tell your friends to read it too. As I said, the digital version is available online. I'm going to check back with you in a few weeks." The vice principal stood and took a book from the pile. He handed it to Sam, then picked up the note and conversation.

"I'm going to keep these in your electronic file, as a reminder of what can happen when you're not a good digital citizen. I believe that if you read my book, and try very hard, we won't have any more trouble."

He picked up his phone, snapped a picture of the conversation and Ms. Snell's note, then crumbled up the pages and threw them away.

"There. I just sent them to the central database. Head back to class, Sam," he said cheerfully, "and don't forget to tell your friends about my book. We don't want them to make the same mistake you did. Copies are available online!"

Sam was so relieved to avoid punishment, he didn't ask any questions. He walked out the door, the book under one arm.

7

Students filled the lobby outside the office. It appeared to be some kind of transition time for seventh and eighth graders. They moved through the lobby in packs, waving cell phones at one another and exploding in laughter at whatever appeared on the screens. The packs broke apart then came together again, scattered and reassembled. Max, the boy from the back of the bus, leaned against one of the brick walls with his friend Trent. Sam spun around and headed in the opposite direction before the eighth graders noticed him.

He found his homeroom without much trouble and went in cautiously. All the students still sat at the computer terminals. Before he could join them, Ms. Snell summoned him to her desk.

"Back so soon?" She was smiling again. "Did you speak with the vice principal?"

"Yeah."

"And?"

Sam held out the book. "He gave me this."

"Good," she said, apparently already familiar with the

book. "I hope you'll read it carefully. We don't want another…incident."

"I'm sorry. It's just—"

Ms. Snell held up a hand. "Let's not make excuses. Let's move forward. Take your seat Samuel. The other students are selecting electives."

"What are those?"

"There are instructions on the portal. Click the *Academic Adventures* tab." Sam nodded blankly and returned to his seat.

"What happened?" Henry whispered.

"I had to talk to the vice principal."

"Really?! Whoa! What did you do?"

"I don't know. I said I found a slingshot yesterday and that girl Missy got all upset." Sam nodded to the other side of the room.

"A slingshot? Marvelous! Why did she get upset?"

Sam shook his head. "I just said I found it. That's when she told the teacher."

Henry looked puzzled. "Really? That's strange."

"Yeah. I'll tell you more later. What are we doing now?"

Henry frowned. "Picking something called 'electives'."

"What are those?"

"Classes we go to every other day, in the afternoon."

"Like art and stuff?"

"Kind of…"

"But?"

Henry gestured to his computer. "They sound…well, I don't know. I'm just not finding one that suits me."

Sam looked at the screen. Three course titles blinked in bold yellow letters, each with a description below it.

1. Cooking for Body Wellness

Learn how to pick foods and prepare them in the best way possible for a healthy body and mind.

2. Social Superstars

Discover the exciting world of social media. Build your online footprint and share it with friends and family.

3. Cooperation Over Conflict

Become trained in solving potential problems through cooperation. Improve your communication and relaxation skills.

He finished reading and turned back to Henry. "Those are the only choices?"

"It seems that way."

"What are we going to do?"

Henry shrugged. "I guess we need to pick one."

"They meet twice a week for the whole *year*?"

"That's what Ms. Snell said."

Sam turned to his own computer, X'ed out of the conversation with Missy and clicked *Academic Adventures.* He scrolled down the page, rereading the course descriptions. *Social Superstars*? Did kids really want to do this?

As if reading his mind, Henry spoke. "Ms. Snell said that's one of the most popular."

"What do you learn?"

"I have no idea."

Sam scrolled further down, hoping he'd missed something. As it turned out, he had. "Hey what's this?" At the very bottom of the page, after a long blank space, a fourth course was listed. No description. Just a title: ***Industrial Arts***.

"I don't know," Henry said. "I didn't see it. Ms. Snell

didn't mention that one, which is quite strange, because she talked about all the others in great detail."

"'Industrial' sounds kind of cool."

"I like art," Henry added. "Let's do it." They each highlighted *Industrial Arts*, and hit *Submit.*

Almost immediately, Ms. Snell spoke.

"Samuel. Henry. My desk please."

Sam looked at Henry. He shrugged. They walked wearily to the teacher.

"I've just received your elective selections, and I think you may have *accidentally* made a mistake." She looked from the boys to her computer.

"Really?" Henry asked, leaning over to try and get a glimpse of the teacher's screen. "What does it say?'

"It says you both chose Industrial Arts, but that wasn't one of the courses I went over. Samuel, you were talking to Mr. Throxon, but Henry, you were here. Which one did you intend to select?" She blinked repeatedly while waiting for a response.

"Err," Sam said. "We thought Industrial Arts sounded good."

"I like industry," Henry said.

"And I like art," Sam added.

"Me too," agreed Henry.

Ms. Snell smiled at them for a moment. "No," she said. "I'm afraid not. That subject is outdated and will soon be removed from the curriculum. Samuel, I'm going to sign you up for Social Superstars and Henry, I think you'll enjoy Cooking for Body Wellness." She hit a few keys on her desktop and clicked the mouse.

Frustration rose in Sam's stomach. "I thought we got to choose."

"Students get to choose unless they make the wrong choice. Then, it becomes my job."

"But…"

"Go sit down boys. I think you're really going to enjoy your new electives. I'm excited for you!"

8

"This day has been a disaster," Sam said, when at last it was time for lunch.

"You're right about that," Henry agreed. "I know *convicts* who've had better first days in prison."

"You know convicts?"

"Well…no. But I bet there are some."

"I can't believe she wont let us take Industrial Arts."

"Makes me want to take it even more. Wonder what it is?"

"Guess we'll never know."

They found the sprawling cafeteria and sat down at a table near the back. Sam spotted Roger sitting with a group of unfamiliar boys. They made eye contact for a moment, then Roger looked away.

Sam turned back to Henry. "What comes after lunch?"

"Phys Ed. We have it every other day, in between electives."

"Thank goodness. I can't take another minute on the computer."

"Think we'll play dodgeball? It's the first day after all."

"I sure hope so," Sam said. "We always played it on the first day in elementary school."

"That's true. But I'm getting the feeling middle school is different. There's not even any recess."

"Really?" Sam asked with surprise. "Who said that?"

"Ms. Snell mentioned it while you were in the office. She said recess is a 'breeding ground for competition and conflict'."

"What? Was she being serious?"

"I think so," Henry said. "She doesn't seem like much of a joker. Come on; let's go look for the gym. My sandwich tastes like an old shoe anyway." He tossed it into the trash and the two boys wandered out of the cafeteria.

They found the gymnasium on the other side of the school and waited awkwardly for the P.E. teachers to arrive as dozens of sixth graders filed in behind them.

"There are a lot of kids here," Sam whispered.

"Must be two or three sixth grade sections," Henry replied.

All the students from Ms. Snell's room were there, along with quite a few others. Roger was one of them. Sam watched as he and another boy began talking to a pair of girls. Sam couldn't help noticing that they were very pretty. One had shining black hair that hung down to her shoulders. She wore glasses and neon yellow sneakers. The other had long copper colored hair. Sam had never noticed a person's eyes before, but hers were such a brilliant blue, it was hard not to. Henry had seen the girls too. "Who are *they*?"

"No idea," Sam replied softly. The girl with red hair glanced in his direction. He snapped his gaze away, before she could notice him staring.

"Well," said Henry, "I think it is essential we make a

strong showing this afternoon…so as to win their hearts." Both girls laughed at something Roger had said. Sam found this peculiar because Roger had never said anything funny that he could remember.

"Hey," Henry said, gesturing towards the rafters. "What are those?"

High above them, two thick rope ends protruded from the ceiling. A bronze bell with an inverted Y-shaped clapper hung down between them.

"Could they be climbing ropes?"

"They're awfully short."

"I think they may lower down. Here come the teachers. Maybe they'll tell us."

A man and woman strode into the gym and over to the sixth graders. They both carried iPads.

"Good morning," the man said. He was bald and wore a tight sweat suit. "Welcome to P.E. I'm Mr. Montero and this is Ms. Fischer. We're your teachers."

"Hi guys," Ms. Fischer said. She had blonde hair pulled back in a ponytail.

"Physical education," Mr. Montero said. "What do we mean by that? What do those words mean to you?"

At the front of the crowd, two girls raised their hands. One of them was Missy. Sam thought he recognized the other one too. Henry stuck his hand in the air and waved it violently, trying to catch the teacher's attention.

Mr. Montero pointed at him.

"Sports," Henry said proudly.

The gym teacher frowned. "What do you mean?"

"Sports," Henry repeated. "Basketball, football, soccer. Demonstrations of athletic prowess!"

"Wellll…No, not really. Physical education is not a competition. Anyone else? How about you?" He pointed to the girl next to Missy.

"Physical education is a study of the body and how to keep it healthy."

"Yes! Excellent," Mr. Montero sad. "Excellent. What's your name?"

"Margot."

"Whose class are you in, Margot?"

"Ms. Snell's." Her words overflowed with pride.

"Margot, you're exactly right. In Physical Education, we will learn about our bodies and how to take care of them."

"Oh no," Henry whispered. "Not that."

"Before we can improve our physical performance. We must understand what's happening in our bodies right now. We need to take baseline readings of our vital signs."

The woman held up the iPad. "Technology will help us do it. Each of you will be linked to one of these devices. It will keep track of your heart rate and the number of steps you take."

"No," Henry whispered. "Please no."

The woman pointed across the gym to a gray box with wheels. "Inside that cart are tablets with applications to track your progress. All of it is uploaded to your student portal. You'll be able to view the data from home…at least, very soon you will."

"Unfortunately," Montero said. "The gym isn't getting a Wi-Fi signal right now, so we won't be able to use the equipment until next time."

"That's good news," muttered Henry.

"So today, we're going to play a game called Keep Ball-ieving. It's a lot like a game called dodgeball, but we don't call it that."

"Yesssss," Henry hissed.

"We're only doing this because the monitors aren't

ready yet. I'll give a quick summary of the rules and then we'll get started."

Keep Ball-ieving, as it turned out, was *exactly* like dodgeball. Except the jails were called "waiting stations" and it wasn't called "getting knocked out", it was called "going to wait". The name changes didn't seem to fool anyone. Every kid in the gymnasium knew what game they were playing.

The teachers divided the students into two teams. Sam and Henry were on one side, Roger on the other.

Before the game began, Henry nudged Sam. A few feet away, the girl with red hair stood alone. Sam felt butterflies rise in his stomach. "Are you going to talk to her?" he asked.

"No way," Henry said. "I'll simply demonstrate my skills on the dodgeball court and with any luck she'll want to talk to *me*."

Sam rolled his eyes.

The game began. Two balls were in play and before long, they both whizzed through the gym at lightning speed. Mr. Montero yelled, "It's not about competition, it's about team work," but no one seemed to notice. Sam didn't see much action for the first few moments, but did catch one ball hurled his way, sending the thrower to jail, or the waiting station, as it was known. Henry was hit a few seconds later.

"Can you believe it?" he muttered on his way past Sam. "Slipped right through my fingers. Someone must have covered it with oil or grease or something. Don't worry, I don't think she saw."

The game raged on, with neither side able to gain a true advantage.

"Nice effort!" Ms. Fischer yelled at no one in particular.

A tall boy had the ball now. He'd been sitting with Roger at lunch and had already sent at least half a dozen players to the waiting station. He wound up and heaved the ball in Sam's direction. It shot from his hand like a rocket, much too fast to catch. Sam instinctively dove out of the way.

It sailed over his head and smacked, with a terrible THWAP, into someone behind him. Sam turned and saw with horror that it was the girl with red hair.

She glared at him. "You blocked my view."

He tried to speak. "But, I didn't mean…" She trotted away before he could finish. "I'll get her out of jail," he thought. "I've just got to last until the end."

WHIZZZZZZ…another ball rocketed past his ear, just missing him. Only a few players remained in the game. Sam grabbed a ball near his feet and whipped it back across the gym. The boy who'd knocked out the girl with red hair lunged to catch it, but the ball was traveling too fast, and it bounced off his fingers.

"Yes!" Sam yelled in celebration. He looked around. No one seemed to have noticed. Within a few seconds his last teammate had been hit. Sam was the only one left.

On the other side of the gym, Roger and a girl wearing a yellow headband remained. She scurried forward, grabbed a ball as it rolled across the dividing line, and flung it at Sam. Her aim was off and the ball sailed high. Sam leapt up and caught it.

Roger and Sam were now alone on opposite sides of the floor, each with a ball in hand.

Over the years, the pair had played a lot of dodgeball together. Both were strong players and they had always been good friends. In fourth grade, they made a pact. If ever the last two players left, they agreed to throw the balls to someone in jail rather than try and knock each other out.

Sam thought of the pact now with relief. He could throw the ball to the girl with red hair. That would certainly make up for blocking her view. The gym was loud with cheering from both sides. Ms. Fischer tried to quiet the crowd, but was unsuccessful. Roger moved back and forth across the floor. Sam did the same.

"Throw to jail?" Roger yelled.

"Of course," Sam said with a smile. He glanced across the gym to where the girl with red hair stood with the other prisoners. She stared back at him with eyes like blue sapphires.

"On three," Roger yelled. "One…two…three…"

Sam ran forward and heaved the ball toward the jail. It sailed high into the air toward the girl with red hair. But before it reached her, Sam realized something was wrong. Roger's arm was too low. His eyes were on Sam.

It was a trick.

The ball hit him before there was time to react. The gymnasium erupted simultaneously in cheers of triumph and cries of defeat.

Sam watched in astonishment as Roger's lips twisted into a grin. "Oops," he mouthed, and trotted away.

9

Sam didn't feel much like talking on the ride home and was thankful that Henry didn't bring up the dodgeball game. When the bus stopped, he headed straight into the house, avoiding Roger completely. He went to bed that night sad and discouraged.

The next day, Ms. Snell announced that electives would begin in the afternoon. Sam's heart sank at the thought of Social Superstars. He logged onto the student portal, clicked the *Electives* tab and reread the description. *Build your online footprint.* What did that even mean? It sounded like something from Mr. Throxon's book.

"Do you see a room number?" Henry asked. "I can't find anything."

"Me neither," Sam replied.

"Hmmm...It says I'm *not* enrolled in Cooking for Body Wellness. That's good. Maybe we're both in Social Superstars."

"I don't think so," Sam said. "That would be too good to be true. Wait a second...no way."

At the bottom of the page, *Industrial Arts* had turned

from yellow to blue. Sam scrolled to the right. *Enrolled-Room 110.*

"Henry," he whispered. "I got into Industrial Arts."

Henry looked at him in disbelief. "Me too."

They turned to the teacher's desk. Ms. Snell had been watching them, but quickly turned away, her smile even more forced than usual.

"How did it happen?" Henry asked on the way to lunch. "She told me I was going to be in the food class."

"No idea," Sam replied.

"Maybe she likes us after all," Henry suggested.

"Are you kidding? Did you see her as we were walking out?"

"I did," Henry answered solemnly. "She looked like a wasp after its nest has been kicked."

Sam laughed.

"I wonder though," he continued. "She was the only person, except you, who knew I wanted to take Industrial Arts."

"It's weird," Sam agreed.

"Look," Henry said once there were seated. "It's those girls from gym class."

He was right.

The girls sat a few yards away, at a table with several others. Roger and his new friends sat nearby. As Sam and Henry watched, Roger leaned back in his chair and said something to the girls. A second later, he spun completely around and joined their table.

"Isn't that the kid who knocked you out yesterday?" Henry asked. "He seems to think he's pretty cool."

"Yeah," said Sam. "That's him."

They watched in disbelief as two eighth graders approached Roger. Sam recognized them from the back of the bus. Max held his shiny golden phone. Trent walked beside him.

"How does he know those older fellows?" Henry asked.

"No idea," Sam muttered. "They must think Roger is friends with the girls."

Max and Trent high-fived the younger boy as if they were old pals, then they too, took seats with the girls.

Henry sighed. "Don't worry. We'll have our chance. The year is young."

Sam chuckled. "Right. I'm sure we will."

After lunch, the two friends hurried to the Industrial Arts room. "I bet there will be loads of students in this class," Henry said.

Sam nodded. "We should have left earlier."

At the end of a deserted hallway, they found a set of double doors numbered 110.

"Should we go in?" Henry asked.

"I guess so."

"Are you sure? It could be a trap."

"You think?"

"It's pretty suspicious that we were suddenly enrolled."

"Let's risk it."

Henry pulled open the door and they walked inside.

Sam marveled at what he saw. The classroom, if it could be called that, was massive. It had an exceptionally high ceiling and was filled with the most marvelous collection of apparatus imaginable. Machines stood everywhere; saws, drills, welding equipment and thick clamps for holding and bending metal. Tools of all kinds covered the walls.

"Holy—"

"What is this place?"

A gruff voice spoke behind them. "It's a shop, of course. What does it look like?"

They spun around. An ancient, gray-haired man with horn-rimmed glasses and sky-blue eyes stared at them with an expression of amusement. His face was a tapestry of wrinkles and part of his left ear was gone. He wore a faded lab coat spotted with stains.

"It's…well…we didn't know," Sam stuttered.

"You must be Sam and Henry."

"We are. But? How did you?"

"Got a printout of the selections yesterday. Got two actually. The first one had you signed up for my class. Second one didn't. Something didn't add up. I had you re-enrolled. But don't worry, we can get you back in Social Superstarters, or whatever it's called, if you want."

"No!" they shouted in unison.

"Good. Welcome to Industrial Arts. I'm your teacher, Mr. Arthur."

"I'm Henry. Henry Delmont. This here is Sam Torwey."

They shook the teacher's callused hand.

"Is there anyone else coming?" Sam asked. He and Henry were the only students in the room.

"One more," the shop teacher said. "Used to have to make a waiting list for this class. I guess times change, huh? Here he is now."

The door behind them opened and a boy slipped through. Sam had seen him before. They'd been in the same tour group. He was even tinier up close and his clothing appeared even more tattered.

"You must be Milo," Mr. Arthur proclaimed.

The boy nodded timidly.

"Hiya, Milo," Henry roared. "I'm Henry, Henry

Delmont. This is Sam Torwey."

Milo nodded again, but remained silent.

"Nice to meet you Milo," the shop teacher said. "I was just about to give these gentlemen a tour. Follow me. Time's a wastin'." He started off across the shop, moving with a stiff limp.

"We build things in this classroom boys, and trust me, with all this equipment, you can build just about anything. Might even learn something along the way. I know some teachers, don't give me good reviews…dangerous and outdated and all of that." He held up his hand. "But look, I've only lost a couple fingers." Two of his fingers were only nubs.

Henry gasped.

"Just kidding," he said, extending the fingers that had merely been folded over. Henry exhaled in relief. The shop teacher held up his other hand. The pinky was gone. "Only lost one."

Sam didn't know whether to laugh or run for the door.

"I've been teaching at Perkinsville Middle School Public since…well, since before it was even Perkinsville Middle School Public. They keep trying to shut me down, but here I am, back for another year."

They walked along a row of towering machinery, all very old, all in perfect condition. Every saw blade was polished to a shining silver; every drill bit a sharp spiral of gleaming black.

"This is amazing," Henry murmured.

"Glad you're excited," the shop teacher replied. "There's a lot of good stuff in here."

He showed the boys where they could find wood, nails, glue and paint. Then he hobbled to the other side of the shop and through a set of metal doors. Inside, a huge mound was piled high with what, at first glance, appeared to be junk. But it wasn't junk at all. It was the most fantastic collection of items Sam had ever seen. There were old bikes and scooters, lawn mowers and snow blowers, at least half a go-cart, a pile of wheels, pulleys, gears and an ancient looking refrigerator. It all sat beneath a grimy sign that read *Juniper Tools.*

"This," Mr. Arthur proclaimed, "is the Pit. If you can't make something from scratch, chances are you can get it here. Take anything you need. Just do me a favor, if you're trying to start one of those motors, take it outside so the fumes don't kill us." He gestured to another set of doors behind the enormous pile.

"I'll tell you how my class runs," he said, limping out of the Pit. "*You* think of a project and *you* build it. I'll help along the way. Nobody quits until it's done." All three boys, even Milo, smiled excitedly.

"You're going to start the year constructing a piece of furniture. Not too exciting, but I need to make sure you can use all the tools without cutting off an arm. There are some examples over there." He pointed to the far wall. "Take a look. I want you to pick something today. Finish the furniture, and you can start working on a bigger project."

For the next ten minutes, Sam and Henry discussed all the things they intended to build, while studying the furniture examples. Milo did the same, but Sam got the impression he was paying more attention to their conversation than the furniture.

"What a class!" Henry said. "We really lucked out, didn't we? I plan to get the woodworking done quickly. Then I'll move on to something a little more complicated— an atom smasher, or maybe one of those rocket-propelled backpacks."

"Do you have much practice working with your

hands?" Sam asked.

"Oh sure," he replied confidently. "I made a paperweight for my dad last year. The principles are the same." Sam noticed Milo smile.

"So boys," Mr. Arthur barked, walking back to the table, "what are you thinking?"

"I'm going to try a foot stool," Sam said.

"I was thinking about a bookcase," Henry added. "I'll save the jetpack for later in the year. No one likes a show-off."

"Probably a good idea." Mr. Arthur turned to Milo. "And what about you?" Milo didn't answer. Sam noticed a patch of skin showing through a hole in his shirt. "Any ideas?" the shop teacher prodded.

Milo raised a hand and pointed to a nearby wall. A replica of a Victorian mansion hung between hammers and chisels. It took Sam a moment to realize the mansion was actually a birdhouse.

"Oh," Mr. Arthur said, "I didn't make that. It's been here since before my time. Always meant to hang it somewhere on the grounds." He limped towards the house. "But it's bolted to the wall. Beauty isn't it?"

No detail had been spared. It had small balconies, chimneys, a porch and tiny shingles. There were posts for birds to stand on and holes for entry, all disguised perfectly as flagpoles and windows.

"No," the teacher said. "I think this is a little advanced for sixth grade. It takes years to learn to shape wood like this."

Milo kept looking at the birdhouse. Mr. Arthur studied him. "I *suppose*," he said after a moment, "you could build *a* birdhouse and use this one as inspiration."

The boy smiled again, but when he noticed Sam and Henry's stares, the smile vanished.

"Alright then," Mr. Arthur declared, "let's get started."

For the next forty-five minutes, he led the three boys around the shop and demonstrated each piece of machinery. He cut a piece of oak on a table saw, then removed the middle using a drill and jigsaw. He made fancy corners with a band saw and inlaid a pattern with something called a router. When the demonstrations were over, Henry and Sam headed to the supply room to get some wood.

"By the end of this year," Henry said, "I really will be an expert craftsman."

Sam laughed. "Think you'll be able to make a birdhouse like that Milo kid?"

"Hmm," Henry said. "That might be a little advanced, even for me."

"I know," Sam agreed. "Is he crazy?"

"He's awfully quiet," Henry said, "and a tad odd."

"Yeah, and he looks like he needs some new clothes." Sam turned to leave, but stopped short.

Milo stood in the doorway with Mr. Arthur.

"I mean…" Sam stuttered, "I was…kidding." Milo pretended to study a shelf for a moment, before walking quickly away.

"Be careful, Sam," Mr. Arthur muttered. "You'll hurt someone's feelings. He seems like a nice enough kid." Sam didn't know what to say. The teacher sighed. "Well, we're late. Why don't you two put the materials aside and walk back to class. Ms. Snell doesn't like tardiness."

Sam and Henry piled their wood on a table near the sink and headed for the door. As they left the shop, Milo continued to study the birdhouse, his expression blank.

"I wish I hadn't said that," Sam said in the hallway.

"Yes," Henry agreed solemnly, "me too."

They walked the rest of the way in silence, Sam

thinking all the while of Milo's face in the supply room.

By the time they arrived at room 220C, five minutes had passed. An assignment had been projected onto a wall and the students dutifully typed it into the homework section of their student portals. Margot and Missy scowled at Sam and Henry when they entered, but Ms. Snell said nothing. Sam sat down at his computer and began copying the assignment.

At 2:15, the teacher stood up. "I hope you all have a pleasant afternoon. Class dismissed." Sam gathered his things and stood to leave. "Not you, Samuel. You and Mr. Delmont will be staying with me." Sam's heart sank.

Henry spoke. "We have to catch the bus."

"I'm afraid this is more important." Sam and Henry remained seated. The room cleared and the teacher approached them. "Your tardiness is becoming a real problem. You were late yesterday and now you're late again."

"We lost track of time," Sam muttered.

"My job is to educate you, to prepare you for…for…*life*. The world moves fast. You'll never survive if you're tardy."

"I agree," Henry pleaded. "If I miss this bus, I'm definitely not going to survive—"

"Please don't interrupt. You both owe me the time you missed, plus a penalty. I'd like you to sit in your seats and think about what you can do to be more punctual."

Sam opened his mouth to protest, but a glare from the teacher made him think better of it. They sat in silence for five minutes, Ms. Snell standing awkwardly between them.

"Now," she finally said. "What have you learned?"

"Uh…" Sam turned to Henry.

"Not to be tardy."

"What else?" she asked.

"If we're tardy, we miss the bus," he continued. "Ms. Snell does this have anything to do with us signing up for Industrial Arts because it really is a good class. It's about—"

Her smile vanished. "No. Nothing at all. You enrolled in an elective that will do nothing to prepare you for the real world. It's a terrible shame. However, the teacher in charge has been here longer than me. The matter was out of my control."

She started to walk away, obviously shaken by the reference to Industrial Arts. "Now good day to you both. Do not be late again."

The boys hastily departed the classroom.

"What was that about?" Henry asked when they got to the lobby. "She got kind of mad."

"No idea," Sam said. "What a terrible end to the day. Between Ms. Snell and that stuff we said about Milo…I feel horrible."

"Me too," Henry agreed.

"What are we supposed to do now? The buses are gone."

"I suppose we'll have to call for rides."

"Do you have a phone?"

Henry shook his head.

"I do, but it's not charged."

Henry pointed to the office door. "Maybe in there?"

"Good idea."

They went into the office and Sam introduced Henry to Miss Partridge, the secretary. She was happy to let them use the phone, but neither of their parents would be out of work until five. They had almost two hours to kill.

"What shall we do now?" Henry asked.

"We could start our homework."

"We need computers for that. Maybe in the library?"

Sam shook his head. "I saw it on the tour. No computers there."

"That's okay. We can do some reading. Besides, I haven't seen it yet. Come on."

They set off to find the library, Sam still upset about how the day had ended.

"I can't get over how big this school is," Henry said as they turned down a vacant corridor.

"It was probably nice when it opened," Sam added.

"I wonder why they never updated it. Those cables for example, shouldn't they be in the wall?"

Above their heads, blue ethernet cables had been secured to the ceiling with zip ties.

"Maybe it's cheaper that way."

"Who knows?"

They climbed a set of stairs, then another. They walked down several more hallways.

"I could have sworn it was around here somewhere," Sam said. "Maybe around this corner… oof!"

He slammed into a figure coming from the opposite direction. It was the teacher with the greasy skin and jagged scar. He crumpled to the ground.

"I'm sorry," Sam stuttered. "I didn't see—"

"Watch where you're going!"

Sam leaned down and tried to help him up. He was breathing heavily, almost wheezing.

"Don't touch me!" he snapped.

"Sorry, I just—"

Before he could finish, the man stood and walked quickly away.

"That's that other sixth grade teacher," Sam whispered, "Mr. Dean."

"That fellow gives me the creeps," Henry said with a

shutter. "Let's keep moving."

They found the library a few moments later. Sam pulled the door opened dramatically and Henry marveled at the size of the space.

"Wow," he said. "This is unbelievable. Look at all these books! And we have the whole place to ourselves!"

The library did indeed appear to be completely empty.

"Let's go back this way," Sam said pointing into the stacks of books.

"Good idea," Henry said. "Seems like a great place to read a mystery. I'll bet there are tons—Wait, is that someone back there? Isn't that…"

"… Milo," Sam whispered.

Tucked in the far corner, peering down at a book, he looked especially small in the grips of a tattered satin armchair.

Sam glanced at Henry, who nodded. They walked over to Milo. He didn't seem to notice, apparently engrossed in whatever he was reading. Unsure what to do, Sam gave a slight cough. Milo looked up, noticed the boys, and looked away.

"Err…" Sam started, "We're sorry about what we said."

"Really," Henry added. "It was unkind. Please accept our apology."

"It's okay," Milo said quietly. "My clothes are old."

"No. They're… fine," Henry said awkwardly.

They stood in painful silence until Sam noticed Milo's book.

"Hey," he said, "is that *Sherlock Holmes*?" The small boy nodded.

"Really?" Henry asked. "That book is great! Have you read it before?"

Milo nodded a second time.

"My favorite story is *The Speckled Band*," Sam said.

"I like *The Blue Carbuncle*," Milo replied softly.

"Oh yes, that one's great," Henry agreed. "With the goose and all."

Sam couldn't be sure, but it seemed like a grin had flickered across Milo's face. The conversation stopped there, and he and Henry sat down at nearby desks.

Henry took an enormous volume from a nearby shelf and started to read. Sam sat in silence. He glanced at the book Milo held, then looked around the cavernous library. The dusty chamber would be a perfect setting for a Sherlock Holmes adventure. He wondered if he'd ever have an adventure of his own. It seemed unlikely.

With a sigh, he gazed out a nearby window to the tree line at the edge of the lawn. It gave him an idea.

"Hey," he said. Milo and Henry looked up. "It's a beautiful day outside. Maybe we should go explore those woods behind the school? I've never really done that before."

Henry seemed interested, but waited for Milo to respond first.

"I mean, it's no big deal if you don't want to," Sam said.

"Okay," Milo said softly, the smile creeping across his face again. "I'll go."

"Sounds great!" Henry exclaimed.

They left the library in a hurry and exited the school through the lobby.

"I think I saw a path into the woods in the back. Let's try there."

They crossed the lawn to a break in the thicket where a narrow path wound its way into the woods.

They followed it for several minutes before stopping at a fork. The trees around them were huge, their branches woven into an elaborate web. A thick canopy of leaves blocked direct sunlight from reaching the forest floor, preventing smaller plants from growing. Without them, the boys could see deep into the forest. It seemed unending.

"Can you believe we're in Perkinsville?" Sam asked.

"I was thinking the same thing," Henry answered. "It's amazing no one has built here."

Milo nodded, silently.

"Which way?" Sam asked.

"*Two roads diverged in a yellow wood*," Henry said.

"Huh?"

"This way." He pointed to the path that was a bit less worn. "It may make all the difference."

They walked on through the forest, up a steep hill and down the other side. They rambled through a knoll of thick pine trees and came to a clearing where huge wedges of granite jutted out of the earth.

"Amazing," Henry said. "It looks like a boulder graveyard. I've never seen anything like it."

They passed between the rocks and reentered the woods on the other side.

"We might never find our way back," Sam said.

"I'm not too worried about it," Henry replied. "I have an excellent sense of direction."

"Really?"

"No."

Milo giggled. Sam was about to laugh along with him, but stopped. "Do you hear that?"

The faint gurgle of moving water drifted through the trees.

"Yes!" Henry said. "Come on!"

They ran toward the sound. Around the next bend, a wide river came into view. The water rushed downstream at a furious pace.

The boys stopped and stood on the bank, several feet above the river. At the other side, a sharp cliff rose straight up from the water. Like a great rock wall, it ran in either direction as far as the eye could see. To their left, a large slab of stone jutted out above the river, interrupting the cliff face. Perched on top of this jagged pulpit was the most magnificent tree Sam had ever laid eyes on.

It was a huge beech, rising from the stone as if by magic, the great trunk anchored in place by a tangle of knotted roots. From this, dozens of limbs extended over the water, their leaves waving gently in the breeze.

"Wow," Sam said, noticing the thick heavy weight of the branches, "that would be perfect for a…"

"…tree house." Milo finished his sentence.

They walked along the bank until they were directly across from it. "Do you think anyone else knows about this?" Henry asked. "Look at the size of it. It must be three hundred years old."

"I don't know," Sam said. "We're a long way from the main path, and I don't think anyone walks in the woods anyway."

"How can we get to it?" Henry wondered aloud.

"Good question." Sam scratched his head. "I doubt you could get up there from the water, even if you had a canoe or something."

"You're right," Henry said. He got down on his knees to get better look at the rock holding the tree. "I bet no one has ever climbed it…we shall be the first."

Milo walked to the edge of the water and considered the situation in silence. Sam picked up a stone and hurled it over the water. It snapped against the cliff and bounced back into the river. Milo looked to see what had made the splash.

After watching a second rock bounce into the water, he smiled and turned to the others. "I know how we can get there."

10

"We'll meet inside the woods at exactly 2:30," Sam said the next day at lunch.

He sat with Henry and Milo near the back of the cafeteria. Around them sixth, seventh and eighth graders munched on sandwiches and snapped pictures.

"Best to infiltrate the forest one at a time," Henry said. "Less chance of detection."

"Yeah, I get the feeling Ms. Snell wouldn't be too happy about us being in the woods," Sam said.

"Why?" Milo asked quietly.

"I don't know. I think she's...more of an indoor person."

Henry nodded in agreement.

"I'm really excited," Sam continued. "We just have to get through gym."

"Speaking of gym, can we head there a little early?" Henry asked. "I've got a bit of a problem."

"What is it?"

"Well...there used to be quite a bit of gum on the bottom of this table."

"Used to be?"

"Yes," Henry replied flatly. "It now resides on my left palm." He held up a hand covered in purple gunk.

"Yuck," Sam said.

Henry frowned. "Yuck indeed. Let's go find a sink. See you later, Milo."

They walked out of the bustling cafeteria and down a deserted hallway.

"There," Sam said pointing to a restroom door.

"Perfect," Henry said. "If I'm going to strike up a conversation with those two girls from gym, I certainly can't do it like this." He pulled open the bathroom door and went in.

"Are you just going to start talking to them?" Sam said, "Seems like—"

They both froze.

Several boys huddled together in front of the sinks. Cigarette smoke hung in the air. Sam's heart began to race. At the sound of the door closing, the group turned around. Max was at its center. Trent stood to his left, and to his right, to Sam's disbelief, was Roger.

The smokers glared coldly at Sam and Henry. Max took a step forward, placed a smoldering cigarette between his lips and inhaled deeply. He held the smoke in for a moment before blowing it forcefully into Sam's face. The hot, dirty air filled his nostrils, and he coughed violently.

"Get out," Max breathed. "Now."

They didn't need to be told twice. Henry opened the door with his gum-covered hand, and they rushed away.

"Were those the guys from the back of the bus?" Henry asked nervously.

"Yeah…and my used-to-be best friend."

Before going more than few paces, Mr. Fiddlesbee, the

ancient principal, turned down the hallway. Seeing their expressions of dismay, he stopped.

"Hello, boys. Is everything all right? Why aren't you at lunch?"

"We…ummm….er…" Sam mumbled.

"We were just using the bathroom," Henry said.

"Oh," Mr. Fiddlesbee nodded. "Great minds think alike. Have a good day boys." He smiled and strolled past them.

"Great minds think alike?" Sam whispered. "What does that mean?"

"It means," Henry, said grimly, "he's headed to the bathroom himself." Mr. Fiddlesbee pulled open the restroom door and disappeared inside.

"They'll think we told him," Sam said.

"Most likely," Henry agreed. "Oh well. Nothing to be done about it now. Serves them right. Come on. Let's go along."

Physical Education passed with no sign of Roger.

"You think they got in trouble?" Sam asked at the end of the period.

Henry nodded. "You got in trouble for *mentioning* a slingshot. I think smoking in the bathroom is a little worse. How many steps did you take?"

Sam looked down. The gym's Wi-Fi signal had been fixed and all the students now wore wristbands to monitor their heart rates and movements. The results were being transmitted, in real time, to the iPads. The class had been doing laps around the gym for 30 minutes.

"2754 steps," Sam answered.

"I got 2760," Henry said proudly.

"So?"

"That means I'm the better athlete."

"Why?"

"More steps. Hey, here they come."

The two girls from the first day approached.

"They must want to talk to us," Henry said.

"I think they're just putting their wristbands and iPads away."

The girls were only a few feet away. Henry suddenly spoke loudly. "DID YOU HEAR I TOOK 2760 STEPS TODAY, SAM?"

Sam stared at his friend in horror.

"THAT'S RIGHT, *2760* STEPS!"

The girls walked past without slowing down.

Henry lowered his voice. "You think they heard me?"

"It would have been hard not to."

"Excellent. I'm sure they were impressed. Next time, we figure out their names. Come on let's go."

The boys went back to Ms. Snell's room and typed the nightly homework assignment into their portals without incident.

"The hour is finally upon us," Henry whispered, as they left the classroom. "Let's take a few laps around the building while people clear out. Throw off any tails."

"You think someone might be tailing us?"

"Seems unlikely. But, you never know, Sam. You just…never know."

Fifteen minutes later, when the hallways were empty, the boys slipped out a back door and crept towards the woods. Inside the forest, Milo was waiting with a bulging backpack.

"Hey," Sam said with a grin. "Sorry we're late. Henry's paranoid."

"*Cautious*," Henry corrected him. "Henry is cautious. You need me to carry anything?"

Milo smiled and shook his head.

"Alright then," Henry murmured. "Off we go." They

crept into the shadowy forest without another word.

There was crispness in the air that hadn't been there the day before and every few steps a dying leaf spiraled down from above. By the time they reached the river, the sun had started to set.

Milo put the pack down on the riverbank and gazed across the water to the beech tree. He knelt, unzipped the bag, and reached inside.

The green canvas was faded and several patches were sewn into the sides. Along one strap the letters M-I-L-N-E-R were written in faded letters. His last name, Sam realized. Milo rummaged around for a moment before pulling out a ball of twine and a baseball so old and filthy, Babe Ruth might have used it.

"Couldn't we just use a rock?" Henry asked.

Milo shook his head. "Baseballs have cork centers. They float."

Henry looked puzzled. "I must confess, I find myself confused. It made sense earlier. Can you go over the whole thing again?"

Milo sat down and placed the baseball in his lap, then took up the string and lassoed the ball in a complex web of knots.

"Okay," Sam said. "I'll explain. As you can see, Milo is tying a line onto the baseball."

Henry nodded his understanding.

"I'm going to throw the ball across the river and when I do, the line will trail behind it."

"Yes," Henry said. "I understand that. How do we retrieve it though?"

Sam gestured across the water. "If we're lucky, the ball will loop over that branch, bounce off the cliff and come back. If we can fish the baseball out of the river, we'll have a direct link to the tree."

"But what good is a string? It won't hold us."

"That's just part one. I'll explain part two if we get that far."

"Alright," Henry said. "Onward we go."

When the last knot was tied, Sam took it and walked to the edge of the water. Behind him, Henry unwound a long length of string. The ledge of rock holding the tree was about fifty feet away, roughly eight feet above the water. Sam studied it carefully and trained his eyes on a low hanging branch adjacent to the cliff face.

"Ready when you are," Henry reported. "All systems go."

Sam focused on his target and heaved the ball with all his might. It sailed high into the air, out over the water, the long tail of twine racing behind it. Halfway to the tree it started to fall. "Come on, come on," Sam whispered, "come onnnn….YES!"

The ball just barely cleared the branch before colliding with the cliff. With a loud crack it ricocheted off the rock and shot back towards the boys.

"Here it comes!" Henry yelled. The ball landed in the middle of the river, diving into the dark water like a torpedo. At first, Sam was sure it was lost. Then the buoyant force of the cork center took over and the white sphere popped to the surface. With the momentum of the collision still propelling it, the ball drifted through the water, back towards the boys. The strong current was also at work, forcing it downstream.

Milo bolted past the floundering ball, to a place where the riverbank sloped toward the water, and laid out on his stomach. "Grab my legs," he commanded.

Sam and Henry did as they were told, holding tightly to Milo's jeans as he wriggled forward and hung out over the water. The ball churned toward them, only a few feet away.

"Lower me more," Milo urged. Sam looked at Henry, whose face was already getting red. He was afraid they would drop Milo into the river. "I'll be okay, just a little further."

Using all their strength, Sam and Henry inched Milo further down the bank. He stretched out over the swirling water, his arm extended to its fullest. The ball was inches away. Milo lunged forward dragging the boys to the edge of the bank.

Sam was losing his grip. He couldn't hold on any longer.

"Pull me up! Pull me up!" Milo cried.

Sam and Henry threw themselves backwards and yanked Milo up over the side of the bank where the three of them collapsed in a heap.

"Did…you…get it?" Henry managed to gasp.

Milo stuck his hand in the air. It clutched the swollen ball. The string was still there, held by a single thin thread.

The boys ran breathlessly back up the riverbank until they were opposite the tree. The thin strand of string now ran from the coil at their feet, up and out across the river, around a branch and back again. It was a direct link to the beech tree. Water droplets shimmered on the thread like crystals.

"Part two?" Henry asked.

"Part two," Sam answered. "Do your work, Milo."

Milo handed the ball off to Henry and walked over to his backpack. He reached inside and produced a coil of thick white rope.

"Where in the world did you get all that?" Sam asked. "There's got to be 100 feet there."

Milo shrugged. "I just had it. Can I have the baseball back?"

Henry handed him the ball and watched with fascination as Milo untied the twine and retied it to one of the rope ends.

"Okay," Sam explained. "Right now we have a string that goes from here, out around that branch and back. We're going to use it to get this rope in place. Let's give it a try."

The rope was laid carefully on the ground and slowly, very slowly, Milo began to wind up the free end of the twine. As he pulled one end of the string in, the other end was pulled out taking the rope with it. It was the same setup as the line and pulley on a flagpole. With each tug, the rope slithered further down the riverbank until it disappeared into the water.

The twine cut through the swirling current, dragging the rope behind it. Milo continued to carefully wind until the strangled rope breached the surface. It climbed slowly from the depths, higher and higher, finally making contact with the smooth bark of the tree.

The string was so taut now, with the weight of the rope, Sam was certain it would snap. But with one smooth pull, Milo sent the rope over the branch and back towards the swirling currents below. Sam and Henry cheered loudly. Milo continued to wind and, remarkably, the end of the rope was soon securely in his hands.

"What now?" Henry asked.

They watched as Milo tied a loop at one end of the rope and fed the other end through its center. As he continued to pull, the looped end was forced back towards the tree where it constricted around the limb.

Henry shook his head. "Brilliant."

The design worked perfectly. Within minutes, one end of the rope was in Milo's hands and the other attached securely to the beech tree.

"Let's tie it off," Milo said, unable to mask the excitement in his voice. But when the boys tugged the rope backwards towards the nearest tree, they discovered, to their horror, it was too short.

"So close," Sam said with disappointment.

Henry slumped to the ground. "Curses! What are we going to do now?"

Milo, who was still holding the rope, looked back across the river to the beech tree. "If we could move the other knot out a little further on that branch, we'd have enough."

Henry sighed. "Milo, you've done some amazing things here. But I don't think there's any way we can move that knot from way over here."

"Nope," Milo said shaking his head. "You're right. Two of us need to hold the rope while the other goes over and moves it."

"Are you mad?" Henry said with wide eyes. "If one of us fell in that current we'd never get out. We'd drown."

Milo nodded slowly. "It's the only way."

Henry stared at him in disbelief, then looked to Sam, who said nothing.

"I can't do it," Milo said. "The rope is going to sag and I won't be able to pull myself up the last few feet. I'm not strong enough." He stared down at the ground. The boys were silent. The only sounds came from the river in front of them and the forest at their backs.

Sam looked at the rope in Milo's hands. For years he'd dreamed of the chance for an adventure. Here it was. "I'll do it," he whispered.

Henry opened his mouth to object, but seeing Sam's expression he stopped and considered his new friend carefully. "Yes," he said, "Yes! *Our doubts are traitors, and make us lose the good we oft might win by fearing to attempt!* On my sacred honor, Sam, I shall not let go of that rope. You will not fall!"

Sam grinned and saluted the others.

The plan was simple. Henry and Milo would hold the line while Sam shimmied across the river. He decided it would be easiest to cling to the rope using both his hands *and* feet. At the edge of the riverbank, he laid down on this back. "Okay," he said, "Pull it tight."

Henry and Milo struggled backward with the rope until it was taut.

"Try that," Henry said.

Sam wrapped his legs around the line and pulled up with both hands, lifting himself off the ground. The rope sagged, but didn't give way. He tipped his head back and surveyed the tree upside down. It looked miles away. His heart began to pound.

"You can do it, Sam!" Henry declared.

With great concentration, he released his left hand and moved it further along the line. He repeated the process with his right, then his left again. His head was over the river, then his torso, then his whole body. He could hear the water rushing by only a few feet below.

Sam continued until he was halfway across. By then, his arms and legs ached. He stopped to catch his breath, but it did little to help his tired muscles. He had to keep going. As he slid his hands further along the line, he happened to look back to the riverbank. What he saw made his heart sink.

Henry and Milo had turned shades of dark red. Even from his position over the water, it was clear they were in pain. Both their chests heaved in and out.

And then he felt it. A nearly imperceptible movement. Just enough to register in his fingertips. The rope was beginning to slip.

For a split second he glanced down at the dark water. It looked eager to swallow him up, to pull him relentlessly downstream to the rapids. He considered going back, but then he saw the tree. Basking in the afternoon sun, it seemed to challenge him forward. He somehow knew that to turn back would mean losing the tree forever.

Sam focused every ounce of concentration on the rope above him and once more began to move. Hand over hand he pulled himself along the thin line. He could sense with every movement, the rope slipping towards the water, but he did not look back. He was dimly conscious of a change in angle as he moved upward, away from the water, towards the branches.

Then, with a sudden jolt, the rope dropped from beneath him. His body swung forward and he knew all had been lost. But he was jerked violently to a stop, as if the loose end of the rope had found some new anchor.

He dared a glance back to the far shore, realizing immediately what had happened. Milo's legs had given out and he'd gone down. Henry had been jerked forward, but had somehow managed to stop himself. He now held the weight of the entire operation in his hands. Henry was no longer looking at the ground. His head was up. His eyes were locked on Sam, and his entire body was shaking. There wasn't much time left.

Sam went faster, moving up the line by the force of will power alone. He was level with the rock ledge, then the roots of the tree. He moved higher. The rope itself was now twitching.

On the riverbank, blood trickled down Henry's hands, burned from his flesh when the rope had been ripped forward. He looked crazed, drained.

Milo opened his eyes and tried to stand and help his

friend, but he was too late. Henry collapsed, his muscles finally giving out. He held onto the line, like he'd promised, as it dragged them over onto the ground. Exhausted, they tried to get up, eager to pull their friend from the water. But the sound of a splash never came.

They looked up and across the river.

Sam Torwey sat on a thick branch of the beech tree, grinning from ear to ear.

11

By the time Sam regained enough strength to climb up to where the rope was tied, the sun was low in the sky. It took a great deal of yanking to loosen the knot and slide it further out.

"Try it now," he yelled across the river.

"Yeah!" Henry called back. "It'll work!" His voice still sounded weak.

"Okay. Tie it off. Should I try and come back?"

"No!" Henry yelled. "Milo has a plan!"

Sam watched as Milo removed something that looked like a playground swing from his backpack. It wasn't a normal playground swing. A large pulley had been secured to the top.

"What's that for?!"

"You'll see!"

Milo slipped the pulley onto the rope before tying it off. Sam realized what he was up to. "Zip-line…"

Milo and Henry squeezed onto the seat and, hand over hand, pulled themselves across the river. A few minutes later, they stood next to Sam. "Unbelievable! What a great idea!" He raised his hand for a high five. Milo slapped his palm, but when Henry held back, Sam noticed the bubbling blisters covering his hands.

Seeing Sam's expression, Henry laughed. "It was worth it. What's more, I don't have any good scars."

"Thanks for holding on," Sam said.

"Don't mention it."

"Where did you get that swing and pulley?"

"I dunno," Milo said. "I just…had it."

"Is there some way to move the seat from one side to the other, or does one of us have to bring it each time?"

"We'll use the twine for a recall line. We can tie it to the seat and then pull it back and forth."

"Awesome." Sam looked up. The branches seemed to rise above them forever. "You want to do some climbing?"

"Maybe not today," Milo said quietly. "It's getting late."

"I guess you're right. Henry's hands need some rest anyway."

"I have a few more layers of skin," Henry said. "But if you insist, I suppose it can wait."

Milo tied the recall line in place, got up on the swing and glided across the river. Henry pulled the seat back and did the same.

"That's much easier," Sam said when they all had crossed.

"And really fun," Henry added.

Before they left the riverbank, Sam looked out over the water again. The line hung like the lone filament of a spider's web, a thin black silhouette in the hollow twilight of the canyon. He smiled and followed his companions into the woods.

The lawn outside the school was completely vacant

and the building was dark. "How are you getting home?" Henry asked.

"I was gonna call my mom," Sam replied, "but it looks like the school's closed."

"We can give you a ride."

"Are you sure?" Sam asked.

"Of course. What about you Milo?"

Milo looked down. "I have my bike."

"You ride your bike to school?" Henry asked in astonishment. Noticing Milo's reddening cheeks, he added, "That's cool. But it's getting dark and my mom has a van, so we can fit your bike in. No problem."

"It's okay. Don't worry about it."

"Really. I insist."

Milo shrugged. "Alright."

There was a lone van in the school driveway. "There she is," Henry said. "Do you know what time it is? I think I'm really late." He was right. When they got to the car, the driver's door opened and Henry's mom got out.

"Henrrrry," she said with raised eyebrows. "You're half an hour late. Is anyone else even here? Please tell me you were doing homework."

"Errrr…sorry about that," Henry said sheepishly.

His mother frowned. "I don't like it. I don't like it one bit. Who are your friends?"

"This is Milo and Sam. I offered them rides home."

"Oh, wonderful," she chirped, face brightening. "Hello boys. It's a pleasure to meet you. Climb on in."

Milo looked at Henry with an expression of uncertainty.

"Oh right. Yes. We just have to load Milo's bike," Henry said.

Mrs. Delmont raised her eyebrows again and sighed. "Okay, well hurry up. It's getting late, and I need to start dinner."

Milo walked over to a forlorn rack beside the school and retrieved a bike with a ripped seat and no grips. It was covered in rust. Sam and Henry helped him lift it into the van before piling in themselves.

"So, how was school today?" Mrs. Delmont asked.

"Oh fine," Henry answered casually. "Nothing much out of the ordinary." He winked at his friends.

"Why do I even ask? Milo, where do you live?"

Milo hesitated before answering.

"Over near Hidner Park," he said finally.

"Oh," Mrs. Delmont said. "Okay."

Sam had never been to Hidner Park but he'd driven by it a few times. The park itself was overgrown with an old slide and some swings. He remembered hearing his dad say it was no place for kids anymore.

As they got closer, the buildings became increasingly dilapidated and Mrs. Delmont again asked for directions.

"It's just up here on the left," Milo said softly. "That blue one."

Henry's mom stopped the van in front of a small blue home. Though rather tired looking, it was the nicest house on the block. Sam and Henry started to get up to help with the bike, but Mrs. Delmont raised a hand in protest. "That's alright," she said. "I've got it."

Milo climbed out and helped unload the bike. He turned to Henry and Sam and gave them a wave. "See you guys later."

Mrs. Delmont got back in the van and started the engine, but didn't drive away. Sam noticed her looking out the window at Milo, who still stood at the curb. He raised his hand and waved a second time, but Mrs. Delmont stayed put. She reached for the door latch and looked like she was going to get out again, when Milo suddenly turned and wheeled his bicycle slowly down the narrow driveway. This seemed to satisfy her, and they drove away.

"What was that about, Mom?" Henry asked.

"Hmm?" she murmured. "What was what about?"

"Never mind," Henry said. Sam had been wondering the same thing.

"Now, I'm not exactly sure where we are," she said, "but I think we want to go this way." They turned down an abandoned street. A few moments later, they turned down another. Soon they were lost.

"There should be a sign for the freeway around here somewhere," Mrs. Delmont said. "We can take that back to the other side of town."

They turned again. "Henry, get my phone out and plug in our home address"

"Siri" began to talk and directed them down another deserted street. Sam looked out the window and studied the crumbling buildings, hoping they were close to the freeway. As they stopped at a traffic light, he glanced down a side street and was shocked to see a small boy riding a rusty bike along the darkened sidewalk. He had a huge canvas backpack slung over his shoulders.

Milo turned down off the sidewalk and down an alley. A sign of twisted metal hung overhead. It was meant to be illuminated, but all the bulbs were smashed or missing. Sam could just barely make out what it said: Milner Auto Salvage.

By the time the light changed, Milo had disappeared into the darkness.

12

"Are you sure it was him?" Henry asked the next morning on the bus.

"Positive," Sam replied. "He still had the backpack on."

"That's strange. I wonder why he didn't just have us drop him off there?"

"If you had seen it," Sam said, "you'd understand. It was kind of creepy. It looked like it was going to fall down."

"I guess maybe his family doesn't have a lot of money. Don't mention it to him. He would have said something if he wanted us to know."

Sam nodded.

"Anyway..." Henry went on, lowering his voice, "are we going back out there today?"

Sam was happy to change the subject. "Definitely. We need to figure out how to get supplies across the river so we can start building the tree house. We should tell Mr. Arthur our plan and see what he says."

Henry looked concerned. "Do you think he'll tell us

it's against the rules?"

Sam shook his head. "For some reason I think he'll really like the idea."

"Not if he knows we've been dangling over a rushing river," Henry countered

"You're right. Even he might say that was a little dangerous."

"Luckily," Henry said coolly. "Danger is my middle name."

"Really?

"No. It's Alfred."

Sam laughed loudly.

Suddenly, a voice spoke from somewhere behind them.

"Sounds like we got a couple of comedians up there!"

Sam stopped laughing and looked nervously at Henry. They waited a moment, before deciding the comment had been intended for someone else.

"My mom can pick us up later," Sam said. "Since your mom picked us—"

"Hey!" the voice called again. "Tell us the joke funny guys!"

"I think they're talking to us," Henry said quietly.

Sam turned slowly around.

"Yeah, you!" Max sat high on the back of the very last seat. Trent smiled evilly beside him.

The bus fell silent.

"I mean, I knew you were tattle-tales," Max called, "but I didn't know you were tattle-tale comedians… until I heard all that laughing. I like to laugh." He turned to his friend. "Trent, do *you* like to laugh?"

"Yeah, Max. I *love* to laugh."

Sam's heart began to pound.

"What's the joke, boys? What's so funny?"

"We love jokes!" Trent shouted.

Sam and Henry sat frozen in the vinyl seat. The whole bus was silent.

Sam started to sweat. "What are we going to do?" he whispered to Henry. "We can't just sit here."

"Maybe we can make them laugh? Do you know any hilarious jokes?"

"Are you nuts?! We're not going to make them laugh."

"Do you have any better ideas? They think we reported them for smoking yesterday."

"Oh boyyyys," Max called again, "everyone is waiting."

"Maybe we could just stand up and say we didn't?" Sam suggested.

Henry considered the idea. "Yes. That might at least get them to back down. Let's give it a try."

Slowly, they stood. Only six rows separated them from the eighth graders. Roger sat at Max's feet, grinning.

"Oh look, the funny guys have a joke ready," Max announced. "You gettin' this Trent?"

Trent had his cell phone pointed towards the front of the bus. He was recording the whole thing.

Sam opened his mouth, but no words came out. Henry came to his rescue.

"We didn't tell on you," he declared in a surprisingly steady voice, "and we're completely out of jokes. You'll have to…to ask someone else." They turned to sit down, hoping the standoff was over.

"Whoa, whoa, whoa. That's it?" Max cried. "I thought you were funny." Sam looked, again, to the back of the bus. The eighth grader reached into his bag. Trent handed the cell phone off to Roger and did the same.

"These kids wanna see something funny." Max glared at Sam. "You're not gonna show them something funny?"

"No. And we didn't tell on you." Sam forced the words out as loudly as he could.

"Okay, okay," Max said calmly. "I guess I gotta do it. You know what's funny?" Sam and Henry remained silent. "This," Max said, "is funny."

The eighth graders' arms shot forward.

From the blur, two projectiles were released. They flew over the heads of the students like missiles and slammed into their targets.

SLAP! SLAP!

Sam's chest was suddenly wet. He looked down to find what had once been a tuna fish sandwich smashed into the top of his shirt. Oily goop seeped onto his skin. Chunks of mayonnaise-covered fish were everywhere.

The bus erupted in laughter. The driver stared straight ahead, earbuds in, rocking back and forth to the music.

Sam turned to his companion. Henry looked like he'd been hit in the face with an egg salad water balloon. It filled his mouth and nostrils. It dripped down his glasses in yellow rivulets. A soggy bun stuck to his hair.

The roar of laughter was deafening.

"Told you it'd be funny!" Max yelled.

Sam and Henry slumped down into the seat.

Henry took a sweatshirt from his backpack and mopped up as much of the egg salad as possible, before handing the shirt over to Sam. They sat in silence until arriving at the school. Snickers and pointing followed them off the bus and into the building.

"You can bet they won't mess with me again," Max boasted.

"That was hilarious," Trent added. "Losers!"

Sam spotted the sunken face of Mr. Dean in the lobby, bobbing between the heads of students.

"Over there," he said. "Maybe he can help us?"

"Isn't that the guy you crashed into the other day?" Henry asked weakly.

"Yeah, but he's still a teacher."

Mr. Dean spotted the filthy pair, recoiled in disgust, and continued on without a word.

"Did you see that?" someone said from behind. "Even the *teacher* doesn't want to go near them."

"Get a picture!"

The taunting finally subsided when they reached the second floor. They stopped to assess the damage. Sam's white shirt was a collage of stains, most of them varying shades of yellow. Henry's looked the same.

"You have something on your nose," Sam said.

Henry frowned and wiped away a brownish glob. "What do we do now?"

"I don't know. What *can* we do? Go in I guess."

Henry pulled open the door and walked into the classroom. Sam sat at his computer terminal and stared down at the keyboard, not wanting to see or talk to anyone else.

"Samuel." Ms. Snell's voice made him cringe. "May I see you at my desk please?" He decided to pretend he hadn't heard her.

"Samuel," she repeated. "My desk." There was no avoiding it. He walked wearily to the desk. She looked him over and shook her head. "You need to go down to the nurse's office and change into different clothes."

"But Ms. Snell, it wasn't my fault—"

"We are working with expensive pieces of equipment. I can't risk you ruining them with this…this mess."

"I didn't come to school like this! Look at Henry…We—"

"There are spare clothes in the nurse's office. You can take Henry with you." She smiled. "Once you've cleaned up, we can discuss what happened."

At the nurse's office, a flat-faced woman sat staring at a computer screen. A placard on her desk read *Nurse Francine.* Her expression instantly turned from boredom to disgust at the sight of the boys. Without a word, she pointed to a cardboard box at the other side of the room. It was labeled *SPARE CLOTHES.*

Sam and Henry wandered over and peered into it. A lump of faded clothing lay at the bottom. Henry leaned down and took it out.

"Oh dear," he said quietly, peeling apart the mound and handing items to Sam.

On top, were a pair of bright red sweat pants, a plaid skirt and a sweater that Nurse Francine might have once knitted. Below these, a pink tee shirt bearing the words *Perkinsville Flower Show-1989* sat beside an enormous flannel shirt. A white tank top with mold stains on the neck lay wrinkled at the bottom.

Henry shook his head. "This is turning into a catastrophe of monumental proportions." He turned to the nurse. "Excuse me Nurse Francine, do you have any other clothes? These aren't going to…err…fit."

"That's all there is," she said with disinterest. "It's not a fashion show."

Henry gritted his teeth in frustration. Sam picked up the red sweatpants. They would only go down to his knees.

Henry suddenly leaned in and spoke in a whisper. "I just had a brilliant idea. Follow my lead." Sam nodded.

"Err…Nurse Francine?" He hobbled to the desk. "I'm still not feeling very well. I think I might *vomit* again."

Sam's eyes lit up in amazement. At the word 'vomit,' the nurse sprang from her chair and backed into a corner.

"Yeah me too," Sam groaned. "I knew I shouldn't

have come to school today."

"*That's* what's all over you?!"

The boys nodded weakly.

"Why didn't you say so?! You have to leave! Immediately! You're going to get me sick! Why would you come to school like—"

Sam and Henry stared at her in surprise.

"I…I mean… I mean…I'm *so* sorry you're not feeling well…but you *cannot* be at school after…after vomiting."

"Oh…yes," Henry moaned turning to Sam, "we should go home."

"What are your names? I need to call your parents. We really do need to act quickly."

Henry looked at her with despair. "My mom drove us in. She's probably still outside."

"Well does she have a cell phone?" Francine asked desperately.

"Yes… yes…can I call her?"

"Of course! Of course! Quickly!" she waved wildly to a phone on a table near the boys.

Henry picked it up and dialed a number. He hunched over, as if standing were too much for him.

"Mom," he whispered, after a few seconds, "it's me… Henry. I couldn't make it. I got sick again." He coughed weakly. The nurse recoiled. Henry looked sadly up at her. She tried to force a sympathetic smile, but failed.

"Sam must have caught it, Mom. He…well… I'm not sure how to say this…he *upchucked* all over himself." Sam stuck a finger into his mouth and bit down on the knuckle to stifle a laugh.

"Thanks, Mom. Can you take Sam, too?" Henry looked at his friend. "You'll try not to spew all over the car won't you?"

Sam nodded innocently.

"He won't," Henry went on. "No, that's okay. Don't come in. We'll wait outside, just in case the nausea seizes us again. We don't want to leave Nurse Francine with a mess."

Henry hung up the phone and the nurse began to douse it with disinfectant. "Better…uh…move along now boys. Time to go."

"We will," Henry moaned. "We will. But there's another sick student who should come with us. We were together last night."

The nurse looked very pale.

"Who? What's his name? Did he throw up too?!"

"I'm not sure," Henry whispered. "If he hasn't yet, it won't be long. He's in sixth grade, not sure what class." Henry started to convulse.

"I'll call him! I'll call him! Just get outside! What's his last name?!"

Henry turned to Sam.

"Milner," Sam said, remembering the backpack. "Milo Milner. Please hurry." He hunched over in feigned agony.

"Go! Go! I'll tell him you'll be outside. Just go!"

Sam and Henry limped from the room. Outside they burst into laughter before sitting down at the base of the huge statue to wait for Milo.

"That," Sam said, "was incredible."

"One of my more brilliant ideas," Henry agreed.

Before long, Milo wandered out the front door, backpack bulging on his shoulders. He looked utterly confused and scanned the driveway for an explanation. When Sam and Henry stepped out from their hiding place, his eyes widened in amazement.

"To the tree!" Henry proclaimed, raising a fist in the air. "We'll explain on the way."

Milo didn't need to be convinced. He hopped down

the steps and followed his friends around the side of the school without any questions.

As they made their way through the woods towards the path, Sam relayed the morning's events. Milo didn't say anything, but looked angry when he heard what had happened on the bus.

"They filmed the whole thing. That's the worst part."

"How?" Milo asked. "And why? Why would they do that?"

"Cell phone," Henry said. "They think we told on them for smoking in the bathroom. We walked in on them yesterday."

"Did you?"

"Of course not," Sam said. "Mr. Fiddlesbee, the principal, just happened to find them."

"It was rotten thing to do," Henry said. "Literally rotten, judging by the way I smell. But at least it got us a day away from Ms. Snell and the Student Portal. You think the rope will still be there?"

"It'll be there," Sam replied. "No question."

They quickened their pace and a few moments later walked off the path towards the sound of the river. The zip-line hung in place.

"Let's add another length of twine," Milo said, taking off his backpack and reaching inside. "That way we can pull the seat back and forth both ways."

With the new recall line in place, Sam crossed the river first. Henry pulled the seat back, and followed. Milo went last.

"Come on," Sam said. "Let's climb up and find a spot for the tree house." Together they moved up through the thick branches until they were high above the water.

"I'm going to stop here for a second," Henry said halfway up the tree.

"Me too," Milo said. "I need a rest."

Sam was too excited to stop and continued skyward until he could go no higher. The view was incredible. A mosaic of treetops spread out before him in all directions. The highest spire of the school was just visible in the distance. It seemed miles away.

"You guys gotta get up here," he shouted down to the others.

"I'm quite comfortable here," Henry called back.

Milo gazed up through the branches, but didn't move.

"Suit yourselves, but you're missing out! It's a perfect place for a tree house!"

Two thick branches forked out from the tree at exactly the same height. They were perfectly smooth except for a single round knot protruding from the branch nearest Sam. He climbed onto it and started out towards the knot.

"What on earth are you doing?" Henry shouted.

"I just want to check something out." He crept further out and looked down at the knot. "That's weird…"

The bark between his thighs was gray and smooth. Smoother even, than the bark on the trunk. The knot, however, was darker and covered with gouges and cuts.

"The wind must have torn a smaller branch right off," he thought.

"Sam," Henry called. "Come back down here. We're going to discuss the fort!"

"Okay!" he yelled. "I definitely found the spot for it!"

13

The boys spent the rest of the morning high in the tree, planning the fort and laughing about their escape from school.

"I wonder what Ms. Snell did when she found out we got sent home?" Sam said.

"Let's hope she did nothing," Henry answered. "We aren't exactly her favorites. I bet she just went on with her day. Milo, what did your teacher say?"

Milo shrugged. "I don't think he noticed me leave. I don't even think he knows my name. I have Mr. Dean. Do you know who he is?"

"Yeah," Sam said. "We saw him this morning. He didn't even care about all the kids making fun of us."

"He doesn't seem to like kids," Milo replied. "Makes you wonder what he's doing here."

"Hey," Henry said, looking down at his watch. "It's almost time for Industrial Arts. Want to sneak in the back way and tell Mr. Arthur about the tree house?"

"Hmmm," said Sam, "I don't know if that's such a good—"

"Let's do it," Milo said suddenly.

Henry grinned. "Off to Industrial Arts we go!"

They crossed the river and headed back to the school.

"This is my kind of school day," Sam said. "Tree house in the morning, Industrial Arts in the afternoon."

"Me too," Henry agreed. "Maybe we should ask Max to throw food at us more often. Look, there's the school. How are we going to get in?"

"Not sure. Let's get a little closer." They crouched on all fours and crawled through the underbrush to the edge of the lawn.

Sam pointed to a set of double doors at the back of the building. "I'm pretty sure those lead to the Pit. See? There's some scrap metal piled beside them."

"Do you suppose they're open?" Henry asked.

"I hope so. If we run out there and can't get in, someone will probably see us. It's the middle of the day."

"What do you think, Milo? "

Milo didn't answer. He had unzipped his backpack and was rummaging around inside.

"Let's go for it," Sam said. "We've had good luck so far."

Henry grinned. "*Fortune sides with him who dares.* Milo, are you ready?"

"Almost," he said. "I just have to find—here it is. I'm ready."

Milo pulled a twisted piece of wire from the depths of his backpack and slipped it into his pocket.

"What's that for?"

"Just in case."

"In case what?'

"Never mind. Let's just go."

"Okay," Henry said. "On three. One…two…three…"

The boys burst from the shrubbery and sprinted

across the lawn. They skidded to a halt in front of the double doors. Sam grabbed one of the handles and pulled. The door didn't budge.

"It's locked," he whispered.

Henry tugged the other handle. Nothing happened. "We've got to get back to the forest!"

A bell rang inside the building. Hundreds of students and teachers would be moving between classes. "Let's go!" Henry cried. "Someone is going to see us!"

"Wait!" Milo jumped in front of the others. He pulled out the twisted piece of wire, bent the ends together and stuck them into one of the knobs.

"What the—"

He moved the wire back and forth until there was a soft click, then twisted the wire to the right and, miraculously, pulled open the door.

Sam and Henry dashed into the building behind him. They slammed the door shut and slumped to the ground.

"We made it," Henry gasped. "We made it."

"How…" Sam said, "How did you get that door opened?"

"That's…what I was wondering." They froze. Mr. Arthur stared at them from the entrance to the Pit.

For a few seconds, no one spoke. The boys looked up in terror. He looked right back with a frown.

Then, his face relaxed. He sighed, took out a key, and relocked the door. "Nobody's talking huh? Well, I guess it's better not to answer some questions. Come on now, time to get to work." With that, he turned and limped back into the shop.

"I have no idea what just happened," Sam said.

"Nor do I," agreed Henry. They both looked at Milo. He grinned, shrugged and walked after Mr. Arthur.

Sam and Henry managed to measure and cut exactly one piece of wood in the sixty-minute period that followed. Milo worked much faster.

"Where did he learn to use all these machines?" Sam asked.

Henry shook his head. "How did he learn to pick locks? That's what I want to know. You think he'll teach us? I mean it's a good skill to have. Great for a résumé."

"I bet he'd teach us. Let's ask him."

Before they could, Mr. Arthur shuffled over. "Looks like things are moving right along gentlemen. Any questions?"

Henry nudged Sam. "Tree house," he mouthed.

"Oh right…yeah…well, we were wondering about our next project?"

"Next project? You just started your footstool. You have a long way to go. Finish that and then we'll talk about your next project." He started to hobble away, but stopped. "Just out of curiosity, what did you have in mind?"

"A tree house," Henry said.

Sam looked at Mr. Arthur's face, trying hard to read his expression. He couldn't.

"Tree house, eh? Now where'd you get an idea like that?"

No one answered. "Why do I get the feeling this is somehow tied to your bizarre entrance?"

No one spoke.

"Well, let me think. There's no question every kid your age should have a tree house. Not a bad project. But there aren't any trees in here, and it needs to be done during school. Where you plan on building it?"

Sam and Henry looked at each other. "We found a tree in the woods that would work," Henry said.

"Oh yeah? Been exploring the grounds have you? Hmmm, well I suppose there's plenty to explore. Doesn't happen near enough."

The boys waited for him to continue.

"You know? I kind of like the idea. You could build the tough parts here, then bring them out to your tree." He looked up. "I don't suppose you want to tell me where it is?"

Again, no one spoke.

"Didn't think so. I guess it's probably better that way…okay…that's what we'll do. You work hard on these projects. If they turn out halfway decent, we'll see about a tree house. Now get back to class."

The boys didn't move. They couldn't go back to class.

"What's the matter?" Mr. Arthur studied them with narrowed eyes for what seemed like an eternity. "You know," he finally said, "I just remembered, I actually need to leave that backdoor unlocked. Just in case there's a delivery or something." He took a key from his pocket and handed it to Henry. "Would you unlock it for me? Just leave the key in the knob. I need to go to my office now. I'll see you boys later." He limped away.

"Did he just give us permission to slip out the backdoor?" Sam whispered.

"I think so," Henry said. "Come on. Let's get out of here before the bell rings."

14

As the days marched on, Mr. Arthur's class and the tree house were the only beacons of hope in an otherwise dismal school year.

The mornings began with taunting on the bus.

"What's for lunch today boys?" Max might yell, or "How about a little more egg salad?"

After that, they headed to homeroom, where things weren't much better. They sat at their desks during Ms. Snell's boring lessons, then moved to the computer terminals, completing assignments and uploading them to the student portal. Next, they reviewed work done by others and posted comments for everyone to see.

"Have you noticed that Missy15 comments on everything we do…and it's always bad?" Sam asked Henry one morning.

"Yeah. Ever since the slingshot conversation, she's been out to get you. Her friend Margot isn't much better. Look at this." Sam leaned over to Henry's screen. He'd just posted an essay entitled *Why Winter is the Best Season.* Below it, a comment blinked red.

Margot24: Henry, in this essay you mention going sledding at the town golf course. Are you even a member of the golf course? Have you considered what would happen if you got hurt? Who would be held responsible? You need to remember that actions have consequences.

Missy15 had liked the comment. So had Ms. Snell.

"I've never even gone sledding at the golf course. I simply suggested it might be fun."

Sam looked across the room. Margot and Missy pounded furiously away on their keyboards. "Probably posting more comments," he muttered.

"Yup," Henry said. "Look."

Below Margot's comment, another had appeared.

Missy15: I agree with Margot24. Henry needs to think more carefully about his actions.

"What an idiot," Sam whispered. "Here, I'll like your post." He clicked the like button. "There. I did it."

Henry frowned. "You liked Margot's comment."

In gym class, they continued tracking their exercise with fitness bracelets. They had graduated from walking laps and moved on to floor exercises. These, as it turned out, were just as boring. Some of the students asked for group games but were quickly discouraged.

It had taken a great deal of eavesdropping, but Henry had finally learned the names of the girls they'd noticed on the first day. Unfortunately, that was all.

"We need activities that can be tracked by fitness apps," Mr. Montero declared one afternoon. "You can track sit-ups. You can't track Keep Ball-ieving."

"How am I supposed to get Ali to notice me," Henry said softly, "if all we do is sit-ups? I mean, yes, my sit-up form is perfect. Don't get me wrong. But she just doesn't notice."

"Which one is Ali again? Does she have the red hair?" Sam pointed across the gym.

"No. No. That's Candace. She's a much better match for you. Ali is the one with glasses. I think I may be in love with her."

"You've never spoken to her."

"It's love at first sight, Sam. Not first sound."

All in all, Sam was disappointed with the way things were going at Perkinsville Middle School Public. But the tree house kept him going, that, and Industrial Arts.

He'd managed to finish the footstool, and though it wasn't perfect, he was proud of the result. Henry felt the same way about his bookshelf. "Sure it's crooked. No big deal. Gives it character," he said. "I think it's actually better that way."

Milo's birdhouse was a different story. Though infinitely more complex than the other projects, it was perfect, a true work of art. The flagpoles, the turrets, all of it was flawless.

Even Mr. Arthur was impressed. "Where did you learn to do that? I never taught you to inlay patterns."

"I don't know," Milo said quietly. "Just kind of figured it out."

With their furniture complete, the shop teacher began explaining the basics of tree house construction. Each class began in front of a big rolling chalkboard, with the shop teacher drawing diagrams and explaining building concepts. When he finished, the boys went to work.

For weeks, Henry and Sam measured wood for Milo to cut and drill. Every afternoon, they snuck it into the forest and down to the riverbank. When they had enough material, they began the process of ferrying it across the zip line to the tree. It was painstakingly slow work, but

Sam loved every second.

He and Henry talked the whole time, with Milo listening intently. They stopped to skip rocks, chase squirrels and explore the riverbank.

"No fish in here," Sam said one day. "At least none I can see."

"Yes," Henry agreed. "My dad says there used to be rainbow trout in this area, some of the best around, but they're gone now."

"What happened to them?" Milo asked.

"I don't know."

They began construction of the tree house on the highest branch in the tree, the one with the strange knot Sam had discovered. By mid-October, the frame was in place. A week later the floorboards were secured, and when Halloween rolled around, the platform was complete.

"Not bad," Henry said. "Not bad at all."

"We've been working hard," Sam said. "Maybe we should take tomorrow afternoon off and celebrate with a little trick-or-treating. My neighborhood is great. The houses are really close together. You guys should come over."

"An excellent idea," Henry proclaimed. "Milo, are you in?"

"Maybe. Do I need a costume?"

"It's hard to trick-or-treat without one," Sam said.

"Oh, then I better stay home. I don't have a costume."

"Nonsense," Henry replied. "I'm sure we can find you something."

"I have tons of masks," Sam said. "It'll be fine."

Milo grinned. "Okay. Sounds great."

The air was brisk on Halloween morning. In the

school lobby, students wearing outrageous outfits clustered around phones and snapped photo after photo.

"They sure take a lot of pictures," Sam remarked as he and Henry waded through the chaos.

"I wonder where they all go?"

"Online I think."

"Every single one?"

Sam nodded.

"But look, most of them aren't even wearing real costumes. Like what's that kid supposed to be?" Henry pointed across the lobby. A boy with white face paint, dyed green hair and a basketball jersey had flipped his phone around and was snapping a picture of himself.

"Maybe he's the ghost of a basketball player?" Sam suggested.

"Wouldn't the ghost eventually just want to be regular ghost? He must have *really* liked basketball if he's going to walk around like that for all eternity. They should take a picture of us. Our masks are awesome." Henry beamed with pride.

"Should we put them on?"

"Not yet. I can barely see though mine. Let's wait until we get to class."

"There's Mr. Throxon," Sam said. "What's he supposed to be? The Cat in the Hat?"

The vice principal leaned against a wall at the opposite side of the lobby. He wore a puffy red and white hat. Sam noticed a pile of books at his feet.

"Looks kind of goofy," Henry said.

"He is kind of goofy," Sam answered. "I think he's handing out copies of his book."

"His book?"

"Yeah. *Building a Better Digital You!* He gave me a copy on the first day. Didn't I tell you that?"

"Oh yeah," Henry said. "I forgot. Doesn't look like anyone is too interested." Students walked by the vice principal without a glance. "Come on, we don't want to be late."

Outside room 220C, the boys slipped on their masks and pulled open the door. Sam expected the entire class to gasp in horror, but most of the students were already at their computer terminals.

"I thought we'd get more of a reaction," Henry complained as they sat down.

"Me too. Did anyone even notice us?" Sam turned around. Margot and Missy whispered together at the other side of the classroom. Neither wore a costume. Missy pointed at Sam. Margot nodded, then rose and approached the teacher's desk. A moment, later Ms. Snell summoned the boys.

She smiled at them. "Please remove the masks."

Sam and Henry looked at one another then back at the teacher. "But it's Halloween," Sam protested.

"Inappropriate."

"I'm just a swamp monster—"

She held up a hand, still smiling. "Remove the masks and begin your morning work."

"Unbelievable," Sam fumed on the way to lunch. "Inappropriate. Does she think I'm the *real* swamp monster? And why does she listen to Margot and Missy?"

"Margot and Missy are the worst," Henry said. "That morning was about as much fun as trying to make a jack-o-lantern out of a tomato."

The boys met Milo and spent the lunch period discussing plans for trick-or-treating.

"We want to start just as it's getting dark," Sam said. "There's really only a two-hour window before people start running out of candy and turning off their lights."

"Do you know which houses give out the quality candy, you know, the big bars?" Henry asked.

"Yeah, we'll hit them first. We don't want to get stuck with any apples or toothbrushes."

After lunch, Sam and Henry headed to gym. They waited in the line for fitness monitors. Candace and Ali stood a few feet away.

"Ask her where she's going trick-or-treating," Henry whispered.

"You ask her," Sam replied.

"Fine. I will." He left the line and cautiously approached Candace.

"Err…excuse me ladies," he said awkwardly. "I was just wondering…" Before Henry could finish, Roger cut in front of him.

"Where you guys going tonight?" he asked coolly. Henry looked back at Sam, who beckoned him to retreat.

"Hmmm…I dunno," Candace replied. "Where are you going?"

"Probably over on Davis Drive, near my house. Lot of us are going there. It's gonna be pretty sweet."

Candace rolled her eyes. "Pretty sweet, huh? Well, maybe you'll see us."

"That didn't go very well," Henry muttered.

"Don't worry," Sam said. "I overheard Roger invite her to my neighborhood, so maybe we'll see them out anyway." Seeing the despair on Henry's face, he added, "I don't think they even realized you walked over. You're good."

After school, the boys took the bus to Sam's house and set to work assembling costumes. They found a cape in the closet and some lint covered fangs under the bed.

"These are cool," Henry said. "But Milo needs a

mask."

"I think the one I wore last year is in my desk." Sam pulled open a drawer and looked inside. Henry examined the collection of books shelved nearby. He picked up one book and then another.

"Hey," he exclaimed, when the safe behind the books was revealed. "What's this?"

"Oh," Sam said. "Nothing really. I found that in my grandparent's attic."

"Any treasure in there?" Milo asked.

"Nah," Sam said. "Actually, there is one cool thing in there. Check this out." He dialed in the combination and swung open the safe's door. His friends peered inside.

"Whoa!" Henry said. "What's that?" He reached into safe and removed the slingshot Sam had found on the last day of summer. He and Milo stared at it in amazement. "Look at it," Henry breathed. "It's…"

"Perfect," Milo finished his sentence. "Where did you get that?"

Sam too, was struck again by the slingshot's craftsmanship. He had almost forgotten about it. "I actually *found* that on the last day of the summer. It was the weirdest thing."

"You found this?"

"Right out in the street."

"Have you tried it?" Milo asked.

"No. I couldn't find anything to use as the elastic."

"Oh, we have to try it out," Henry said. "Can you imagine shooting this from the tree house? It would be incredible. Wait a second! Is this what you were talking to Missy about on the first day of school?!"

Sam nodded.

"Why not bring it in Monday? Maybe Mr. Arthur has something we can use as an elastic."

"Good idea," Sam took the slingshot and slipped it into his school bag. "Now, let's find that mask for Milo."

For the next hour, they rummaged around until they found the mask behind Sam's dresser.

"What about something to hold the candy?" Henry asked. "Do you have any pillowcases?"

They raided the linen closet and were soon ready for the evening ahead. At 6:30 they put on their masks and crept into the darkness.

The trio zigzagged across the neighborhood, ringing doorbells at one house after another. Before long, their sacks bulged with candy.

"This is going quite well," Sam said. "Shall we head home to feast?"

"We haven't seen Candace or Ali," Henry lamented. "We'd better hit a few more houses, just in case they're still out."

They wandered down a darkened cul-de-sac.

"I hear laughing," Henry said. "It could be the girls. Come on!"

"Is it?" Sam asked. "Sounds like boys to me."

At the end of the cul-de-sac, seven or eight figures stood together under a streetlight. Three held up cell phones.

"They're filming something," Sam whispered. A roar of laugher erupted. "But what?"

It was hard to tell in the darkness. As they got closer, Sam suddenly realized what was going on. Two members of the group hurled eggs at a darkened house. One after another they smashed into the windows creating a dripping, gloppy mess. The group howled with laughter at each impact.

"Let's turn around," Henry said, but it was too late.

"Hey," yelled one of the boys, "looks like we have

company."

The other members of the group turned. In the dim glow of the streetlight, Sam recognized several faces. Max stood with Trent and two other eighth graders from the back of the bus. Roger stood next to them. Ali and Candace were there too. The boys were smiling, but the two girls looked nervous and uncomfortable.

"We're all wearing masks," Sam told himself. "They won't know who we are." Before there was time to retreat, the crowd had surrounded them.

"Doing a little trick-or-treating kids?" Max asked in a baby voice.

"Getting some *cannnndy*?" another taunted.

"Hey," said Roger. "I recognize that mask." He pointed at Milo. "This must be Torwey, the joke teller from the bus."

Max's eyes lit up. "No?!" he said. "It can't be. You picked the wrong street funny man."

Sam didn't know what to do. His heart began to pound.

"Come on, Ali," Candace said urgently. "We're going home. Now." The girls started to leave, but Max held up a hand.

"Wait! Don't leave yet. We're just about to have dessert." He turned back to Sam. "Hand over the candy, big guy…or we're gonna use the rest of these eggs on your face."

Sam didn't move.

"We're not handing over anything," Henry said, his voice quiet, but steady.

"Oh no?" Max stepped forward and shoved him backwards. "And who's gonna stop me from taking it? This little runt?" He pointed to Milo. "I'm surprised he can even carry that bag on his own." The crowd burst into laughter again. He shoved Henry a second time.

Sam was shocked by what happened next.

As the eighth grader moved in for Henry's candy, Milo, who had been standing like a statue, came to life in a whirl of motion. With incredible speed, he turned on his heel and whipped his bag of candy through the air like a wrecking ball. It completed one full rotation before slamming into Max's gut with a thud.

The eighth grader doubled over in pain. In the same motion, Milo leapt forward, snatched up the fallen bag of candy, and turned to his friends. "Run," he said.

Sam and Henry spun around and took off down the road. They didn't stop until safely inside Sam's kitchen. There, all three slumped to the floor out of breath and unable to speak.

"That," Henry managed to exclaim, "was incredible!"

15

Sam woke on Monday feeling very apprehensive. They had humiliated Max, embarrassed him in front of his friends and the two girls. Retaliation seemed likely. But the day began in a suspiciously normal fashion.

"He hasn't done anything out of the ordinary," Henry said when Sam sat down beside him.

"Really? That's good." Sam dared a glance to the back of the bus. Max sat in his usual seat. He noticed Sam and grinned.

"He just smiled at me."

"Maybe we're friends now."

"I don't think so. Something's coming."

But nothing did. The bus ride passed without incident.

"Think he forgot about it?" Henry asked on the way to room 220C. "He doesn't seem particularly bright."

"Let's hope so."

Ms. Snell greeted the students and instructed them to begin the day by logging into their portals and completing a math assessment.

"I hate math first thing in the morning," Henry

muttered.

"I hate math all the time."

They'd been working for just a few minutes, when a chime suddenly sounded at all twenty computers.

"What was that?" Sam asked.

"I don't know."

Ms. Snell stood. "It sounds like you've all just received a school-wide message. Those can be read by clicking the mailbox icon."

"Maybe there's a burst pipe or something and we can go home early," Sam whispered. He clicked the mailbox. Immediately his heart began to pound. The message had not been sent by a teacher, or a secretary, or anyone like that. The sender was Max212.

"Henry did you get something—"

"Yes."

"What is it?"

"I don't know, but it looks like everyone else got it too."

Sam clicked on the message and a video began to play.

"No," he whispered. "Please no."

"Where did he get this?" Henry stammered.

Sam looked around the room. The video played on every single screen. It showed him and Henry standing side by side on the bus, looking nervous and confused. "This," someone said off screen, "is funny." And then two sandwiches sailed through the air and slammed, horribly, into the defenseless boys. The bus exploded in laughter.

Around the classroom, students turned from their screens and stared at Sam and Henry. They snickered and whispered to one another.

"How do we get it to stop?" Sam said. "Can we delete it?" He looked for some kind of delete button on the screen. He didn't see one. What he did see was the comments section below the video. There were already twenty-eight, no thirty, thirty-two comments.

Mark3094: Losers!

SamanthaK 6022: HAHAHAHA

Amandatheswimmer60 : Ewwwwww

Tylerbasketball4ever: Hope they like egg salad!

KellyP4688: SOOOO FUNNY LOL

JoeS63390: Idiots!

More appeared every second.

"There has to be some way to stop it!" Sam cried.

Henry shook his head. "I don't think so."

TM84ZZZ: Don't bother coming back to school!

MayaG400d: OMG dying!!!

SB50219: Check it out!!!

"Why?" Henry whispered. "Why are they doing this?"

Sam was speechless.

Laughter began to rise around them.

"Stop it," Henry snapped, turning to the class. "Turn that off! It's not funny!"

Ms. Snell spoke sternly from her desk. She was looking at her computer. "I expect everyone to be working only on the math assessment. The school-wide message is inappropriate and will be reported to the administration."

Sam looked back to his screen. The video had been deleted. But it was too late. It had gone to every student. It was out there. Sam and Henry were the laughing stock of the entire school.

In the hallways, everyone stared. At lunch, everyone pointed. When they got to gym, it was the only topic of discussion.

"How about their faces when they got hit?"

"I think they started to cry!"

"Imagine how bad they smelled after being covered with egg salad?"

"Probably doesn't matter. Ever see the little kid they sit with at lunch? He's filthy. I bet they're used to it."

It went on and on. Sam didn't know what to do. Even Henry, who always seemed to have a plan, was at a loss. The jeering continued the next day, and the day after that. Everywhere they went, it followed.

"There go the funny guys!"

"Yuck. Do you smell that? Here they come. Get a picture!"

Even at home, there was no escape. It continued, all the time, online. Try as he might, Sam couldn't resist checking the video, in hopes that the comment section would start to die down. He borrowed his mom's computer, created an account and logged onto Facebook.

It was the first thing he saw. Thousands of views and almost that many comments. There were even edited versions. Ones with music, ones with commentary, ones where Sam and Henry had been given thought bubbles that said things like "Can I have some of your sandwich please? Just smash it into my face!"

An *Acceptable Behavior Online* message had been sent out to all the students, but as far as Sam could tell, Max hadn't gotten in trouble.

By Thursday, he couldn't take it anymore. He didn't want to ride the bus. He didn't want to go to school. He thought about telling his mother the whole story, but was too embarrassed.

Sam and Henry became as quiet as Milo. Unsure how to respond to the jeering, they didn't react at all and moved through the school like ghosts.

"What's wrong with you guys?" Mr. Arthur asked during Industrial Arts. "You've been like ghosts all week.

No one's talking. No one's fooling around. I don't like it."

Henry looked down at the workbench. Sam stayed quiet. Milo knew what was going on, but he too was silent.

Henry got picked up early on Friday afternoon for a dentist appointment, leaving Sam to endure the bus ride home alone. The thought of it was more than he could bear. He waited in a deserted hallway until the noise from the lobby subsided. When the building was silent, he went cautiously to the front door, intent on walking home alone. He looked out to make sure the coast was clear. One student remained on the gravel driveway: Milo.

"What are you still doing here?" Sam asked, plodding down the granite steps.

Milo ignored the question. "Do you want to go down to the tree house for a while?"

Sam looked down. He hadn't thought of the tree house in days. They'd finished the main platform just the week before, but now it seemed like ages ago.

"I don't think so, Milo. I missed the bus. I gotta figure out how I'm going to get home. Maybe some other time."

"Oh, yeah, okay, never mind," Milo said quietly, and turned to leave.

Milo had stood by his friends all week, sat with them at lunch, walked beside them in the halls. Before long, some of the worst jeers were aimed at him. Kids made fun of his clothing, his size, his shyness; took pictures of him. Yet, he never left them.

"Wait," Sam said. "Let's go down there for a while. See how everything's holding up."

A smile flickered across Milo's face.

They walked across the back lawn and entered the woods. Leaves crinkled underfoot as they left the path and headed in the direction of the river. When the water came into view, Sam couldn't help feeling a bit better.

He crossed the river first and began to climb. Up and up he went, until at last he reached the platform. Sam climbed onto it and sat beside the scarred knot with his legs dangling down.

Milo settled in next to him. "Nice view today," he said. The treetops were awash in deep reds and yellows. Sunlight danced on the river far below. "You know those kids at school? Don't let them get to you."

"Yeah," Sam said, "I know."

"Really," Milo continued. "They think it makes them cool. Some of them aren't even bad kids, just followers. They don't think for themselves. It'll stop eventually." He paused. "Bad things happen…usually to undeserving people… you can't let it get you down…really… because it'll get better soon. I know it will."

Sam glanced at Milo. He looked like he'd been fighting battles for a long time, probably bigger battles than viral videos. "You're right," he said slowly. "I've been feeling sorry for myself." Sam stared out over the trees to the roof of the school, just barely visible. "I'll try not to do that anymore. There are things to be sad about, but not this."

Maybe it was Milo's words, or maybe it was being out in the woods away from it all, but Sam felt better than he had in days. Before long, the two climbers were talking and laughing together high above the forest floor.

"You should have brought the slingshot," Milo said. "It would be fun to shoot up here if we could get an elastic."

"I know," Sam agreed. "We really need to do that."

Then he remembered his backpack.

"Wait a second. I actually have it with me! I put it in

my bag on Halloween!"

Sam opened his backpack, took out the slingshot and handed it over. Milo held it up and closed one eye, locking a distant tree in his sights.

"It's gonna be tricky to find an elastic that fits," he said, passing the slingshot back.

"Don't worry," Sam replied confidently. "We will."

Milo nodded, then pointed to the knot protruding from the branch between them. It stuck up between two planks. "Aren't these markings strange?"

He was right. The bark around the knot was covered with deep cuts.

"Yeah," Sam said. "You think it happened when the branch broke off?"

"I'm not sure," Milo replied. "It doesn't look natural. It almost looks like carving…wait a minute…can I see the slingshot again?"

Sam gave it to him. Milo balanced the polished handle on the knot. A shiver ran up Sam's spine. Milo shook his head in disbelief. The grooved pattern on the slingshot aligned perfectly with the cuts on the knot.

"This slingshot," Milo said quietly. "It came from right here." He turned it over slowly.

Carved into the base were three letters: J.R.J.

"What does J.R.J. mean?" Milo asked.

"I don't know," Sam replied. "It must be someone's initials. I can't believe I didn't notice it sooner."

"Whoever it was," Milo said slowly, "They were here before us." He pointed to the branch. The gray bark around the knot was different than the rest, as if it had been worn down.

"You know what?" Sam said. "I'm just remembering something. The slingshot fell out of a garbage truck, and I might be crazy, but I'm pretty sure one of the guys said something about the stuff in the truck coming from a school." Milo looked at Sam with raised eyebrows. "I bet some kid made this years ago, lost it on the school grounds, and it got picked up in the summer cleanup!"

"I don't know," Milo said. "Look at it. It's perfect, like something from a museum. And it's been stained to protect the wood. I don't think most kids would do that. Look at the way it's carved. I like to carve wood, but I couldn't make smooth grooves like those."

"Hold it for a second," Sam said, handing the slingshot off.

He hunched down and studied the knot. The cuts suggested the slingshot had been carved while still attached to the tree. But a few of the notches were different. They appeared deeper, deliberate, as if added later.

"That's strange," he said. Sam hung out over the water to view the groves from the side. "What the…"

The carved lines on the slingshot came together with those on the branch to reveal what was unmistakably an arrow pointing straight down. Sam and Milo looked at each other and then to the water far below.

Something rectangular shimmered between the rocks on the riverbed.

16

The next morning Sam took a seat beside Henry, eager to tell him about the discoveries. He and Milo had studied the object in the water for nearly an hour, but could see no way of getting to it. They planned to return to the tree that afternoon.

The usual chorus of taunts drifted up from the back of the bus, but Sam ignored them. Instead, he gave his friend a pep talk like the one Milo had delivered the day before.

"It hurts to know everyone is talking about you. It hurts to think it's going on all the time, even when you're supposed to be safe at home. It's even worse when you realize the video will always be out there. That's just the world we live in." Henry nodded sadly.

"But it's only part of the world we live in, and we can't let it get to us. We can't waste our days thinking about it. There are things to be sad about, but those idiots," he nodded to the back of the bus, "aren't on the list."

Henry considered these words for what seemed like a long time. Finally, he smiled. "You're right. I've lost days feeling sorry for myself. *Days*. Life is too short for that. *Gather ye rosebuds while ye may* as the saying goes." His face brightened. "Thank you my friend. I …I will not make that mistake again!"

"Errr…good," Sam said with half a smile. "Anyway, I've got some incredible news. Listen to this…"

Henry's eyes widened as Sam explained the revelations from the day before. "You're joking," he said in astonishment.

"I'm not. We don't know what it could be, but we're going to try and get it."

"Excellent," Henry said. "Excellent."

The seats in room 220C had been rearranged to foster what Ms. Snell said was a "more productive atmosphere." The new configuration had Henry and Sam at opposite sides of the room, so there was no opportunity to discuss the mysterious object further. Sam now sat next to Missy, Henry next to Margot. Sam suspected this was intentional.

Nevertheless, when Ms. Snell announced the start of a social studies unit on exploration, Sam's ears perked up. He'd read about Magellan's voyage around the world and was excited to revisit the shipwrecks and mutinies.

He quickly realized that Ms. Snell's idea of exploration was a stark contrast to his own. They spent two hours using a computer application to draw a scaled map of the classroom to learn, as she put it, "about their surroundings."

"So much time is devoted to learning how to use new apps," Henry said when they escaped to the lunchroom. "We never seem to learn any actual content. It's really pretty bad."

"I know," Sam said, taking a seat next to Milo. "Is Mr.

Dean any better?"

Milo looked up from a sandwich. "No. We do pretty much the same thing. Mr. Dean doesn't pay much attention."

"Enough about school," Henry said. "Tell me more about what happened yesterday. How are we going to get that thing out of the water?"

They spent the rest of lunch trying to come up with a plan.

"We'll think of something," Sam said as the bell sounded. "Let's meet in the woods after school?"

Milo nodded. "See you then."

Sam and Henry headed in one direction, Milo in the other. A few minutes later, they stood in the gymnasium. Several students pointed in their direction and snickered.

"There they are," someone whispered. "The sandwich suckers."

"That's a new one," Henry muttered.

"Yeah," Sam agreed. "Has a nice ring to it. Where are the gym teachers?" Mr. Montero and Ms. Fischer were not in the gym.

"Not sure. Wait, that must be them now."

The door at the back of the gym opened and a man walked in. It wasn't Mr. Montero. It was Mr. Fiddlesbee, the principal.

"What's he doing here?" Henry whispered.

Sam didn't answer. The principal ambled across the gymnasium floor with his hands behind his back and paused before the group of students. Then he bowed.

"Good afternoon," he said grandly. "Your teachers are attending a conference today. I'll be… filling in. It's been a while since I ran a gym class but I guess it will come back to me."

There were stifled giggles, but he ignored them.

"Now then," he said. "Your teachers asked that you each sign out something called a 'fitness monitor' so your progress can be recorded, but I cannot seem to find the key to the cart, so you'll have to do without."

"Uh Mr. Fiddlesbee, sir…what are we going to do today?" someone asked.

The man produced a slip of paper from his pocket.

"It says here…stations…pushups…sit-ups…stretching and calibration. I'm not entirely sure what that means."

A girl raised her hand. Henry nudged Sam. It was Candace. "That's where we put on our fitness monitors and get them programmed correctly."

"Ah yes. Thank you. I'll have to come up with something else for you to do. Let me think… shouldn't be too hard. I've taught gym classes here before…many years ago…but let's just see…" He looked around the gym, then up at the ceiling. "Perfect."

He crossed to a nearby wall where two cranks stuck out from the stone. He began to spin them, one with each hand. An ominous clicking echoed through the gym and the students turned to look for its source. Slowly, the two dark ropes Sam had noticed on the first day, slithered down from the rafters at the center of the gym.

"No…way…"Henry whispered. "Awesome." The ropes continued their descent until at last making contact with the hardwood floor.

Mr. Fiddlesbee returned to the group. "I used to the love the ropes. Have you had much practice with them?"

The group stared blankly at him.

"No? Well then, no time like the present. I'll tell you what, there's a bell up there." He pointed up to the rafters. A bronze bell with a Y-shaped gong, hung between the dangling ropes. "We used to use that for racing. In fact," he chuckled, "back in my prime I used to be able to get up there pretty quick, but today, since it's your first time, we'll say no racing. How's that?"

Margot raised her hand. She looked very pale. Mr. Fiddlesbee pointed to her. "Yes?"

"Mr. Fiddlesbee, there's no safety harness. No pad. I don't think we're suppose to be using those ropes."

"Yes," Missy said from beside her. "They're dangerous."

Mr. Fiddlesbee looked at them with confusion. "Dangerous? You're kids aren't you? You'll be fine. I'll tell you what. I'll stay by the ropes and help you through it." He bowed again. Missy frowned. Margot shook her head.

"Now, let's break into groups. You go over to stretching." Fiddlesbee waved his arms at a group of students near the front of the crowd. "You all head over to that corner of the gym and do some sit-ups. You guys over there to push-ups. Stretching is that way, and the rest of you… over to the ropes."

Sam and Henry walked to the sit-up station.

"Mr. Fiddlesbee may be a little crazy," Sam murmured as they crossed the gym.

Henry nodded. "I love it."

At the sit-up corner, the boys sat down on the floor and dropped to their backs.

"You think," Sam said, lifting his torso off the mat, "you'll be able to climb that rope?"

"Probably not," Henry answered. "I'll likely get about halfway up, then fall off and die."

Sam choked on a laugh as he rose again. "Maybe not, though. We've been doing a lot of climbing this fall. There's a chance we make it to the top."

Henry shrugged. "I hope you're right. Hey, let's climb

at the same time and if one of us can't make it, the other will just stop. That way we won't look like jack-a-lopes."

"Yeah, okay." Sam wasn't sure what jack-a-lopes were, but the strategy made sense.

Mr. Fiddlesbee brought his fingers to his lips and let fly a tremendous whistle. It was time to move to the next station. Sam inspected the rest of the group on the way across the gym. No one looked particularly athletic, which was a relief. After a few rounds of half-hearted pushups, he heard the whistle again.

Henry stared across the gym to the ropes, their next destination. "Listen to the bell, Sam," he said. "*It tolls for thee.*"

The ropes seemed to rise much higher when viewed up close. The bell between them was at least thirty feet in the air. A Y-shaped gong hung from its center.

"Alright," Mr. Fiddlesbee said, "who's going first?" No one in the group moved. "Are you scared? Why, in my day we climbed these kind of ropes in first grade."

Sam stared down at the ground.

"Okay, fine," he said. "Looks like I'm going to have to choose. How about…you…and…you? Come on up here and give it a shot."

Sam looked up. To his relief, a boy and girl standing next to Henry were chosen. It was clear the boy didn't stand a chance. There was too much of him, and not enough of it muscle. He gripped the rope high and hung wiggling in the air for a few seconds, before letting go and falling to the mat. The girl fared slightly better. She shimmied up a yard or so, then stalled and slid back to the ground.

"This is going to be harder than I thought," Sam whispered.

"Yes," Henry agreed. "Like teaching a snake to do a

handstand."

One after another, pairs of students attempted the climb and failed. The boy in front of Sam made it fifteen feet up and then ran out of energy.

"Not bad, not bad. But I need someone to get to the top," Mr. Fiddlesbee said. "So far only one student has gotten all the way up." Fiddlesbee waved at a nearby mat where Roger lay doing sit-ups. "Isn't anyone else going to step up?"

After one more failed attempt, it was Sam's turn. He stood opposite Henry at the base of the ropes, not sure where to start. "Get moving men, we don't have all day," Fiddlesbee barked.

Sam gave Henry a nod, reached up, wrapped his hands around the rope and pulled down hard. Surprisingly, he rose off the ground with relative ease. He curled his legs around the rope, pulled down again, and moved higher. To his left, Henry did the same. Up they went, side by side, until they were well above the crowd.

"Nice work, boys!" Fiddlesbee shouted from the floor. "Keep going."

The ceiling was getting closer. They were twenty feet in the air, then twenty-five feet. With a final tug, Sam pulled himself up the last stretch of rope and grabbed a rafter.

"I guess those trips across the river paid off," Henry called.

"I guess *so,*" Sam replied. "Nice view from up here."

"Alright boys. This isn't a tea party. Get back down here. It's almost time to go."

When they were back on the ground, Fiddlesbee whistled and called all the students over. "Nice work today. I saw some good effort at most of the stations."

"The ropes didn't go as well. Only three students

made it all the way up. I'm going to have two of them show you how to climb. Watch what they do, and next time, do the same thing. It's that simple."

Sam's heart sank.

"Where are they?" Fiddlesbee looked over the group. "Mr. Regerio." He pointed at Roger. "Andddd…there. You." He pointed at Sam. "Show them how it's done."

Everyone in the gym turned and stared in his direction, Candace and Ali among them. Slowly, Sam walked to the front of the crowd. Roger sneered at him.

"That's the kid from the video. Sammy Sandwich," someone whispered.

"Loser."

"Alright boys. It's not a race. I just want the rest of the class to see your technique."

Sam, Roger, and every other person in the gym, knew it was, in fact, a race - a race Sam was certain he'd lose. Roger had always been strong. He was bigger than Sam and had been resting most of the gym class.

"What are you waiting for? Get up there!" Before Sam knew what was happening, Roger jumped into the air, grabbed the rope, and began pulling himself skyward.

"Gooo!" Henry screamed from somewhere in the crowd.

Without wasting another second, Sam lunged into the air and snatched the rope. Roger was already six feet off the ground and rising quickly. Sam tore after him in hot pursuit. Hand over hand he rose higher. The crowd began to cheer. His callused hands slid over the thick rope and the gap between the two climbers began to close…three feet…two feet. Then they were even, twenty-five feet off the ground. Sam moved faster, inching ahead. The rafters were only a few feet away. With his last ounce of effort he stretched his right arm as high as it would go and managed to brush the ceiling with an outstretched finger.

"I won," he thought. "I won." But next to him, Roger, only a second behind, lunged for the bell between the ropes.

"No," Sam thought. "No…"

Roger grabbed one arm of the gong and slammed it into the bell, sending a loud clang through the rafters. Sam looked at him in horror. "You…you weren't supposed to ring the bell."

Roger met his gaze with a grin. "Dude," he said, "don't even worry about it," and then began to lower himself back to the mat.

Sam looked at the bronze bell two feet from his head. The thick Y-shaped gong still wobbled back and forth below it. How could he have been so stupid? Of course Roger would use the bell. He sighed and began climbing back down the rope.

"Well boys, nice display," Fiddlesbee said. "It wasn't supposed to be a race, but I guess you were the winner after all." He gestured to Roger. "I'm glad you stopped that cigarette business before it affected your health!"

"Sam got to the top first!" Henry protested.

"I don't know about that. I saw him ring the bell. Anyway, you all did a good job. Your regular teachers should be back next time. Good day." With that, he walked across the gym and disappeared through the door. No sooner was he out of earshot than Roger started recounting the climb.

"Smoked him. Knew I would. That kid is such a loser. Sammy Sandwich Sucker." The designation of "that kid" annoyed Sam more than "Sandwich Sucker."

"Looked like you were barely trying," a tall blonde boy piped in.

"They seem to be living in some kind of fantasy

world," Henry said when he found Sam. "You clearly made it to the top first."

Sam shrugged.

"We can't let him get away with this," Henry went on. "Let's go tell the real story."

"Nah," said Sam. "What's the point? Let's go." Henry opened his mouth to protest, but someone else spoke first.

"You really did win." It was a *girl's* voice. Sam and Henry turned around to find Candace standing right behind them. Ali was beside her.

"That kid is a jerk. You won," she said again. "Everyone saw it." She looked at Ali for a moment. "It was cool." The girls smiled and walked away.

17

"Milo, you should have seen it. He won the race *and* the heart of a fair lady in a single gym class. Remarkable."

Milo giggled and covered his face.

"I don't know about winning any hearts," Sam said, smiling. The three boys were rambling through the woods en route to the tree house. The sky above them was dark gray, the forest dim and quiet.

"Contraire," Henry replied. "Not only did she declare you victorious, but she went out of her way to mention how cool it was. Furthermore, she correctly classified Roger as a jerk, which is a great sign. I don't think they cared for his Halloween antics." Henry's logic was hard to argue with. He was definitely back to his old self.

"Who are these girls?" Milo asked. "Are they in your class?"

"They're in our gym class," Henry answered. "Quite beautiful and very smart. Oh, and also funny."

"How do you know they're smart and funny?" Sam asked.

Henry ignored him.

"So you're friends with them?" Milo said.

"Mmmm, friends might be an overstatement," Henry conceded. "Today was the first time we talked to them." He scratched his head. "Well actually, we didn't say anything…but one of them definitely talked to us."

Milo giggled again. "So you're nearly married?"

"Patience," Henry stated calmly. "These things take time. *Rome wasn't built in a day.*"

It wasn't long before they were across the river and high in the branches of the beech tree.

"Can you see it?" Sam asked.

"No. I think it's too cloudy." Henry peered down at the river in search of the mysterious object.

Sam looked up at the sky. Gray clouds covered the sun. "Darn it," he muttered. "I think you're right. It looks like it's going to rain." A low rumble of thunder drifted across the treetops.

"Are you sure this is the right spot?" Henry asked.

"Positive," Milo answered. "This is the knot the slingshot was cut from. It was right underneath."

"We need to get closer," Sam said. "Did you bring any rope?"

Milo nodded. "Yeah, I'll get it." He crept back to the tree trunk where his pack was tied, removed a long length of rope and crawled back to his friends.

"Alright," Sam directed. "Tie that off and throw it down."

Milo whipped the rope around the branch, tied a series of knots, and flung the remaining heap down to the water. It uncoiled with a whir and snapped taut just above the rushing current.

"Perfect," Sam said. "Who's going down?" Milo and Henry stared at him innocently. "What. Me?" They nodded. "Why me?"

"You're the best climber," Henry remarked. "Remember? The champion of sixth grade?"

"I don't think I want to."

"Hmmmm…" Henry said. "Well I suppose we could ask Roger on the bus tomorrow. I'm sure he would love to try."

"Fine. Fine," Sam grumbled. "But what should I do when I get down there?"

"Just check it out, see if you can see anything," Milo said.

"Here," said Henry. "Take this." He reached into a pocket and took out a small black cylinder.

"What's that?" Milo asked.

"It's a penlight, a small flashlight I carry for situations like these. Maybe you can shine it into the water?"

Sam took the light. "Are you sure you don't want to go down yourself?"

Henry shook his head.

"Okay," Sam replied. "But if I fall in, you'll have to jump down and rescue me." Thunder rumbled through the river canyon again. Milo and Henry looked at him blankly.

"Just kidding. I'm not going to fall in." With that, he reached down, grabbed the rope and rolled off the branch.

Even with the light drizzle that had started, going down was simple. The rope was easy to hold and Henry kept yelling words of encouragement from above. Near the bottom, Sam stopped and peered into the water. It was hard to see more than a few feet below the surface. He wiggled down the last bit of rope and looked again.

"I can't see anything," he called up. "It's too dark."

"Okay. Better climb back up—" BOOM. A clap of thunder muffled Henry's words.

"WHAT?!" Sam called.

"I SAID, BETTER CLIMB BACK UP. IT'S GETTING BAD FAST!"

He was right. The drizzle had turned suddenly to a steady stream of rain and an army of black clouds had formed above the cliff. Another clap of thunder rattled through the canyon. Sam looked up to his friends. They turned to silhouettes as a jagged shard of lightning cut through the sky.

"HURRY!" Henry screamed.

"One second!" Sam stared down at the water, concentrating on the area just below the rope. Another bolt of lightning exploded overhead and in that instant, he saw it: a metal container between the rocks on the river floor. It was visible for just an instant. The riverbed vanished with the lighting and Sam was left dangling below his friends, the storm bearing down upon them all.

"ARE YOU NUTS?" Henry screamed. "WE'RE GOING TO GET KILLED!"

Fighting the urge to wait for another lightning bolt, Sam pulled his eyes from the water and began to climb. Wind whipped along the river sending raindrops into his skin like a swarm of bees. The rope was drenched and slippery. For every four feet up, he slid back two.

"Come on, Sam," Milo pleaded. Something in his voice was different. Sam realized it was fear. He continued the battle upward, inch by inch, toward the branch.

"Hurry!" Henry called. With the last of his strength, Sam reached up and took hold of the limb. The boys leaned down and pulled him onto the branch. "C'mon," Henry said. "We have to get down from here. We'll be struck by lightning!"

One after another, they slid across the branch and

began climbing down. The smooth bark of the beech was slick and Sam nearly tumbled out of the tree. The roar of thunder was constant and lighting ripped the sky into panes of shattered glass. Even in the chaos, Sam couldn't stop thinking about what he'd seen on the riverbed. They'd never get it. It was too deep, the current too strong. If they went into the water, they'd surely drown. Whoever put it there, wanted it to stay.

"Where's the seat?!" Henry yelled, over the howl of the wind and rain.

"What?" Sam called back.

"The seat… to get across the river. It's gone." He was right. The pulley and seat were missing.

"There," Milo said, pointing out over the water. The seat swayed in the wind halfway across the river. Another deafening clap of thunder echoed through the canyon. It was so loud, all three boys covered their ears.

"Grab the cord and pull it back! Hurry!" Henry screamed.

Sam reached down and gripped the recall line. He gave one quick jerk, and the seat shot back towards the boys. He pulled again. The seat came closer. He stopped and stared at the string. An idea had occurred to him. Pull it.

"WHAT ARE YOU DOING?" Henry yelled. "KEEP GOING!"

"Milo, you do this!" Sam said tossing him the line. "I'll be right back." Without another word, he dropped to his knees and began climbing further down the slippery tree.

"SAM!" Henry screamed, "Come back!"

"Just get the seat ready!" Sam yelled. "I have to check something."

He jumped from the lowest branch down to the tangled mass of roots that gripped the rock. Frantically, he ran his hands up and down the tree. In the darkness it was difficult to tell root from shadow.

"Come on…come on…" he whispered. "It has to be here." He shined the penlight on the base of the tree. And then he saw it. A thin gray wire wrapped around one of the roots. "I found something!"

"WHAT?!"

"I said I found—" BOOM. Thunder drowned his words.

Sam followed the wire to the edge of the rock ledge where it disappeared into a small crack that zigzagged down to the water. He pulled up, freeing it from the crevice. Lightning spread out like a fan overhead. He continued to pull until the wire went taut, one end in his hand, the other disappearing into the river. Sam's heart beat rapidly. The rain poured down. *This is it*, he thought, and gave a yank. It didn't budge.

"SAMMMMM!" Henry screamed. "THE STORM. WE'RE NOT GOING TO MAKE IT!"

Lighting struck again and again. Thunder was constant. Sam turned to climb back up the tree, when he remembered the rocks surrounding the sunken container. "Straight up," he whispered. "That's the only way. It has to be pulled straight up."

He scampered back across the roots, untied the wire and wrapped it around his ankle. Then he leapt into the air, grabbed hold of the lowest branch and climbed up to the others.

"Get on," Henry shouted. "We're all going at once!"

Sam took a seat next to Milo. Henry squeezed in on top of them.

"Let's go!" Sam yelled. Henry reached up and began pulling them across the angry river.

"Stop!" Sam shouted. "Stop!"

Henry looked at him like he'd lost his mind, but let the

seat come to rest. Sam stretched down to his ankle and took hold of the wire. He leaned out over the water and pulled upwards. Nothing happened. He pulled again, harder. The wire started to wiggle.

A lightning bolt sliced through the canyon and hit a tree fifty yards down stream, blowing the trunk apart.

"SAM! WHAT ARE YOU DOING?" Henry screamed.

"Hold on!" Sam said, "just one more... GOT IT!" With a final tug the object came loose, and Sam pulled it out of the water and up to the suspended seat. "GO!" he yelled, the treasure clutched in his hands. "GOOO!"

"YOU GOT IT? HOW?!"

"NO TIME! JUST GO!"

Hand over hand, Henry hauled them towards the shore. The raindrops bit into their faces. Wind tore their soaked clothes. At one point, lightning fired into the water upstream, causing it to glow an eerie yellow. With a shudder, Sam realized what would have happened if the wire around his ankle had still been in contact with the river.

They reached the opposite shore, jumped from the seat and took off through the forest. Waterlogged branches broke apart overhead and leaves sliced through the air like razors. Together they barreled forward through the mayhem, twice losing the path. Finally, they broke through the underbrush and tumbled onto the lawn as thunder roared overhead. The school was dark, except for a few forgotten lights on the upper floors. Sam thought he saw a silhouette standing at one of the windows, but was too concerned with the lightning to give it a second thought.

"We're almost there!" Henry shouted. "Come on!" They skidded to a halt in front of the shop room door.

"Please be unlocked. Please be unlocked. Please be unlocked," Sam whispered. Milo turned the knob, and miraculously, the door opened. They rushed inside and slammed it shut.

The shop room was dark.

"I guess Mr. Arthur's gone," Henry said breathlessly.

"Guess so," said Sam. "Turn some lights on so we can see what this is."

Milo flipped a switch, flooding a nearby workbench with light. Sam placed the object on the bench. It was a slimy, metal box. That was all. There were no markings of any kind, just a thick padlock and the wire Sam had used to retrieve it.

"What do you think is inside?" Milo whispered. No one answered.

"How are we going to get it open?" Henry asked, examining the lock. "Milo can you pick this?"

He shook his head. "Doubtful. The bottom's filled with dirt and rust. We need to find something to break it open."

Sam looked around the room. "What about those?" he said, pointing to an enormous pair of clippers hanging on the wall.

"Yes," Milo said. "Bolt cutters. They should work."

The bolt cutters were so heavy, Milo needed help getting them off the wall and over to the table. There, he positioned the beak-like blades around the heavy shackle. "Okay, now push those ends together as hard as you can." Sam and Henry pushed with all their might, but the lock wouldn't break.

"Stop, stop," Henry gasped. "It's not working."

"Here let's try this." Milo swung the handles around and positioned them between a large vice anchored to the table.

"Now let's just tighten the vice and hope nothing slips."

"What happens if something slips?" Sam asked.

"One of us would probably lose a finger," Milo answered matter-of-factly.

They twisted the vice around and around, until the long handles of the shears were bending under the tension.

"Should we keep going?" Sam asked. "It looks like the handles are going to snap."

Milo studied the apparatus. "You're right. Something's about to give. Try one more turn."

Henry slowly spun the vice around until suddenly, with a crack, the lock split in two. The shears tumbled to the ground with a clatter that echoed into an ominous silence.

They looked at each other, then back at the box. Goosebumps covered Sam's arms.

"This is it," Henry said. "Open it."

Milo scraped away a waxy substance that had been used as a sealant and pried open the lid. The boys peered inside.

At the bottom of the box, a wooden bracket held something thin and metallic. Sam reached in and pried it out. He placed the object delicately on the workbench, and they peered at it in silence.

It was an ornately carved rod, about eight inches long, with rectangular tabs protruding from either end.

"What the heck…" Henry whispered.

At the center of the rod, the letters J.R.J. had been pressed into the metal.

He leaned in further. "It looks like some kind of double sided…"

"…key." Milo finished his sentence. "And it's solid

bronze."

Sam didn't hear his friend. He had noticed additional writing. Two words. One on each tab: *Choose* and *Wisely*.

18

The search to determine the identity of J.R.J. began in earnest. It occupied all their spare time. Every day, the boys met in the deserted school library and poured over books looking for some clue, any clue, as to who had left behind the mysterious key.

They looked through local history books, New England history books and United States history books. They flipped through volumes on the founders of Connecticut and the settlers of the town.

No one with the initials J.R.J. could be found.

At one point, Henry discovered an ancient looking book on notable Perkinsville residents, but the J pages were missing.

Their luck was no better the next week, or the week after that. They tried searching the public library, but found nothing.

Thanksgiving came, then Christmas, then the new year. No progress had been made.

It wasn't all work. Snow fell in early January and they went sledding in Henry's backyard. During a lengthy cold spell, they hiked out to the tree house, hoping to skate on the river. Unfortunately, it wasn't frozen.

On Valentine's Day, Henry made an elaborate card for Ali, but couldn't work up the courage to present it. "What happened?" Sam asked when he retreated to the lunch table, card still in hand.

"I just feel we need to develop our relationship before exchanging gifts."

All the while they kept searching.

"We *need* to figure out this person's name," Henry said as they left Ms. Snell's classroom one day in early March. "Initials aren't enough."

"You're not considering giving up are you?"

"Of course not. Perseverance, Sam, is the secret to all great triumphs. Come on, let's head back to the library. There's got to be something we missed."

But there wasn't.

"Frustrating," Sam said.

"Really frustrating. Any other ideas?"

"What about Mr. Arthur?" Milo suggested. "He's been here a really long time. Maybe he remembers someone with the initials J.R.J.?"

"Actually," Sam said, "that's not a bad idea. Let's go ask."

They left the library and crept through the quiet school to the shop. Sam threw open the door in excitement. "Mr. Arthur, we have kind of a weird question. Do you know anyone—"

Mr. Arthur stood by the sink. He wasn't the only one. In front of him were three others, and they were the last people Sam wanted to see in the Industrial Arts room - Max, Trent and Roger. They held boxes of paper. The shop teacher turned around at the sound of his name.

"Hi boys," he said pleasantly. "We have some visitors

this afternoon." He motioned to the others. "I found these gentlemen smoking in the bathroom earlier today. I don't think it's the first time they've been caught either."

Max muttered something under his breath, but Mr. Arthur ignored it.

"To help take their minds off cigarettes, they're helping me with some recycling. I collect the paper from all the classrooms and it's been piling up. There's a lot of scrap metal to get rid of too. These fellows have their work cut out for them."

The old man noticed unfriendly gazes passing between the two sets of boys. "You guys know each other?"

Silence.

Mr. Arthur chuckled knowingly. "Well, I'm going to be pretty busy with these three for a while. Have a good weekend boys."

"Those were the guys from Halloween, right?" Milo asked when they left the shop.

"Yeah," Sam said. "And the ones who threw the sandwiches at us."

"And the ones who put up the video," Henry added.

"I guess we'll have to wait to ask Mr. Arthur," Milo said.

"I was really hoping to crack the case before the weekend," Henry said.

"Me too," Sam agreed. "It's frustrating."

"We could go back to the library for one more search?" Milo suggested.

"Eh," Henry said. "I think we checked every single book."

"Just one more look," Milo urged.

So they went back to the library and looked through a dozen more books. Nothing turned up.

"Let's call it a day," Sam finally said. Milo nodded, but Henry kept reading.

"You guys go ahead," he said absently. "I'm almost done. I just stumbled upon this book about caves…it's really interesting…nothing to do with J.R.J. but I just want to finish this chapter."

"Should we wait?"

"That's okay. I'll be right behind you. Just meet me outside. It's a beautiful day."

Sam and Milo exchanged glances, shrugged and left the library.

Henry was right. It was a beautiful day. The snow had melted and the temperature edged steadily past fifty degrees. It seemed spring might be coming early.

They shuffled down the steps outside the lobby and wandered over to the statue that towered above the driveway loop. Milo leaned against the red *Perkinsville Middle School Public* sign. Sam paced back and forth, deep in thought.

"Are we missing something obvious?" he asked. "We've been looking so hard, we should've found something by now."

"You would think so," Milo said quietly.

"Maybe it's staring right at us, and we're just not seeing it. J.R.J….J.R.J…. who could it be?"

"I wish I knew," Milo said.

Footsteps sounded on the gravel behind them.

"Here comes, Henry," Sam said without looking up. "Who knows? Maybe the cave book gave him an idea."

Milo shook his head in dismay. "It's not Henry."

"It's not? Who is it?"

Milo nodded back towards the school. Max, Trent and Roger were coming towards them.

"Well, well, well," Max said, an evil grin spreading over

his face. "What have we here?"

"Come on Milo," Sam said, "let's go." As they started to leave, Max stepped in front of them, blocking the path.

"Not so fast," he said. Sam and Milo spun around, but the others had moved in from behind. They were surrounded

"You know," Max said slowly, "moving paper for that old guy isn't how I like to spend my Friday afternoon."

"Me neither," Trent growled.

"We wouldn't have to," Max continued, "if teachers weren't checking up on us every five minutes. You know why they're doing that? Because you ratted us out." He smiled.

"We didn't tell on you," Sam said in a low voice.

"No, I'm sure the principal just happened to walk in right after you ran out." Max looked at Milo. "What? Not such a big man without your sack of candy, are you runt?" He turned to the others. "Hold them."

Trent lunged forward, grabbed Sam's arms and forced them behind his back. Roger did the same thing to Milo.

"Let go of me!" Sam gasped, struggling to free himself. It was no use. The eighth grader was too strong. Milo wriggled helplessly beside him.

Max stepped towards Sam and looked him straight in the eye. "You know, when your idiot friend hit me with that bag, I'll admit it stung a little. I've been meaning to pay you back. There are always so many teachers around. But look…" He waved at the vacant school grounds. "No one here to protect you now. Brace yourself." Max cocked back his arm and clenched his fist. "This is *really* going to hurt." His expression glimmered with delight. Sam closed his eyes.

"NOOOO!"

The scream came from a few feet away. Sam opened

his eyes just in time to see Max knocked to the ground by a charging figure.

It was Henry.

He spun around and without a moment's hesitation, dropped a shoulder and ran at Trent. Sam dove out of the way as Henry plowed into the eighth grader's chest, sending him sailing into the *Perkinsville Middle School* sign, which cracked at the force of the blow. Roger was so shocked he let go of Milo and tore off down the driveway. Max and Trent followed, hunched over and groaning.

"Yeah…you better run!" Sam yelled after them, with a shake of his fist. "Henry!" he said, spinning around, "That was amazing! You saved our lives!"

Henry didn't answer. He and Milo were frozen in place, eyes fixed on the same thing.

"Guys?" Sam said. "Guys? What's wrong?" He followed their gaze to the remnants of the crushed sign that hung at the base of the statue. The red plastic had fallen away revealing a slab of polished stone. A deep engraving had been cut into the rock: *The Jacob R. Juniper School.*

"J.R.J." Milo whispered.

All three boys looked slowly up to the statue. It was a tall man with a beard and deep-set eyes. His expression was one of sly amusement, as if he knew something no one else did. He wore a long coat and Stetson hat.

Clutched in his right hand was a slingshot.

19

With J.R.J.'s name revealed, the search had renewed momentum. On Saturday morning, the boys met at the public library and scoured the books for any trace of Juniper. Despite hours of searching, they came up with nothing.

"I don't get it," Sam said. "Every one of the other schools in town is named after someone, and all *those* people are mentioned in these books. Why not him?"

"Yes, it's quite vexing," Henry agreed. "There's nothing on the internet either and everything's on the internet. *I'm* on the internet."

"You are?" Milo asked.

"Well…yeah….if you count the video of me getting hit in the face with an egg salad sandwich…"

The results were no better the next weekend or the weekend after that.

"It's like someone erased him from history," Sam said.

"I need a break," said Henry. "Let's call it a day and start fresh tomorrow. There's still a lot of books we haven't checked."

"Sounds good to me," Milo said, closing a copy of *Unsolved Mysteries of New England.*

"Do you two think you can sleep over tonight?" Henry asked. "Then we can come back early tomorrow."

"Sure," Sam said. "I think that would be fine. I'll have to call my mom."

"What about you, Milo?"

"I have to ask my dad."

"Can you call him?" Henry asked.

"I can try, but he's probably not home right now."

"Why don't we walk over and wait for him to come back?" Sam suggested. "I would love to see what a scrap yard is like."

Milo stared at him in disbelief. "You know about the scrap yard?"

Henry nodded. "Yeah. We saw you ride in there. It seems really cool. We never understood why you didn't want to tell us."

"It's not really a normal place to live," Milo said softly.

"Seems like an excellent place to live," Sam countered. "At least now we won't have to drop you off down the street."

"Okay, we could walk there from here. It's not too far."

The sign for *Milner Salvage* swayed in the breeze when they passed below it. Milo told them to wait outside while he went into a small trailer to look for his dad. He came right back out. "Not here. Must be out on a job."

"Can you give us a tour?" Henry asked, looking at a huge forklift in amazement.

"Yeah," Milo said proudly, "sure."

Sam and Henry quickly learned the salvage yard was a fascinating place. Damaged cars of every shape and size were stacked as far as the eye could see. Most were older models Sam had never seen before. Engine pieces were piled everywhere, and Milo showed them the powerful electro magnet that was used to move things around.

When they got back to the trailer, a rusty Chevrolet pulled into the driveway. It stopped beside them and a man got out. Milo's father.

He was only a few inches taller than Henry and wasn't much heavier. His hair was gray and cut so short, he appeared bald from a distance. He wore brown coveralls and work boots. When he spoke, his voice was soft.

"Hi boys," he said, walking over to greet them.

"Dad," Milo said. "This is Sam and Henry."

"Of course," he replied sticking out a hand for Sam to shake. "I've heard a lot about you two. It's a pleasure to meet you both." Sam shook Mr. Milner's hand and was immediately struck by how thick and callused his small fingers were.

"I gave them a tour."

"Oh good," he said. "Well, why don't you come inside so we can talk?" Mr. Milner opened the door to the trailer and the boys followed him in.

There was a small office set up near the entrance, with a desk and two folding chairs. A board on the wall was covered with papers, most of them bills. Beyond the office, a sink stood between a small stove and another table. Against the back wall were two bunk beds. That was all. Sam wondered which was Milo's until he noticed a picture taped beside the top bunk. It was a detailed drawing of an enormous tree by a river. Three figures sat in the branches.

"Dad," Milo said, "is it okay if I sleep over Henry's tonight?"

Mr. Milner smiled. "Sure, sure. That'll be fine."

"Do you need help unloading the tires tomorrow?"

He laughed. "No, I think I can manage. Besides, sleepovers are a lot more important than tires. Can I give you a ride?"

Milo turned to Henry. "Do we need a ride?"

"Thanks, but we can just walk back to the library. My mom's going to pick us up there. It's a nice day for walking."

The evening at Henry's was filled with pizza, soda and ice cream sundaes. They played poker for pennies and told ghost stories by flashlight. Sam brought along the slingshot, and they searched Henry's basement for something to string it with. Sam couldn't remember falling asleep, but when he woke up, it was still unstrung in his hand.

At ten o'clock the next morning, they piled into Henry's dad's car and headed, once more, to the library. Mr. Delmont looked a lot like his son. He had the same straight brown hair, and like Henry, wore thick glasses.

"Back to the library again?" he asked. "True scholars. So many books and so little time. That's what I always say." He spoke with great diction. Sam thought he might begin to spout off quotations just like his son.

A cell phone buzzed from the center console.

"Ah," he sighed, picking it up, "you try to get away, but they can always find you. Hello?"

A muffled voice on the other end began to speak.

"Whoa, whoa slow down. Just take it easy, Otis. Put it aside, and I'll get it straightened out."

The voice on the other end said something in reply.

"I assure you, it won't be a problem. Yes, I know you have a system. I understand that." He smiled at the boys. "Well, I'm just about to make an important delivery. Can it wait? What are you doing working on Sunday? Alright.

Alright. I'm on my way." Mr. Delmont hung up the phone and frowned. "Boys, we have to make a stop. It won't take long."

"Who was that, Dad?" Henry asked.

"That was Otis, from the town hall. He needs me to come down and help him with something."

"Is that the guy with the beard?"

"The very same. Have you met him?"

"I said 'hello' to him at the Christmas party last year. He told me Christmas parties were no place for children."

"That sounds like Otis alright," said his father. "He's overseen the town archives for as long as anyone can remember. Does *not* want to retire. He can be a little tough to work with."

Henry turned back to his friends. "My dad's in charge of the tax department at Town Hall. All the tax records get sent down to the archives in the basement."

"It would be much easier to store it all online, but Otis won't hear of *that*," Mr. Delmont said. "He's a bit obsessed with record keeping, and it's not only tax records. He's got everything down there: newspapers, birth certificates, deeds, wills…all under lock and key. Won't let anyone inside. He's really quite a character." Mr. Delmont laughed. "Apparently, my assistant didn't catalog something correctly. Otis is a little upset. I'm going to run in quickly and calm him down. You can wait in the car."

"Can we come in and see?"

"I doubt he'll let you see much, but you're welcome to take a self guided tour of Town Hall."

Otis waited for them in the lobby. Old and hunchbacked, his beard hung down to his waist in wispy silver strands.

"Henry," he barked in a raspy voice, "this assistant of yours, he's got to go." It took Sam a moment to realize Mr. Delmont was also named Henry.

"Oh, I don't know about that, Otis. He seems to be doing a pretty good job."

"Not with the filing. Wait until you see what he's done." He looked at the boys. "What are they doing here?"

"This is my son Henry and his friends. They—"

"Humph," Otis interrupted. "This is no place for children."

"They won't be any trouble," Mr. Delmont replied, giving the boys a wink. "Where are the files?"

"Downstairs," he barked. "Follow me."

They took an elevator to the basement. A chain-linked cage blocked the archives from general access. Otis approached the door and began to open the first of three padlocks protecting it.

"High security down here," Mr. Delmont said with a hint of sarcasm.

Otis grunted. "My father ran these archives before me, his father before that. The reason they're in good order is because of security and diligence. I take weekly inventory. Nothing goes in or out unless I say so. Follow me. The boys stay here."

"Aw, come on Otis. They want to see what goes on down here." Otis studied the boys. His eyes lingered on Milo and his backpack.

"Alright," he grunted. "The bag stays outside."

Milo put down his backpack, and they followed Otis into the shadows of the archives.

Tall shelves spanned the basement, each lined with books, boxes and folders meticulously labeled in black marker. They walked to a metal desk at the end of the corridor. On top of it were three sheets of paper. Otis pointed at them

"There are no dates on these," he snarled. "How can I catalog them without dates?"

Henry's dad looked at the documents. "They're from this past summer. June, I think. Does June work?"

"No," Otis shot back. "June is not a date. I need the exact dates."

"All right. If we go up to my office, I can probably find them."

"Let's go," the archivist replied, snatching the undated forms. They went back to the elevator and Otis locked the cage door.

"Boys," Mr. Delmont said, "wait here. We'll just be a few minutes."

As soon as the elevator door shut, Henry spoke in a hushed voice. "Milo, do you have anything to pick those locks?"

"Huh? I don't know. Why?"

"Did you see all the folders? They were labeled with last names."

"Yeah, so?" Sam said.

"This guy holds on to everything. The names on the folders are people who lived in town."

Suddenly, Sam realized what Henry was getting at. "Juniper!"

Milo ripped open his bag and rummaged around frantically. "This might work." He withdrew a tiny screwdriver.

"Hurry," Henry said. "They'll be back soon."

Milo ran to the door and went to work. The first lock was easy. He had it off in ten seconds, the second soon after. The third gave him trouble.

"It's too big. Hold on a second."

"Hurry," Sam said.

"I'm trying. Let me just…here it goes…" The heavy shackle popped open and clattered to the ground.

"Split up," Sam commanded, pulling open the door, "and search for the *J* section."

He bounded down one aisle, Milo the next. Henry scanned a collection of shelves along a nearby wall.

Sam's eyes darted from one folder to the next: *Bates, Barrows*. He dashed down further, *Gillows, Giln*. He ran to the next aisle. Milo was already there. *Topper, Triton*. Too far.

"Back here," he said. They ran towards the front of the room, eyes racing over the folders: *Jacoby, Jules*. And then he saw it, tattered and worn, second shelf from the bottom: J*uniper*.

"There," Sam cried. Milo grabbed the folder.

"What now?" he asked. "If we take it, Otis might find out."

"Here," Henry said, pulling up beside them. "Give it to me." He took the folder and bolted for the front of the room. Next to the cage door, a small Xerox machine stood by the wall. Sam hadn't noticed it. Henry placed the contents of the folder onto the tray and hit *COPY*. Slowly, painfully, the pages slid into the machine for duplication.

"Hurry!" Sam shouted.

"I'm going as fast as I can," Henry said. The first copy came out. Then another and another.

Suddenly, the elevator bell dinged.

"They're coming back," Milo said.

"We can't stop now," Henry stammered. Copies continued to slide from the machine.

The elevator indicator read floor three, then two.

Sam watched the door. "We're not going to make it."

"Done!" Henry cried, tearing the last page from the machine. Without a word he sprinted back into the stacks.

"Quick, put these in your backpack," Sam said passing the copied pages to Milo. The elevator was at the lobby. Henry's frantic footsteps echoed through the chamber.

"Faster!" Sam called. Another ding signaled the elevator's arrival in the basement. The door would open any second. Just in time, Henry emerged through the cage door, out of breath.

"Lock it," he cried. Sam snapped the first lock in place, Milo the second and third.

They turned around as the elevator doors opened.

"Sorry boys. That took longer than expected," Mr. Delmont said. "Otis, now that you have the dates, you don't need me do you?"

The bearded man didn't answer. He glared at Henry. "Why are you out of breath?"

"Oh," Henry stammered, "we were just...."

"Arm wrestling," Sam chimed in. "We were just arm wrestling."

"Humph," Otis grumbled. "This isn't a place for fooling around."

"Sorry about that," Henry said, following Sam and Milo into the elevator. "Won't happen again." The old man eyed them suspiciously until the elevator doors finally closed.

20

"What's with you three?"

"Huh? What? Nothing." Henry's knee bounced up and down nervously.

"You were talking the whole way over here and now, silence. I don't get it."

"We have lots of work to do. We're thinking about that."

Mr. Delmont's eyes narrowed. "Work? On Sunday? You're as crazy as Otis." He left it at that.

The library was nearly empty when they arrived. A woman checked in books near the front desk. Other than her, they were alone.

"There are some study rooms back this way," Henry said, pointing down a hallway. "Come on."

They found a room with a small desk and went inside. Milo shut the door and withdrew the documents.

"This is it," Sam said. "This is what we've been searching for." Milo spread out the papers.

"Looks like a birth certificate," Henry said, picking up one of the pages. "I can't really make it out. Let me stand under the light." He moved in front of Milo, and squinted at the paper. "*Jacob Reginald Juniper*," he read. "*Born July 4, 1838, Perkinsville, Connecticut. Parents - Alfred M. Juniper and Martha A. Juniper.*" Henry looked up. "1838? That's over a hundred and fifty years ago. What else is there?"

Sam was studying one of the other sheets. "I don't know. This could be some kind of property record. It seems like he owned a lot of land. This outline here, I think all that was his. It's bigger than the whole town."

"Wow," Henry said. "Milo, what's that?"

Milo was reading the first page of what appeared to be an encyclopedia entry. Sam looked over his shoulder and read the first paragraph. It was set above the rest of the text.

Juniper, Jacob Reginald. Born 4 July 1838, Died 1909(?). Spouse Juniper, Samantha. Born 29 May 1845, Died 1891. Industrialist, prospector and philanthropist. One of Connecticut's wealthiest residents until disappearance in 1890. Date and location of death unknown.

The narrative that followed went on for several pages. It was a miracle Henry had been able to copy it all.

Jacob R. Juniper was born on the Fourth of July, 1838, in the small town of Perkinsville, Connecticut. From the moment he entered the world, until his mysterious disappearance decades later, Juniper's life might best be described as an unbroken and unabated stream of adventures.

He was delivered during the height of a summer heat wave, and though the temperature never fell below ninety degrees, the streets of Perkinsville were

alive with celebrations of Independence Day. No sooner had the doctor left Juniper's bedside, than a rogue firework sailed through the window and into the newborn's cradle. The infant was showered with sparks, but left unharmed when the primary charge failed to ignite. He was found soon after, clutching the mortar like a teddy bear. Juniper would later joke that no one tempted death so early.

The family's good fortune was short lived. When a smallpox epidemic swept through Connecticut in 1839, Juniper's mother was among the victims. She died before her son's first birthday, leaving his father as sole caregiver.

Alfred Juniper operated a small blacksmith forge in town. It was here that Jacob spent the first years of his life, crawling between the massive anvils and roaring fires. By the time he was seven, it was said he could shape a horseshoe with one hand and bind a barrel with the other.

The boy's talents weren't limited to forging. He was blessed with an extraordinary mind and astonished local schoolmasters with his brilliance. One former teacher remarked, "He knew more about the world at age nine, than I do now. A genius." Others recalled his insatiable curiosity. "He was fascinated by all subjects and destined to be a true renaissance man." Juniper was interested in archeology, particularly legendary treasures lost to history. He penned a book on the subject that was widely circulated.

When not in the forge or the classroom, Juniper spent his time roaming the woods outside Perkinsville. He was an avid fisherman and

especially fond of the beautiful rainbow trout the region was known for. It was during one such fishing trip Juniper carved his first slingshot, a device he would later gain notoriety for. The quality of the instrument was such that it became the envy of every child in town.

Juniper had a strong sense of humor and often planned elaborate ruses to delight his friends. In December of 1853, the owners of a nearby iron mill demanded employees come in on Christmas or lose their jobs. It was Juniper who came to the rescue.

Knowing the factory would be forced to close in the event of a snowstorm, he secretly hijacked the town's telegraph cables and broadcast reports of a terrible blizzard coming in from the west. While the mill owners waited for a storm that would never come, the entire town enjoyed an extended holiday.

After his father's death in 1854, Juniper left Connecticut and set out for the American west. For two years, he traveled up and down the Mississippi River befriending boat hands and learning the trade. By 1856, he had moved on to California where he took employment as courier for a gold mining outfit. There, he worked alongside scouts, carrying secret information about new dig sites through the untamed wilderness.

When the first shots of the civil war were fired, Juniper returned home and enlisted in the Union Army. He saw many battles and received accolades for leadership and valor. Beloved by officers and infantry alike, his charisma gave him an uncanny ability to raise morale.

After the war, Juniper settled in Perkinsville and

converted his father's blacksmith shop into a tool factory. His company produced instruments of exceptional quality, guaranteeing them for life. Before long, it was one of the largest tool makers in the Northeast. Each year, the company raffled off seven slingshots, carved by Juniper himself.

Despite his wealth and success, Juniper lived a simple life. He resided in the same house he'd grown up in and continued to spend much of his time roaming the woods and fishing for rainbow trout with childhood friends. Much of his income was donated to the town library, and he could often be found reading there on winter nights.

In 1870, a large mining company founded by Millious Triton came to Connecticut. The arrival of Triton Industries would have a profound impact on Juniper's life.

Triton came to the state in pursuit of granite. He had developed a reputation as a ruthless and crooked businessman, and his methods were immediately put on display in Connecticut. Excavations were done everywhere, without regard for rules or regulations. Before long, Triton's crews were leveling trees across the state and ripping granite from the earth.

In 1871, Triton arrived in Perkinsville. He set his sights on the rock canyons and cliffs that rose up from the winding river outside town. The land had always been public, but Triton didn't bother seeking a permit or asking anyone for permission. Perkinsville was a small town and he didn't anticipate any resistance. He and his men rolled their equipment down Main Street and headed

straight through the forest. When they reached the base of the first cliff, a voice surprised them from the summit.

"You're not going to be blasting here," a man shouted.

"Get started," Triton yelled to his crew. "This land's public. We can do what we want."

"This is private land," the shadowy figure declared. "You can't dig here."

"Oh yeah? Since when?" Triton called up. "Who owns it?"

"I do," the man said, stepping into the sunlight. It was Juniper.

As it turned out, when Juniper heard Triton was in the area, he exhausted his entire fortune buying the forest around the Perkinsville, nearly 3000 acres.

Triton didn't care. He ordered a worker to unload the equipment. As the man moved toward the wagons, a tiny stone zipped down from the sky, striking him squarely in the head. He fell down, unconscious. The workers looked to the cliff. Juniper stood there, slingshot in hand. Triton commanded one of his thugs to scale the rock. Again, a stone zipped through the air and struck him down.

His team stepped back as Triton fumed. He wasn't used to being pushed around and had no intention of giving in. First, he tried to have the sale of the land reversed. When that didn't work he sent men to threaten Juniper at his home. They were invited in for dinner. Later, the men returned to Triton's hotel room and resigned. Juniper had won them over.

The miner was finally forced to concede. He left the town without any granite. Juniper's victory did not come without a cost. Triton's outfit dumped thousands of pounds of blasting powder into the river. Beautiful rainbow trout floated to the surface as the water darkened. Though it eventually cleared, the trout never returned.

Juniper continued to walk through the woods and visit the river, sad and frustrated at the loss of his beloved fish. One day, he arrived home to find a beautiful young woman sitting on a bench outside his door. She was reading the book he had written years before. They began to talk and found they were both fascinated by the lost artifacts Juniper had described in the book. They formed a connection neither had felt before. By summer's end, they were married.

Her name was Samantha, and she taught the upper grades at the town school. Her pupils adored her. She had a gift for seeing the potential in people and a remarkable ability to help them realize it. She was kind, caring and encouraging; not only to students, but to everyone she met.

For eighteen years, the couple lived happily together. In the winter of 1890, Samantha fell ill. Juniper sent for the best doctors and refused to leave her side. One doctor suspected the illness had started years earlier, from drinking water near the polluted river. Nothing could be done. By springtime, she was gone.

After the burial, Juniper disappeared. The sheriff went to his house and found it empty. No one knew where he'd gone. Juniper was never seen in

Perkinsville again, but his story didn't end.

It was around the time of his disappearance that reports of gold started trickling down from the Alaska territory. Mining companies from all over the country rushed to Fairbanks in an effort to cash in. Among them was Triton Industries.

In the years since leaving Perkinsville, Triton had continued his ruthless tactics, and his company had grown. It had become one of the most powerful in the nation. He took control of huge swaths of land around Fairbanks, driving all the smaller miners from the region. Without competition, he could dig at his leisure, wherever he saw fit. Triton's men laid waste to hundreds of acres of wilderness, leaving behind nothing but destruction.

One day, a stranger wandered into Triton's camp. He had a long silver beard, tangled hair and walked with a cane. Dark glasses covered his eyes. "I've come to dig for gold," he declared in a scratchy voice. "My name is Apollonius Boggleswort."

These words sent Triton's men into a fit of laughter. Clearly they were in the presence of a lunatic. The stranger asked if he might see Triton. Not wanting their boss to miss out on a laugh, they brought Boggleswort to him. Triton looked annoyed. "What do you want?" he growled. "I'm a busy man."

"I beg your pardon sir," Boggleswort mumbled. "But I hear there's gold in these parts, and I've come to stake my claim. Can you show me where to find some?"

Triton's lips curled into a grin. Suddenly, he

understood what his men were up to. "Gold you say?"

Boggleswort nodded.

"Well, certainly. Plenty of gold. More than enough to go around. Why don't you meet us tomorrow morning in the clearing half mile north of camp? We'll see what we can do."

"That would be grand," the old man cried. "Simply splendid!" He departed in high spirits.

The next morning, Boggleswort arrived in the clearing just as the sun rose. Triton was waiting with his men. They were at the top of a deep muddy pit.

"Finding gold is easy," the miner said. "Just climb down there, and you'll be sure to uncover some big nuggets."

Boggleswort's eyes lit up with excitement. "Down there?" he asked.

"Yep. Right down at the bottom."

Boggleswort started to hobble down into pit. As he did, Triton kicked his cane, sending the old man tumbling into the hole. He landed face first in the cold mud. The men doubled over with laughter.

"Sorry about that," Triton yelled. "I must have slipped. Just dig around down there and see what you can find."

Boggleswort got to his knees and began digging. It wasn't long before he let out a cry of joy. "I've found some! I've found some!" He turned and held up a shining yellow rock. Again the workers howled with laughter.

Boggleswort looked puzzled. He studied the rock more closely. It was nothing but piece of sandstone

Triton had dipped in paint. The workers went back to camp leaving Boggleswort to climb out on his own. Triton figured that would be the last they'd see of the old man, but Boggleswort was undeterred. He hobbled into camp and headed straight for the miner's tent.

"You're still here?" Triton asked reproachfully. "Thought you'd had enough."

"I'd like to buy some land from you," Boggleswort said. "My luck is bound to change. I think I just need a pickaxe and a good bucket."

Triton didn't smile this time. "My land's not for sale. Get this old fool out of my sight." Men stepped forward to throw him from the tent.

"Please," Boggleswort cried. "I'm prepared to pay five thousand dollars!"

Triton's eyes narrowed. Five thousand dollars wasn't a fortune, but it was no small sum either. It was more than a year's salary for most men. The tycoon would be happy to take it.

"Five thousand you say? That's not much at all. I'll give you one square acre."

"Only one?" Boggleswort said.

"Only one," the tycoon snarled. "Take it or leave it."

"Okay, okay," Boggleswort said. "One acre. We'll have to go find the land and then sign the papers."

The tycoon rolled his eyes, but agreed to follow the crazy old man into the woods. Boggleswort stopped at a small clearing covered in grass. He staggered around for a few minutes, poking and prodding the ground with his stick.

"This looks good," Boggleswort said, "this is the one I want."

Triton took the five thousand dollars and signed over the papers. He was happy to get rid of the land. There was no gold on it. His best scouts had already assured him of that.

The miners continued to mock the old man that evening. "Is he out there right now?" one asked.

"Sure is," another scoffed. "Just him and a pickaxe. Think he'll dig to China?"

"You better believe he's not finding any gold. That land is worthless. I was there when Triton had the scouts check it."

A few days later, someone suggested they go see how the old man was doing, for a bit of entertainment. When they arrived at the clearing, no one laughed.

Boggleswort hadn't dug to China, but he'd come close. A huge pit had been cut into the earth. It was so deep, the bottom was difficult to make out. There was lift apparatus set up on one side, and deep tire tracks leading into the woods. The men were baffled. Triton was furious when he found out. A search party was sent after Boggleswort, but the old man was gone. For several days, the miners puzzled over what had happened until word drifted back into the wilderness from Fairbanks.

The day after Boggleswort disappeared, a man fitting his description had rolled into the small town on a steel wagon buckling under the weight of a dozen wooden crates. Men were hired to help transfer the cargo into a train. When the boxes had been moved and the train started to roll away, the

men cried out. They'd never been paid. Boggleswort reached into a coat pocket and tossed each of them a heavy chunk of stone. The men cursed the departing train, thinking they'd been cheated. When they returned to the light of the station, they were shocked to find themselves holding gold nuggets the size of chicken eggs.

They rushed to check the train's manifest. Only one name was written in the ledger: Jacob R. Juniper. When the cargo was inspected at the U.S. border, it was determined Juniper had made off with nearly two tons of gold.

Triton came after him with everything he had. He hired gangs to track Juniper down, but they couldn't find him. He hired lawyers to seize his assets, but the accounts were all empty. He hired gangsters to break into vaults that might be hiding the money. He bribed politicians and policemen to declare Juniper a public menace. Nothing worked.

Finally, Triton's gang ransacked Juniper's house. They discovered a document hidden inside a vase. It was a map of California, and on it, was an *X*. The *X* was somewhere deep in the Sierra Nevada Mountains. Triton, like everyone else, knew *X* marked the spot.

He packed up his entire operation and traveled to California. For two years, he'd channeled his resources into finding Juniper. If the man couldn't be found, his gold would have to do. For weeks, Triton's men lugged heavy machinery over the steep trails leading into the mountains. The company coffers had been depleted and no one had been paid, but Triton promised each worker a share of the

treasure. Finally, they reached the spot marked by the *X*, a field of boulders between two mountain ridges. They began to dig and kept digging.

Food ran low, tempers ran high and nothing was found. After weeks of digging, one of the workers cried out. In his hand was a shimmering stone covered in mud. The rock was handed over to the boss. Triton was trembling with excitement as he wiped away the dirt. His expression quickly turned to horror. It was the same shining yellow rock he'd sent Boggleswort after in Fairbanks. One detail had been added. Painted over the yellow, was a rainbow trout.

The whole thing had been a trick.

The expedition into the mountains had cost a fortune. Triton's company never recovered. Back in Perkinsville, people laughed when they heard the story. They suspected Juniper would never make a map with an *X* that actually "marked the spot." He was too clever for that.

For the next twenty years, Juniper was neither seen nor heard from. Then, in April of 1909, a peculiar letter arrived at the Perkinsville Town Clerk's Office. It had no return address. Inside, was a document notarized by a law firm in Egypt: The Last Will and Testament of Jacob R. Juniper.

The first lines of the will left instructions for Juniper's house to be sold at auction, the proceeds donated to the town library system. That was not extraordinary. The next part was. The document stated that the 3,000 acres of forest Juniper owned should be left to the town itself, along with a school at the center. The grounds were never to be altered,

or changed in any way. As the bureaucrats at town hall argued over the document's authenticity, someone had the idea to go out and check the woods. Standing at the middle of grassy clearing, a colossal stone building was discovered.

Hearings and debates followed. The board of selectmen demanded an explanation. None could be found. The school had simply appeared one day. No equipment was found on the grounds, nor any record of supply deliveries, or construction crews. An investigation followed, but no answers turned up. Eventually, the inquiry was abandoned. It was a beautiful school. Why shouldn't it be used? The mayor ordered a statue of Juniper be constructed and school named in his honor. The Juniper School opened in 1910. It stands as a mysterious and magnificent reminder of a mysterious and magnificent man. -W. N. A. 1919

Outside the library, the sun had dipped below the horizon cloaking Perkinsville in shadows. The boys looked up from the article and stared at each other.

"Incredible," Sam finally said. "What does it all mean?"

Milo shook his head. Henry's eyebrows narrowed. "I'm not sure," he said slowly. "What else is there?" Several other documents remained.

"Newspaper articles," Sam said. There were four in total, three from the Perkinsville Gazette and another from the Seattle Chronicle.

"What's the Perkinsville Gazette?" Sam asked.

"Never heard of it," Henry answered.

"It used to be a paper in town," Milo said.

The newspaper columns had been clipped and trimmed to fit neatly onto single pages. The first headline read: ***Perkinsville Men Return from War Victorious-Juniper Receives Highest Honors.*** The next was from the Seattle paper, ***Connecticut Yankee Snatches Gold Fortune from Tycoon.*** After that was another story from the Perkinsville Gazette: ***Triton Chases Juniper, Millionaire Missing***. A faded picture accompanied the headline and the boys saw for the first time what Millious Triton looked like. He was an angry, cruel looking man with sharp features and hair slicked back against his skull. Sam shuddered.

The last clipping was dated 1909. The headline read: ***Longtime Perkinsville resident leaves town 3,000 acres. School discovered on premises. Mayor looks for answers.***

Henry picked up the articles one at a time. "These seem to confirm everything. Unbelievable."

"So what happened to him?" Sam asked. "And where's the gold?"

21

Something was different about Ms. Snell. Sam couldn't put his finger on it.

"She's not smiling," Henry whispered. He was right. The forced smile was gone.

"I wonder what happened," Sam said.

"Maybe Mr. Fiddlesbee told her she actually has to teach us something today," Henry muttered. "I bet that would make her pretty upset."

Sam and Henry separated and took seats at opposite sides of the room. Sam next to Margot, Henry next to Missy. The teacher spoke at once. "I'd like your undivided attention," she said solemnly.

"Maybe we really are going to learn something today," Sam thought.

Ms. Snell crossed her arms and began to pace back and forth between them, her expression grave.

"I'm afraid I have some bad news." She shook her head. "Very bad news."

Next to Sam, Margot's expression mirrored the teacher's.

"Sometime between Friday afternoon and this morning, five computers were stolen from one of the other sixth grade classrooms."

Margot gasped loudly. Missy's lip quivered. The rest of the students were silent.

"The situation is quite serious. Not only were the machines very expensive, but they were, of course, critical to the educational experience of the students who used them."

Margot raised her hand.

"Yes, Margot?"

"What can we do to help, Ms. Snell?"

The teacher gave her a look of deep appreciation. "Thank you for asking. Mr. Throxon is leading the investigation. I am asking each and every one of you to keep your eyes open for any suspicious behavior." Margot nodded solemnly. "An anonymous reporting tab has been added to the student portal. This way, individuals in the school community can report suspicious behavior without risking their own safety. I encourage you all to use it."

She looked from one student to the next.

"I'm afraid there's not much more we can do right now. You may log into your portals and begin the math assignment I have set up for you."

Sam couldn't help feeling a little uneasy. Apparently, the boys hadn't been the only ones sneaking around the school after hours. He logged onto his account and noticed a message blinking in the inbox.

"Oh no," he thought. "What now? Not another video."

But it was only an electronic flier advertising a school-wide dance. Luckily, it was still a few weeks away. He breathed a sigh of relief.

"Samuel," Ms. Snell spoke from her desk. "Henry, I need to see you both immediately."

Sam turned around. "Huh? Me?"

She nodded. He glanced at Henry who appeared just as confused.

They stood and reluctantly walked to the teacher.

"I've just received some very upsetting news."

"Upsetting news?" Henry said. "About what?"

Snell raised her eyebrows. "Maybe you can tell me." She took hold of her desktop monitor and spun it around to face the boys. A message blinked on the screen under the *Anonymous Reporting* tab.

Sam and Henry should DEFINITELY be questioned.

"Who sent that?" Sam demanded.

"Yeah, we didn't do anything," Henry said.

"Lower your voices," Snell said firmly. Every eye in the classroom was trained on the boys. "It was reported anonymously."

"So?! What does that mean? Anyone can just accuse anyone of anything?" Sam was angry.

"We must take each tip seriously. That's the procedure. If you're innocent, you have nothing to worry about."

"But we—" Henry started.

She cut him off. "This matter is not up for discussion. I have forwarded the tip to Vice Principal Throxon. I'd like you both to speak to him."

"Speak to him? You can't be ser—"

"I am very serious," she said. The smile was back, but the teacher's tone was cold. "You need to go down to the office…immediately."

Their footsteps echoed on the tiled floor outside room 220C.

"I can't believe this," Sam seethed. "Can she even—what gives her the right?"

Henry shook his head. "The office… the *vice principal's* office. I never thought I'd be going *there*."

"Who was it?" Sam asked. "Who reported us?"

"Hard to tell," Henry said. "Margot or Missy maybe?"

"But why?"

"They don't seem to like us, for one. Maybe they know we've been hanging around in the library?"

"Or maybe they knew they could report us for no reason at all," Sam said.

"That's more likely."

"Max or Roger?" Sam suggested.

"Could be," Henry said. "If all the classrooms in the school can report anonymously. It could've been them."

"We'll explain the whole thing to Mr. Throxon and tell him we had nothing to do with the missing computers."

"You think he'll believe us?" Henry asked.

"Maybe. He's pretty nice. A little odd…but nice…"

"Odd?"

"Yeah. You'll see. He's got that book I told you about, and these stress balls."

They waited nervously on Miss Partridge's couch for the vice principal. The secretary offered an encouraging smile, but it had little effect. When Mr. Throxon's gigantic silhouette appeared behind his office door, both boys shuddered. But when the door opened, they let out a sigh of relief. Once again, Mr. Throxon was smiling. "Hello boys," he said. "Come on in."

They followed him into the office and took seats in front of the desk. The room was unchanged except for several new stacks of *Building a Better Digital You!* on the floor.

The principal reclined in his chair. He wore a pink

shirt and yellow tie. Sam was reminded of a giant teddy bear. Mr. Throxon took out the two silver stress balls and began spinning them. "So," he said. "What can I help—"

Sam cut him off. "Someone told our teacher we had something to do with stolen computers."

"We didn't," Henry added.

Mr. Throxon leaned forward and studied them. "Hmmmmm....well, before we go any further, I think it would be best if we all did some quick meditation. Follow my lead." He closed his eyes and leaned back in his chair and began to chant.

"Owwwwwmmm....owwwwwmmmmm."

The silver serenity balls whizzed around his palm.

"Owwwmmmm...owwwmmm." His eyes opened. "Isn't that better? Now, what were you saying?"

"Uhhh...we didn't take the computers. There's nothing to support the theory," Henry continued. "We are honorable gentlemen. We don't steal. Someone reported us anonymously. If you could just tell us who it was, I'm sure we could explain. "

Mr. Throxon let out a long sigh, shook his head and looked at Henry. "What's your name?"

"Henry Delmont."

"Henry, it sounds like your friend Sam hasn't encouraged you to buy my book yet. Must be trying to keep the wisdom all to himself, happens all the time."

"Your book?"

The vice principal smiled. "*Building a Better Digital You!* Henry! It's all you need."

Henry looked puzzled. He turned to Sam, who gave him an "I told you so" expression.

"You don't look like much of a reader, Henry."

"Actually, I read quite a—"

Mr. Throxon raised a hand to silence him. "That's okay. I wasn't much of a reader either. But fear not, I've just had the *Building a Better Digital You!* app developed. Now kids can receive the benefits of my self-help program on all their favorite devices!"

"Huh?" Henry seemed quite puzzled. "But what does that have to do with—"

"You got reported online right?"

The boys nodded.

"Well that means someone doesn't trust the digital you. They haven't gotten to know you *online*."

"Digital me? But that has nothing to do with it," Henry said in astonishment. "They reported us for something—"

A phone on the desk rang. Mr. Throxon put down the silver spheres and brought the receiver to his ear. He said nothing. Apparently, someone was speaking on the other end of the line because he picked up a pencil and wrote something on a scrap of paper. "Really?" he said. "And those are the most up to date sales numbers?"

As the call continued, Sam gazed around the cluttered office. The picture on the far wall was the only thing in good order. It hung level in a golden frame.

Sam had noticed it on his first visit, but only now studied the drawing closely. It was a pen and ink diagram on faded yellow paper with the words *JRJ School, 1909* printed across the top. The outline of a building was visible at the bottom.

Concentric lines covered the rest. These showed the contours of the landscape around the school. He could make out the path of the river and the canyon where they'd built the tree house.

Sam's eyes moved to the other side of the map. Something had been added near the top right hand corner. He squinted to get a better look. His eyes widened.

A faint *X* was just barely visible between the contour lines. He nudged Henry, whose mouth dropped open.

"What about the app?" Mr. Throxon murmured into the receiver. He looked frustrated. " Well, we can fix that, can't we? Hold on a second." He put the receiver to his chest and looked up at the boys.

"Go back to class. Henry, take a copy of my book and read it tonight. Sam, read it again and download the app. Tell your friends."

"You saw it right?" Sam asked when they were in the hallway. "On the wall? You saw it."

"I saw it," Henry said.

"Am I crazy," Sam asked, "or was there an *X* near the top."

"I saw that too," Henry said. "And there is very little evidence to suggest you're crazy. The thunderstorm fiasco maybe, but—"

"We need to get our hands on that map," Sam interrupted.

"Yes. It's got to lead to the gold. Any idea how we can get it?"

"No. Not yet. But we'll think of something."

22

It didn't take long to devise a basic plan. They would wait until Mr. Throxon left his office, borrow the map, make a copy and return it.

Of course, putting the plan into effect turned out to be more difficult. Miss Partridge was always at her desk during the school day, and although she liked the boys, they weren't about to ask for access to the vice principal's office.

They tried waiting until the school day ended, but that turned out to be equally problematic. Ms. Snell had taken the anonymous tip much more seriously than Mr. Throxon. She watched Sam and Henry closely as if suspecting they might linger after school. She often followed them to the bus.

Whenever they were able to slip away from her, the office never seemed to be vacant. Late in the evenings, when the school was dark and quiet, a light shown under Mr. Throxon's door, and he could be heard on the phone discussing his book and newly developed application.

"This is harder than I thought," Sam said at the end of

March.

Henry nodded. "Very tough. I feel like a giraffe trying to win a limbo contest."

"What we need," Sam said, "is some kind of diversion. Something big that takes him out of the office for a minute or two. Miss Partridge has a copy machine next to her desk. We could use that. I don't think she would mind."

"How can we create a diversion?"

"Beats me," Sam muttered.

"I have an idea," Milo said quietly, "but it's pretty dangerous."

"Danger is Henry's middle name," Sam said.

"Really?"

"No. It's Alfred. What's the plan?"

"Well," Milo explained, "it seems like Throxon is the only one here in the evening. The school is really quiet, right?" Sam and Henry nodded. "So the plan is pretty simple. I'll hide under Miss Partridge's desk while you two make a whole bunch of noise in the hallway. That should draw him out of his office. I can copy the map, then rehang it before he comes back."

"You think he'll leave the office if he hears noise?" Sam asked.

"Sure he will," Henry said. "If it's yelling or something like that. He's laid back, but not that laid back."

"Sounds risky," Sam said.

"In the pursuit of the exceptional," Henry retorted, "risk is to be expected. If we do get caught, we can just tell him we downloaded his app."

On Friday afternoon, they snuck into the woods, hiked down to the river and crossed to the tree house. There, on the platform, the details of the plan were reviewed. At five o'clock, they crept back through the woods and into the deserted building.

They tiptoed across the lobby and peeked into the office. The secretary's desk was empty.

"Miss Partridge must have gone for the night," Sam said.

Henry pointed to Mr. Throxon's door. A light shown underneath. "Must still be here," he whispered. "I can hear papers rustling. Go ahead, Milo."

Milo tiptoed to the secretary's desk and ducked underneath. Sam and Henry returned to the lobby.

"Put your mask on," Sam whispered. He and Henry slipped the same masks they'd worn on Halloween over their faces. The masks would protect their identities if they were seen from a distance. If, on the other hand, they were caught…Sam didn't like to think about it.

"You ready?" Henry asked. Sam gave him a thumbs up. "Okay. On three we scream. One…two…three…go!"

"AHHHHHHHHH!"

The empty hallway seemed to amplify the sound. It reverberated off the walls as they tore off down the hallway. At the end, Sam turned left, Henry right. They flattened themselves against the wall and listened.

Silence.

"Again," Sam said to Henry. "Now." They screamed.

This time, creaking hinges and the slamming of a door followed. Footsteps echoed down the corridor.

The boys spun around and took off in opposite directions. Sam dared a glance back. A tall figure loped down the hallway in pursuit.

It was not Mr. Throxon.

Sam squinted through the narrow slits of the mask. The man was thin with a waxy, pockmarked face. It was Milo's teacher, Mr. Dean

"What is he doing here?" Sam wondered with a

shutter. Mr. Dean did not seem like one to let them off with a warning.

The teacher's pace quickened.

Sam stopped to catch his breath around the next corner. The footsteps behind him fell silent. Mr. Dean had reached the first intersection and was deciding what to do next. He wheezed loudly.

Sam screamed a third time, hoping to prevent the teacher from turning back. "AHHHHHHH!"

The footsteps started up again, faster this time. Another scream echoed through the building. It was Henry, trying to draw Dean in the other direction. It was no use. The teacher's mind was made up.

Sam raced down the hallway to a stairwell at the end. Two at a time he hurtled up the steps. When he reached the third floor, he heard the teacher start up behind him. Sam pushed open the door and headed down another corridor. He just barely made it around a corner before Dean burst out of the stairwell.

"He's gaining on me," Sam thought with horror. Dean had somehow closed the gap. "I have to do something. I have to throw him off." Another stairwell came into view. An idea occurred, a long shot, but what choice was there? He pulled the stairwell door open causing the hinges to creak loudly. Then, instead of going through, he ducked behind a cabinet a few feet away.

Crouched on the ground, knees tucked into his chest, he waited. The door continued to squeak as Mr. Dean approached.

It slammed shut.

Sam held his breath.

The teacher stood only a few yards away. He wheezed so loudly, Sam wondered if he might pass out. Dean looked from the stairwell door, to the vacant hallway, then back again.

"Please don't see me. Please don't see me." Seconds passed. His lungs ached. Dean didn't move. Sam couldn't hold his breath much longer. His face was dark red. His body began to shake. "This is it. He's got me. I have to take a breath or I'll die."

CREAAAAKK

Dean pulled open the door and started down the stairs.

Sam gasped and sucked in a breath of fresh air, then another and another. He was safe, at least for the time being.

When the teacher's footsteps died away, Sam got up and snuck off towards the back of the school.

At every turn he was sure he'd find Dean lurking in the shadows, ready to pounce, but he reached the Industrial Arts room without detection. He tiptoed across the vacant shop, into the Pit and out the back door.

The cold air bit into his sweat-soaked skin. Sam darted through the shadows to the woods. He tumbled into the bushes and crouched down on his haunches to wait.

"Sam?" A whisper nearby.

"Yeah," he answered, shivering. "Where are you?"

"Over here." Sam crawled across the leaves and bumped into Henry a few yards away.

"You made it," Henry said. "I was really worried."

"Yeah," Sam whispered. "I'm okay. Where's Milo?"

Henry shook his head. "No sign of him."

Sam peered from the bushes with a knot churning in his stomach. The school was shrouded in darkness. He could barely make out the shop door.

Minutes passed.

"This isn't good," Henry said. "He should have been here by now."

Sam nodded. "We have to go back. He may need our help. What was Dean doing in Throxon's office?"

Henry shook his head again. "I don't know. If he has Milo, I don't think there's anything we can do. "

"We've got to at least try. Maybe he's hiding somewhere and needs us to create another distraction. We can't leave him."

"You're right," Henry said softly. "Let's go."

Sam was just about to step from the underbrush when Henry pulled him back. "Look!"

Across the lawn, the shop door cracked open and a tiny figure slipped through. He dashed towards the woods and dove in next to Sam and Henry.

"Sorry," Milo whispered. "I had some trouble."

"What happened in there?" Sam asked.

"We thought you were a goner," Henry added. "Why in the world was your teacher in Throxon's office?"

"I don't know. When Mr. Dean came out, I stayed under the desk. I thought Mr. Throxon would be right behind him. But it turned out he was alone."

"Throxon's probably at a book signing," Sam muttered.

"I tried to take the map down, but it was bolted to the wall!"

"That's probably why it survived all these years," Henry suggested.

"It was really tough to get it down. Every time I loosened one of the bolts, another got tighter. I kept trying, but nothing worked. I finally discovered all three bolts had to be turned at the same time. It was not easy." Milo took a deep breath. "By the time I made the copy and got the map back in place, I could hear someone coming. I had to hide under Miss Partridge's desk until he ran past the office."

Sam was speechless.

"And there was a little problem…I couldn't get the map back quite right. I was rushing…It's crooked. If Dean goes back in the office, he might notice."

"Don't worry," Henry said. "Everything in Throxon's office is a mess. No one would notice a lopsided picture frame."

"Nice job," Sam said. "Really good work." Even in the dim light, he could tell Milo was beaming.

Henry folded the map and tucked it into Milo's backpack. Then the boys crept along the edge of the lawn to the driveway and down to the road. No one was picking them up. That would have been too risky. Someone might see the car. Their parents might ask questions.

Instead, they planned to walk to Sam's house. It was a long walk, more than five miles, but it gave them a good chance to talk about the afternoon's events.

"…and then I ducked behind a cabinet," Sam recounted. "Dean thought I went down stairs. It was pretty lucky."

"Really lucky," Henry agreed. "I still have no idea what he was doing there. We ran into him once before. Literally. Remember Sam? You crashed into him."

Sam nodded.

"Maybe he's looking for the person who stole those computers."

An hour later, in Sam's bedroom, Henry spread the map out on the floor and together they examined it. The *X* lay in the northeast quadrant. It was small, but unmistakable.

"Where do you think that is?" Milo asked.

"Not sure," Henry whispered. "But I bet we can figure

it out. We've come this far after all."

"We'll go after it Monday," Sam said.

"Good idea," Henry agreed. "But fortune favors the prepared. Let's not go into the woods empty handed. Do you guys have flashlights?"

"Flashlights?" Milo asked. "What for?"

"It still gets dark early. We might be out there for a while."

"You're right," Sam said. "And we need some shovels, just in case, and probably some rope."

"You think we're going to be digging?" Henry questioned.

"I don't know. As you said, it's best to be prepared."

"I can bring rope," Milo said. "But we can't take shovels on the bus."

Henry nodded. "Mr. Arthur may have some we can borrow."

"That seems like a suspicious request," Sam cautioned. "Even by our standards."

"Nonsense," Henry replied confidently. "Nothing suspicious about it."

23

"That has to be the most suspicious request I've ever gotten," Mr. Arthur said. "Shovels? What in the world do you need shovels for?" The boys had just arrived in Industrial Arts after a long day in room 220C. "Sure. I got shovels. But what for? Grave robbery?"

"Oh you know, just a little something we've been working on," Sam said nonchalantly. "Nothing too exciting."

Mr. Arthur studied them with narrowed eyes. "Fine. Keep me out of the loop. That way I can plead ignorance if you get caught. I'm in enough hot water over these stolen computers."

"What do you mean?" Sam asked.

"Oh it's nothing," he said. "Throxon came down here asking if I knew anything about the stolen computers. Said he'd gotten an anonymous tip from another staff member. I suspect your teacher there, Ms. Snell, might've put him up to it."

"Really?" Henry asked. "Why would she do that?"

Mr. Arthur laughed. "Oh, she's not my biggest fan.

Last year she tried to take away my funding. Wanted to convert the shop into some kind of cyber lab or something, with computers and iPodes."

"I think they're called iPads," Henry said.

"Yeah, that's what I said. At any rate, I put up a fight. As you may have guessed, I think shop class is important. Kids don't spend enough time working with their hands these days. I know a couple of the old timers on the school board and they ruled in my favor. Ms. Snell wasn't too happy."

"No way," Sam said. "That's unbelievable."

"Well, that's alright. I got nothing to hide."

"So what happened when Mr. Throxon came?" Henry asked.

"He comes in here and says 'You know anything about the missing computers?' I say 'no'. That was it. Then he starts trying to sell me a copy of his eBook. I like the guy, but I'm quite happy without a 'digital me'."

The boys nodded.

"The other fellow was a lot more interested."

"What other fellow?" Sam asked.

"Guy with a pale face, Dean I think his name is. Nervous guy. Wanted to know what Throxon had asked me about, if he had any suspects, that kind of thing. Must be new this year too. I never met him before. Kind of odd."

"What do you mean odd?" Henry asked. "That's Milo's teacher."

"Never mind," Mr. Arthur said. "Follow me." He hobbled off towards the other side of the shop. "Now the thing about shovels is, simple as they are, it's hard to find a good one. The handles break and blades chip." He ducked into the tool closet and reached behind a shelf. "But these," he said, displaying two fine looking shovels, "will never break. Just like all the other tools we have."

"Why not?" Henry asked.

"Because," the old man said with pride, "these were made by Juniper Tools."

Henry dropped a wrench he'd been holding. Sam swallowed hard.

"Juniper Tools?" Milo asked quietly, glancing at his friends.

"That's right," Mr. Arthur said. "Finest tools ever produced." He gestured to the far wall. A huge sign hung above the saws. *Juniper Tools.* Sam suddenly remembered seeing it the first day. He'd completely forgotten.

"They don't make tools like these anymore," he continued. "You know in all my years, I've never had one break? That's the only reason we still have 'em, Juniper Tools closed a long time ago. I should know. My grandfather used to run it."

Henry dropped the wrench he'd just picked up.

"Your grandfather was *Juniper*?" Sam asked, in the steadiest voice he could muster.

"No, no," Arthur said. "My grandfather was William Arthur. He worked for Mr. Juniper and ended up running his company. Will you stop throwing my wrench on the floor, Henry?"

"Sorry," Henry said. "It's just, I never noticed that sign before, even though we were looking for— I mean even though it was right there. It's…an interesting story."

"Yep. When I first started, the school was actually called Juniper School. That was all a long time ago. The company's gone now, and they changed the school name too. Almost all that remains of Mr. Juniper are these tools. See, here's the symbol." He pointed at Henry's wrench. A *Y* had been engraved in the metal. Except it had one added detail: a thin line connected the two outstretched arms.

"That's the emblem. That's how you can tell. It looks like a *Y*, but it's actually a slingshot." Henry gasped, but the shop teacher paid him no mind. "He made slingshots better'n anybody. You'll never find one now of course, but keep an eye out for the tools. If you ever see that symbol on a hammer or a wrench, maybe at a yard sale, somewhere like that, snatch it right up, because it's the only one you'll ever need. Just look for the emblem. Back to work now." He turned and began to limp away.

"Mr. Arthur, wait," Sam called. "Do you know anything else about Jacob Juniper?"

The old man stopped, and turned around slowly. His eyes were narrowed. "Who said his name was Jacob?"

Sam gulped. Mr. Arthur shuffled slowly back to the boys. "How'd you know that?"

"We…just…well…" Henry stammered.

"We saw the statue," Milo whispered, "in front of the building, and we looked him up."

"You did, huh?" The shop teacher seemed unconvinced. "And what did you find?"

No one spoke, each side trying to read the other. Mr. Arthur stared at Henry, then Sam, then Milo. His eyes narrowed. "You really want to know do you?"

They nodded.

"Juniper… was a genius in the pure sense of the word… I mean a real true genius. Everything was easy for him. They say he could read Shakespeare before most children can talk. There was no problem he couldn't solve, no task he couldn't accomplish, and no subject he couldn't understand. Life can get pretty boring for someone like that."

The hair on Sam's neck stood on end. The shop was deathly quiet. Mr. Arthur lowered his voice even further.

"There was only one person who truly fascinated him: his wife, Samantha. Juniper loved her more than anything." He peered at them with unfamiliar intensity. "But her life was cut short."

Sam gulped.

"After she died, things got very strange. There was a rumor… that he found a fortune in gold…bankrupted a crooked tycoon in the process. But the gold…well, it was never actually seen by anybody. Never found in a bank or a mentioned in his will. And Juniper, he disappeared too. Not only from Perkinsville, but from the pages of history. I imagine you had quite a time looking him up."

They nodded dumbly.

"Didn't you find it strange that no one talks about him? That there aren't books written about him? Legends about his treasure, the way there are about Captain Kidd's and the Knights Templar?"

Sam tried to say "yes", but no sound came out.

"There's more to the story. There has to be. But no one knows for sure." Mr. Arthur glanced behind him, as if someone might be listening. "Take the shovels," he said, voice barely audible. "I'm sure that's why you want 'em. But be careful. Jacob Juniper's legacy is shrouded in mystery. I wouldn't start throwing his name around."

"Why not?" Henry whispered.

Arthur stared at him for a moment, then lifted his eyebrows, "Just a feeling…"

They stood together in silence for a few seconds, until finally, the usual expression returned to the shop teacher's wrinkled face. He chuckled. "Now enough about all that. Get back to work. The shovels are in the Pit. Take whatever you need, just don't kill yourselves. I'll be in my office." He limped away.

"Can you believe he knew?" Henry asked.

Sam stared blankly at the huge *Juniper Tools* sign. "I don't know what to believe anymore."

They snuck three shovels into the woods after school and headed straight for the river. They laid the equipment on the bank opposite the beech tree. Sam and Henry had flashlights, Milo a headlamp and his backpack. The key was hidden inside, wrapped in an old tee shirt.

Henry took out the map and the boys studied it together.

"I've never seen so much detail," Sam said. "It's like he knew every bump, every ditch. I think this is the beech tree." He pointed to a spot near the top of the paper. "Which means the *X* would be that way."

They wound their way through the trees in pursuit of the treasure. The detailed contour lines were helpful, but it was tough moving through the woods without a path.

"Look," Henry said, gesturing to an especially dense web of lines, "I think that means a steep hill. The *X* is just beyond it. We should be close."

Sam looked around. "Over there," he cried, pointing to a ridge. "That's it!" They hurried to the base of the slope and scrambled up and over it with their shovels. On the other side, a valley of granite boulders spread out before them.

"We've been here," Sam remarked. "Remember? It was the second day of school."

His friends nodded. "Yeah," Henry said, "the boulder graveyard. I remember. Every single one is drawn on the map."

"It looks like the *X* is drawn *inside* one of them," Sam puzzled. "I wonder what that means. It should be over this way."

They wound between the granite slabs and stopped in

front of what was, without question, the largest one.

"I don't get it. It should be right here."

Milo circled behind the rock. "Guys," he said a second later, "come here."

A massive crack ran down the back of the boulder. He pointed to a triangular chunk missing from the bottom. Carved deeply into the rock, was an *X*. Below it, the jagged entrance to a cave.

24

Together they peered into the blackness of the cave. It was impossible to see more than a few feet inside.

"This is getting crazier and crazier," Sam muttered.

"I never thought…" Henry whispered. "I mean…it's just…wow."

"Well," Milo said after a few moments. "Who's going first?"

Henry didn't say anything.

"I will," Sam said.

"It could be dangerous," Henry warned. "Who knows what's down there?"

"Don't worry," Sam said sarcastically. "I've got *this*." He reached into his shorts and took out a pocketknife. It was smaller than his thumb and had the words *Swoos Army Ages 6 and Up* along the handle.

"Oh wonderful," Henry said. "That'll protect us."

"You know what?" Milo said, kneeling down and removing a length of rope from his bag. "We should tie ourselves together, in case one of us falls off a cliff or something. That's what real cave explorers do."

"Spelunkers," Henry declared proudly. Sam and Milo looked confused. "Cave explorers. I read that book, remember? They're called spelunkers. Never mind…"

Milo knotted the rope around Sam's waist, then his own, and then Henry's. He put on the headlamp. They stood shoulder to shoulder.

"Here we go," Henry muttered. "*Down the rabbit hole…*"

Sam turned on his flashlight, ducked under the rock ledge, and stepped into the blackness. He had seen caves on television, but never in real life. As he crept over and around the jutting rocks, a shiver ran down his spine. He wondered who had been there last.

They moved slowly. It was difficult to see. The shovels were heavy, and they had to stop repeatedly to untangle the rope. Even at this pace, it wasn't long before the light from the entrance disappeared.

Further and further they went.

"Can you see anything?" Milo whispered.

Sam leaned forward and peered into the darkness. "Not really. Wait, I think there's some kind of cavern opening up here."

The dim flashlight beam illuminated the beginning of what appeared to be a large chamber. It rose up before them like a hall.

"Wow," Sam said walking across the expansive space. "Look how high the ceiling is. Let me just…AHHHHH!"

The ground was suddenly gone. Sam tumbled wildly through the blackness, arms flailing. Air rushed past and he realized with horror that he was falling to his death.

He braced for impact.

All of a sudden, the rope snapped taut, jolting him to a halt. His body folded violently. The shovel slipped from his hand and the flashlight spiraled away. It smashed somewhere below. Through the pain, he was dimly conscious of screams from above, and then he began slipping further down.

Sam regained his bearings and heard Henry shouting.

"Grab the rock! I…I…can't hold you!"

He looked up and was able to make out the silhouette of something hanging in the air above him. It was Milo, headlamp still glowing. Sam had pulled him over the edge of the cliff. Henry held them both.

Milo tried to find something to grasp, but it was no use.

"I…I…can't…h…h…hold you," Henry groaned.

The rope slipped, and they dropped another three feet. Henry wasn't going to last much longer.

Sam didn't know how far it was to the ground. Maybe a few feet. Maybe much farther. Whatever the case, one thing was clear: Henry was too far up. There was no way he could survive a fall. Without hesitation, Sam reached into his pocket, withdrew the small knife, and began frantically sawing at the rope.

As he cut through the last of the fibers, he looked up towards his friends, knowing he might never see them again, then once more, dropped into the abyss.

He fell no more than five feet before slamming into the ground.

Realizing he wasn't dead, Sam sprang to his feet and looked up to Milo.

"I'm okay," he yelled. "I'm on the ground. Are you alright, Henry?"

"Y-y-yeah," Henry stammered, "but I'm slipping again. I can't hold Milo much longer!"

Milo was more than twenty feet off the ground, but the rope that had tethered him to Sam hung down much further. "Milo," Sam yelled. "You've got to climb down!

Can you untie yourself?"

"I'm trying," Milo gasped. "The knot is too tight!"

The headlamp dropped another foot. Henry was fading. "You're going to have to cut the rope around your waist," Sam yelled. "Hurry!"

"I don't have a knife," Milo called back.

"I'm going to throw this one up to you!"

Milo looked down. The beam from his light shined into Sam's eyes.

"Ready?! One…two…three…" Using every ounce of concentration, Sam tossed the knife up along the dangling rope. It sailed into the air, illuminated in the beam of Milo's light.

"Grab it!"

As the knife began to fall from the top of its arch, Milo lunged forward and caught hold of it with one hand. Clutching the rope above him, he cut through the loop encircling his waist, leaving the rest of the line intact.

"HURRY!" Henry yelled.

Milo wrapped his legs around the rope and slid down to Sam, hitting the ground just as Henry collapsed in exhaustion.

"Wow," he said after a few seconds. "That was a close one."

"Too close," Sam breathed, heart still thundering.

"Hello down there?!" Henry shouted. "Are you okay?!"

"We're okay!" Sam called back. "Are you coming down?"

"Am I coming down?!" Henry yelled in disbelief. "I thought we were going to try to get you two back *up*. You mean we're still going?"

Sam turned to Milo, received a nod, then looked back up to Henry. "Of course. Tie the rope around one of those rocks and get down here. Oh, and thanks for saving our lives."

It wasn't long before Henry had secured the rope and shimmied down to his friends. "Everyone alright?"

"I think so," Sam said. "How about you?"

"I'm okay, but let's not do that again." He looked around. "So where are we? Did you explore?"

"Nope," Sam answered. "We were waiting for you."

"Well, I'm here now. So let's get to it."

The chamber had straight rock walls like the first. The floor was dirt. It was square shaped, about twenty feet on each side, and completely empty.

"This is the end of the cave," Sam said. "The treasure must be buried right here."

"I think you're right," Henry said examining the walls. "Nowhere else to go."

Without hesitation, Milo picked up a shovel and started to dig. Henry and Sam almost knocked each other over lunging for the other shovels. They dug and they dug, until the edges of the chamber were piled high with dirt.

"I wish we brought some water," Henry gasped. "This is hard work. It's important to stay hydrated."

"That's for sure," Sam said, tossing another scoopful of dirt aside.

"Maybe we should quit for the day. It's going to take us a while to get back out."

Sam nodded. "I think you're right. What do you think Milo?" Milo didn't answer. "Milo…" Sam repeated. "What do you think?

"I think… I think… I found something," Milo said quietly. His shovel had struck something solid and when the boys scrambled to unearth it, they discovered a large flat log. They soon realized there was a whole row of logs, laid down next to each other, as a barrier of some kind.

"It's a platform…or a wall," Milo said.

"There's really something here," Henry said. "Huge logs don't just find their way into caves. Somebody put them here."

"Juniper," Milo whispered.

"I bet something's hidden underneath," Sam said, his voice barely audible. "Let's move these out of the way."

The logs were much heavier than Sam had guessed. Even with the three shovels acting as levers, they were just barely able to dislodge the first one. Moving it to the side of the chamber was an even more difficult process. It took almost an hour to clear away the platform, and when it was finally gone, the only thing beneath it was more dirt.

"Must be right under here," Sam said, and he slammed his shovel into the soil expecting it to strike something hard. It didn't.

"Hmmm…" Henry said. "Let's dig a little more."

They did. After half an hour and several more feet, they had nothing new to show. Sam slumped to the ground. "We've dug like seven feet down. What's going on here?"

"I'm worried," Henry said. "Is it possible we're on a wild goose chase?"

"What? Why do you say that?"

"I've been thinking about it for the last hour," Henry said.

"Why though?"

"Because that's what this Juniper guy was all about. He was so smart; the only thing that amused him was tricking people. He did the same thing with Triton. I want to believe, but I can't stop thinking we're being duped." There was silence. Sam didn't know what to say.

"Wait a minute," Milo exclaimed. "I just remembered something." He jumped to his feet. "I need my backpack. I've got all the information in there. Let's go."

Sam and Henry followed him out of the hole and up the rope to the passageway leading to the surface. Milo darted behind a nearby boulder and retrieved his hidden backpack and the map. He took out a tattered manila folder labeled *Treasure File- Top Secret* and shuffled through it until he got to the article about Juniper's life. "Here," he said, pointing to a line near the end. "I forgot about this."

Sam and Henry leaned in and read the excerpt.

Back in Perkinsville, people laughed when they heard the story. They suspected Juniper would never make a map with an X that actually 'marked the spot'. He was too clever for that.

"You see?" Milo said softly. "It was a trick. This map probably does lead to the treasure…"

"…but it's not where it seems," Henry said.

The *X* in the top right corner of the map was glaring. It was marked in dark ink. "It's so obvious," Sam said. "Too obvious."

"It must be a decoy," Henry added. "But what other way is there to read a map?"

"I don't know," Sam said. "I always thought *X* marked the spot."

"Not with Juniper," Milo said. He reached across the map and pointed to a small marking. "I think with Juniper, *Y* marks the spot." At the tip of Milo's finger, hidden in between a web of lines, was a tiny *Y*.

"Is that what I think it is?" Sam asked in astonishment.

Milo nodded. "The slingshot. Juniper's symbol."

He was right. Even more amazing was that the *Y* was drawn inside the perimeter of the school.

"It's hidden in the building," Sam said. "Just like we

thought."

"Of course," Henry declared. "The article says the school cannot be altered. That's why! That's why it hasn't been updated! That's why the internet cables haven't been put in the walls and everything is run down! There's something hidden! We really should have thought about this more carefully."

"We were too excited," Sam said.

"Where do you think that is?" Milo asked, looking carefully at the *Y*. "The cafeteria?"

Henry shook his head. "I think the cafeteria is on the other side. Must be the gym."

"Yeah," Sam said. "I think you're right."

"We head to the gym then," Henry said. "The treasure awaits!"

"Whoa!" Sam exclaimed. "We can't just leave that mess down there. We have to fill in the pit."

"Why?" Henry asked.

"If it was meant as a decoy, we should leave it as a decoy."

"What are you talking about? We're the ones who fell for the decoy. It was meant for us," Henry protested.

"Even so," Sam argued. "We need to put it back exactly as it was."

Henry shook his head. "I think you're overdoing it, but…. alright. Let's go back and fill it in." They made their way back down the cave and began the painstaking process of replacing the logs and filling in the pit.

Sam took the Juniper file back from Milo and carefully reviewed it that evening. He studied the mysterious key and slowly reread all the articles.

At the bottom of the pile, he discovered something he'd never seen before. It wasn't a clue. It was single sheet of paper on which *Notes* had been written in perfectly formed block letters. Milo's handwriting. Apparently, Milo had been studying the file as well. He hadn't gotten very far.

The only thing written below the heading was *Samantha Juniper born May 29th, 1845*. Milo had drawn an arrow pointing to *May 29th* and written *Same birthday as me!*

Sam smiled and made a mental record of Milo's birthday. He suspected there wasn't usually much of a celebration.

25

A turkey sandwich lay uneaten on the table in front of Sam. Henry stared down at Tupperware container filled with cold pasta. Milo had a peanut butter sandwich. He'd only managed one bite.

"I haven't eaten since we found the cave," Sam said. "Nearly 24 hours."

"Me neither," Henry said, giving the pasta a poke. "Too excited."

"At least you two get to search the gym after lunch. I have to go back for math with Mr. Dean," Milo said sadly.

"I don't know how much searching we're going to do," Sam said. "Too many kids around."

"We're going to try," Henry said. "But it won't be easy."

It wasn't easy at all. The class had moved on to yoga. Sam and Henry were stranded on tiny mats near the center of the gym and there was no opportunity to walk around. They scanned the room for any sign of Juniper's treasure, but it was hard to look thoroughly from the downward dog position.

"That was disappointing," Sam said on their way out.

"It's okay," Henry muttered. "We'll find it after school. I hope Ms. Snell doesn't give us any homework."

"That has never once happened," Sam said flatly.

"I can dream," Henry said, pushing open the classroom door. "Hey, what's going on?"

A line of students waited near Ms. Snell's desk. Everyone looked grim. Margot stood at the front, talking to the teacher. When she finished, she walked back to her seat, glaring at Sam and Henry as she passed.

"Oh no," Henry said. "What now?"

Ms. Snell spoke to the rest of the students in line, then rose to address the class.

"I have some bad news," she said somberly. "While you were at physical education, I was away from the classroom preparing lessons for next week. Something *terrible* happened during my absence: valuable items were taken from the bags of several individuals."

Whispers swept through the classroom as victims made themselves known. Sam realized why so many students had been waiting to talk with the teacher.

"Multiple cell phones vanished, along with two tablet computers." Missy gasped. Margot buried her face in her hands.

"The situation is quite serious," Ms. Snell said. "I contacted Mr. Montero via email and learned that all members of our class were present during physical education. I *hope* this means the perpetrator was not someone in this room."

Sam noticed the teacher's eyes dart briefly to him.

"I want to remind you all about the anonymous reporting tab inside the portal. Please use it if you have any information about the theft."

The students nodded. Ms. Snell nodded. "Now, log on and begin copying down tonight's homework assignment."

"Have you checked your backpack?" Sam asked Henry when they left the room. "Did anything get taken?"

"Not that I noticed. Then again, the only thing in there is an old banana, and they can have that."

"I wonder who it was?" Sam said. "Cell phones and tablets are expensive right?"

"Yes," Henry said. "They are. But we don't have time to worry about that now. Where are we meeting Milo?"

"Lobby," Sam said quietly. "We'll kill some time down at the tree house, then come back to search the gym when the school is empty."

Students filled the lobby, laughing, texting and filming one another.

"I guess the thief didn't get too far," Henry said. "Looks like everyone here still has a cell phone."

"That's for sure. Hey, there's Milo."

Milo leaned against a wall at the opposite side of the room. They rushed over to him.

"Ready?" Sam asked.

Milo nodded excitedly.

"Alright," Henry said. "Let's go out through the Industrial Arts room." The trio turned to start back across the lobby, but two girls blocked their path.

"Where do you think you're going?" It was Margot. Missy stood beside her.

"Mind your own business," Sam growled. "Come on guys."

"Take one more step," Missy hissed. "And we're reporting you to Miss Snell."

"What are you talking about?" Henry demanded.

"You heard me. We both know you're the ones who've been stealing from the classrooms. We tried reporting you anonymously, but that didn't work."

"Now my phone is gone," Margot snapped. "So it's personal. We're taking matters into our own hands."

Henry's face reddened with anger. "We didn't steal anything!"

"Oh no? Then where are you going?" Margot demanded.

The boys glared at her.

"That's what I thought. Turn around and get onto the bus!"

What could they do? If the girls told Ms. Snell they were sneaking around the school, there was no telling what would happen. Sam and Henry had no choice but to follow the other students onto the bus, leaving Milo to ride home alone.

The same thing happened the next day and the day after that.

"What are we going to do?" Sam lamented at lunch on Thursday. "They won't leave us alone."

"We need to figure out who's *really* been stealing from the classrooms," Henry answered. "You know, clear our names."

"Good idea," Milo said. "But how? There are so many kids in the building."

"Well," Henry said. "I know who we can start with."

"Who?" Sam asked.

Henry leaned in and lowered his voice. "The person who thinks it's okay to throw eggs at houses, torture us on the bus and smoke in the bathroom."

"Max!" Sam exclaimed. "You're right. It could be him.

He always seems to have a new phone. That takes a lot of money."

Henry nodded. "Exactly."

"Wait a minute," Sam said. "The day of the first theft, when the computers were stolen…that was the day we found the statue. Max was here after school! He probably left Mr. Arthur's room and then took the laptops. He was with Roger and that other kid, Trent. The computers were probably in their bags!"

"You may be right… but he's innocent until proven guilty. We can't judge him like Ms. Snell judges us. What we need to do," Henry said, "is catch him in the act. That way we can clear our names, once and for all."

"But if he already stole the stuff," Sam protested, "how are we going to catch him in the act?"

"He'll get greedy," Henry said. "Thieves usually do. He'll probably do it during lunch, when the classrooms are all empty. We need to monitor his movements."

For the next week, the boys tracked Max's location. Most of the time, he stayed seated at his usual lunch table. Sam followed him to the bathroom twice, and Milo tailed him to a deserted water fountain. Nothing suspicious occurred.

"We're not getting anywhere," Sam said after a week. "And we can't start searching the gym until those two gremlins leave us alone."

"Don't worry," Henry replied. "If he's stolen this much, he *will* steal again."

"I think he already has," Milo said biting into his sandwich, "or at least, someone has." Sam and Henry turned to him.

"What do you mean?" Sam asked.

"Yesterday a bunch of cell phones got taken from *my*

classroom."

Henry looked across the cafeteria to the table of eighth graders. Max was snapping a picture of himself. His cell phone had a shiny silver case.

"That case looks new," Henry said. "Did we miss something?"

Milo shrugged.

"Did anything of yours get stolen?" Sam asked.

"No. I don't have anything anyone would want. But I do think somebody went into my bag."

"Really?" Henry asked.

"Yeah. When I got home yesterday it seemed like everything in my backpack had been moved around. Nothing was missing, but I don't think I'm going to bring the Juniper File to school anymore. I don't want it to get lost."

"You had the *Juniper* File in there?!" Sam said with alarm. He'd given the file back to Milo a few days before.

Milo nodded. "I've been studying it for clues."

"Do you think someone could have read it?" Henry asked. "It does say *Treasure File-Top Secret* on the outside."

Milo shrugged. "I hope not. I don't think someone looking for a cell phone would have noticed the writing. And if they had, they would've just taken the whole folder."

Sam wasn't so sure. "Maybe. Or they could've made a copy like we did. Better keep it at home from now on." He thought of the file and the note Milo had written about his birthday. May 29th was the next day. Sam and Henry had gotten Milo a new backpack. Sam needed to remember to bring it to school.

"Hey," Henry suddenly blurted. "Where's Max?"

Sam spun around and peered across the cafeteria to the crowd of eighth graders. Max wasn't there.

"He's gone," Henry said, dumbfounded.

Sam craned his neck, trying for a better view. Several of the eighth graders seemed to be looking back at him, but Max was not among them.

"I don't know. He was there a sec— wait, there!" Max lingered by the doorway at the other side of the room. He glanced over his shoulder, and for a fraction of a second, his eyes met Sam's. Then he slipped through the door and disappeared.

"We've got to follow him!" Henry declared. "This is our chance!"

"I'll go," Sam said. "Three people will draw too much attention. Meet me in Industrial Arts." He hurried away without waiting for a response.

By the time he crossed the busy lunchroom, the long hallway outside the cafeteria was empty. But halfway down the corridor, a classroom door stood ajar. "Must be in there," Sam thought, "going through backpacks." He crept to the door and slipped noiselessly inside. The room was dark. Sam reached for the light switch, ready to shout "Gotcha!" But as he turned, the door slammed shut.

Max stared at him through the window. "That oughta stop you from following me," he said with a grin, then raised the cell phone with the silver case. Sam realized he was about to take a picture and dove out of the way just in time. The eighth grader cursed loudly and walked away.

Sam pushed against the door with all his strength. It wouldn't budge. He tried again. Nothing. He pressed against the glass and peered down to the floor. A rubber wedge held the door. Max had planned the whole thing. Sam slammed his shoulder into the oak. It didn't move.

He slumped to the floor in dismay. The room was unfamiliar. Computer terminals lined the walls. If he were discovered alone in the dark with the expensive machines, he'd be in serious trouble. All the thefts would be pinned on him. No one would believe he'd been tricked.

Frantically, he searched for another means of escape. Voices sounded in the hallway, footsteps. Lunch had ended.

At the back of the room, Sam noticed a large vent cover near the base of the wall. He dashed over, grabbed hold of it and pulled. To his surprise, the grate swung forward revealing a rusty air duct. He dove through the opening. As he fumbled to put the vent back, the muffled sound of a woman's voice, a teacher, drifted in from the hall. "That's funny," she said. "Not sure how that doorjamb got there."

Desperately, he tried to force the grate back into place. It wouldn't fit. The doorknob creaked. With all his strength, Sam yanked the vent cover. Just as the classroom door swung open, it snapped into place, catching a piece of his skin in the seam. He bit down hard on his lip to stifle a yell. Blood dripped down his finger. Sam tore his hand away in a quick motion, leaving a sizable chunk of flesh behind. It was clear from the flood of voices that students had entered the classroom. He backed away from the light, turned awkwardly around and disappeared into the darkness.

The ventilation system was a massive network of aluminum ducts that ran through the walls of the school, completely dark inside and deathly silent. Sam crawled along without the slightest idea where he was going. The tunnel was sweltering. In no time, sweat covered his body. He moved along one length of the tunnel and then another, panic rising in his gut. There was no sign of an exit grate.

The suffocating grip of claustrophobia took hold with dizzying swiftness. No one knew where he was. Henry and Milo would realize something was wrong, but even if they came looking for him, they'd never, in a million years, think to search the ventilation system. With horror, he pictured himself stuck in the maze. He imagined dying of starvation, his parents never knowing what had happened.

He decided to go back. Whatever punishment awaited, it was better than perishing alone in the labyrinth. He tried to turn around but found the passage too narrow. He groped his way forward, inch by inch. His hand struck something that protruded out from one of the side panels and for a moment he thought it might be an escape hatch, but when he pulled the object, nothing happened.

Sam's heart began to pound as the metal walls closed in around him. He lay on his stomach, eyes shut, terror coursing through his veins.

"Get it together," he thought. "You're fine. Calm down." He took several deep breaths and began to crawl onward. He made it down three more lengths of tubing, and turned left. He squinted up and down, trying to find a way out, but saw only tunnels of ductwork leading into darkness. Panic gripped him again.

Suddenly, he heard something. A faint high-pitched ringing. It stopped for a moment, then started again. Sam knew the sound. It came from a wood saw.

He crawled forward with newfound determination. At an intersection, he stopped and listened. The sound got louder. He reached another fork and paused again. He waited. Silence. Finally, the banging of a hammer sent him scurrying down another length of piping. A dim light glowed at the end. Sam breathed a sigh of relief. An exit.

A metal grate like the one he'd removed earlier covered the end of the heating vent. He peered through the slats and recognized the familiar tables and stools of the Industrial Arts room. Joy washed over him. Henry and Milo stood nearby.

"Well what are we going to do?" Henry asked, hammer in hand. "You're sure he wasn't in the vice principal's office?"

"The door was open," Milo answered. "No one was in there."

"Max must have him somewhere," Henry said nervously. "Maybe we should tell Mr. Arthur."

At that moment, Sam pushed against the grate with all his might. It sailed forward onto the cement floor with a loud clatter, causing Henry and Milo to spin around. Their mouths dropped open as they watched him spill out of the opening.

"Sooo…" he said, standing up. "What are you guys working on?"

26

"I wouldn't have believed it," Henry said. "If I hadn't just seen you crawl out of the wall… I wouldn't have believed it."

Milo nodded. "I guess Max knew we were watching him."

"Yeah," Sam agreed. "When he trapped me in the classroom, he said 'that oughta keep you from following me.' He almost got a picture of me stuck in the room, but I dove out of the way."

"What a snake," Henry said angrily. "Innocent until proven guilty… but he's looking worse and worse. "

"Don't worry," Milo said. "He'll slip up eventually."

Mr. Arthur limped up to the workbench. He had not mentioned Juniper since their conversation weeks before and things in the shop had returned to normal.

"How's it going?" he asked, glancing down at the small engine the trio was rebuilding.

"Pretty good," Sam said. "Still doesn't start."

"You'll get it." He watched them tinker for a moment before saying something that made all three boys freeze.

It had nothing to do with lost tycoons or buried treasure, but was just as shocking. "I came over to make sure you were planning on attending tomorrow's dance."

They looked up at him in alarm.

"Dance?" Sam asked nervously. "What dance?"

"I take it you haven't heard then."

"I think we'd remember something as alarming as a dance," Henry said.

Mr. Arthur laughed. "Miss Partridge is in charge, and it would sure be nice if you all went. She gets a kick out of it. I'm surprised you don't already know about it. She spent a lot of time making sure it was advertised on the portal."

Sam suddenly remembered the electronic flier he'd received on the *Student Portal* weeks before. "Oh…right… I do think we got something about that."

"She really needs a good turn out because a lot of teachers don't want to have it anymore."

The boys stared up at him blankly.

"Every year, for as long as I've been here, there's been a spring dance. It's held in the cafeteria. I take down the back windows so a breeze blows in, and it always looks real nice. Even got a generator set up to power the speakers because circuits in the cafe tend to short out. " He smiled broadly. "Josh Basserman is the DJ, does a good job with it. Nice kid. He used to be in this class. Pretty good with his hands. Don't know why he didn't keep it up." He shook his head. "Let his friends talk him out of it I guess." Sam remembered Josh. He'd been the tour guide on the first day of school.

"It's tomorrow night. Sorry for the short notice. You don't have to go with anyone, but better decide who you'll ask to dance the last song." He gave Sam a pat on the shoulder and walked away.

"Dance the last song?" Henry said. He'd suddenly gone white. "What's that supposed to mean?"

"I think you know what it means," Sam said uneasily.

"Yes," Henry stuttered. "I know what it means, but…us? We can't…at least I…what are we going to do? We can't go. I don't dance."

"We have to go," Milo said. He seemed oddly amused. "Mr. Arthur is expecting us. Besides, dancing is easy."

Henry stared at him, eyes wide. "Are you mad? What do you mean dancing is easy? Have you ever tried it? We had to do a dance as a class for elementary school graduation. I had a three second solo, and it was *horrible*. Literally. It brought horror to the audience. Even my grandmother deleted the video."

"He's right," Sam said. "Dancing is not easy."

Henry looked queasy when they left Industrial Arts. He looked even worse as they typed the afternoon's homework into the portal. By the next morning, he looked like death.

"What's with you?" Sam asked. There were gray bags under Henry's eyes.

"Oh," he said, "didn't get much sleep. Couldn't stop thinking about it."

"What? The dance?"

Henry winced at the word. "Yes. That."

"Me neither. But, maybe we'll be all right. We don't have to actually dance. We can just hang out there, I think."

"Sam," Henry said, "the kids who just 'hang out' at dances are forever classified as the losers. We have to dance. If we just sit alone, someone will take a video of us, and we'll have to deal with that all over again."

"Hmm," Sam said. "If we dance really badly, they might take a video of *that*. What if we just don't go?"

Henry shook his head, "No good. Then we'll be thought of as the kids who aren't even cool enough to show up. Plus, Mr. Arthur wants us to go."

Henry had a point. Sam tried to convince himself it wouldn't be so bad, that no one would notice them. But if he'd learned one thing during sixth grade, it was that blending into the crowd was far from easy.

"Listen," Henry said as they crossed the lobby. "Everyone is talking about it. We're doomed."

He was right. The dance seemed to be the only topic of discussion.

"You're going, right?" a seventh grade boy asked another.

"Yeah. Everyone is. Look how many people are on this group text." He held up his phone. "They're all going."

"None of the teachers want to have it," a girl whispered to her friend.

"Really? Then who's in charge?" she asked.

"No one. It's unsupervised."

"Did you hear that?" Henry asked. "She said it was unsupervised."

"That can't be right," Sam said without conviction. "Mr. Arthur and Miss Partridge will be there."

Henry didn't seem to hear.

Milo's birthday had arrived, and they presented him with the new backpack at lunch. "Wow," Milo said, after unwrapping the gift. "How did you know it was my…? This is great. Thanks a lot." He stared at the backpack in admiration. It was clear he didn't get many birthday presents.

Sam's mind was elsewhere though. He was so anxious about the prospect of the dance, it was hard to think about anything else. During gym class, he kept falling out of his yoga poses, and back in homeroom he couldn't stop his foot from tapping nervously. Ms. Snell was not amused.

He had taken the Juniper file back from Milo and tried to go over it after school, but couldn't concentrate. At six thirty, he began searching for something to wear. Nothing seemed quite right. He finally decided on a pair of jeans and a red tee shirt. He sighed and headed downstairs.

"Ready?" his mom asked.

"I guess," he muttered.

They got into the car and headed over to pick up Henry and Milo.

Mrs. Torwey tried to chat with the boys on the way to the middle school, but after receiving little in response, she gave up. The car fell silent.

"Are you getting out?" she asked when they stopped outside the school. The faint thud of a bass line drifted out to the car from somewhere inside the building.

"I guess," Sam finally said, reaching for the door. "Come on guys."

Milo hopped from the car, but Henry held back, considering his options. Finally, he got slowly out and Mrs. Torwey pulled away.

Dismay gripped Henry's face when he saw his friends. Like Sam, Milo wore a tee shirt and jeans. Henry's outfit could not have been more different.

He wore a tight fitting silk shirt, deep purple, with bright silver buttons and cufflinks. A thick belt with a golden buckle held up a pair of pleated pants. An elaborately patterned necktie fluttered in the warm breeze.

"Why aren't you two dressed up?!" he demanded. "Where are your clothes? Are you…are you changing in the bathroom?!"

Milo and Sam looked at each other, then back at Henry. "Dressed up?" Sam asked. "Were we supposed to dress up?"

"I don't think we were supposed to dress up," Milo said. "Where did you hear that?"

Henry's face had taken on a yellowish color that closely resembled his tie.

"It's okay," Sam assured him. "You have an undershirt on right? Just wear that."

Henry shook his head. "I don't have one."

"You could go shirtless," Milo said with the slightest hint of a grin.

"Oh no," Henry moaned. "I always do this."

A group of older kids walked past. A few pointed at Henry and another snapped a picture. Not one of them was dressed up.

"Here's what you do," Sam said. "Lose the tie and untuck the shirt. That'll look fine. Cover up that belt buckle maybe…I mean it's nice and all but, maybe just for tonight?"

Henry nodded vigorously. He pulled out his shirt and nearly tore the tie in half trying to remove it. On the way up the steps, he slammed it into a trashcan.

The lobby was vacant and the boys walked across the tiled floor without speaking. The only sound came from the tapping of their shoes and the bumping of music deep inside the school.

"Everyone must already be in the cafeteria," Sam said, looking at his watch. "We're pretty late."

"Maybe no one else showed up," Henry whispered hopefully.

They stopped at the cafeteria doors. Sam glanced at his friends. "Last chance to bail."

Henry shook his head. "No," he replied, voice barely audible, "the only path is forward." He pulled open the door.

Two things became immediately clear. First, they were not the only ones who'd shown up, and second, Miss Partridge and Mr. Arthur had completely outdone themselves. Countless strands of blue and green lights lit up the cafeteria. Each one twinkled to the beat of the music. From somewhere overhead, thousands of silvery bubbles drifted down into the enormous crowd moving at the center of the room. A gigantic disco light spun above the dancers, showering the whole scene in silver rays.

At the far side of the room, a DJ booth had been constructed. There stood Josh Basserman, with earphones, a microphone and several pieces of equipment. A line of students waited to make requests next to him.

"This is awesome," Milo said. "We should dance."

Sam and Henry stared at him as if he'd suggested they dive in front of a train. "You're joking," Sam said.

"Yeah," Henry agreed. "Good one, Milo. Let's head over to those tables and make a plan."

Milo followed them to a line of lunch tables positioned against a nearby wall. They sat down in the shadows and again surveyed the dance floor.

"Look at all those kids," Sam said. "When did they learn to dance? Are they all eighth graders?"

"It looks that way," Henry said. Sweat dripped down his forehead. "There's Max and his gang."

"We look kind of silly sitting over here all alone," Milo muttered. "No one else is sitting down."

"He's right," Sam said. "We shouldn't stay here. Kids are going to start noticing us."

"Alright," Henry said. "Let's try doing a lap. We can take in the scene. You lead."

Sam nodded and strolled casually towards the crowd of dancers, trying to look cool. He didn't know the song playing, but did his best to bounce up and down to the music. It wasn't easy.

"Head that way," Henry said, pointing to the DJ stand. "It'll look like we're trying to request a song."

They didn't get far before Sam heard someone calling his name. It was Mr. Arthur. "Hello boys," he exclaimed with a wide grin. "I didn't see you come in. Enjoying the party?"

"We just got here," Sam said over the sound of the bass line. "But…so far so good."

Mr. Arthur nodded with understanding. "Best to dive right in. I don't know about this music you kids are listening to, but it seems to be good for dancing. What's with you, Delmont? "

Even in the dim light, Henry looked ghastly pale. Sam was concerned he might actually pass out. "Oh," he said weakly, "I'm just getting into dancing mode. Should be ready by the next song."

Mr. Arthur nodded. "Have a good time."

The trio continued on, moving through the crowd slowly. Sam saw several sixth graders he knew, each one swaying in time with the music. As they neared the DJ booth, Henry nudged him on the shoulder and leaned in to whisper something. "Look to your right. Don't make it obvious."

Sam turned his head slowly. Ali and Candace stood a few feet away, dancing and laughing with each other.

"Maybe we should try talking to them," Sam suggested.

"W-W-What?" Henry stuttered. "No way. That would

be crazy."

"Come on," Sam continued. "We look like idiots standing out here alone." Without another word, he stepped toward the girls.

"Wait!" Henry cried. "What are you going to say?"

"I have no idea…" Sam said. It was too late to turn back. Ali had noticed them approaching. He opened his mouth to speak, but before he could, several tall figures stepped into their path. Sam had been walking with such determination that he slammed into one of them. The boy spun around and glared at him. It was Max.

"Get out of here, loser," the eighth grader growled. He shoved Sam backwards into Henry, then turned and looked at Candace. "Hi," he said calmly. "How's it going?" Sam was shocked. What happened next was even more shocking.

"Hey. What are you doing? Don't push him." It took Sam a moment to realize it was *Candace* who had spoken.

"Yeah," Ali added. "Leave us alone. We don't want to talk to you."

Both girls glared at the towering eighth graders. A moment later, Candace brushed Max aside and walked up to Sam. "Hi," she said. "Want to dance?"

"I…err…" he glanced at his two friends. They both looked astonished.

"Come on. It's my birthday, so you have to." She looked past him to Milo and Henry. "They can come too."

"It's m-m-my friend Milo's birthday too," Sam stuttered.

Candace didn't seem to hear. She reached down, grabbed his hand and pulled him into a group of dancers. It happened so fast that Sam had no time to resist. He stumbled after her awkwardly, Henry and Milo in tow.

Max watched them leave, his expression seething.

When they reached the middle of the dance floor, Candace spun around and started to dance beside Ali. They seemed to be familiar with the song and bobbed up and down to the beat in perfect rhythm.

"Come on!" she yelled to Sam.

Sam decided to try and mimic her, but it turned out to be much more difficult than he'd anticipated. Every time the two girls dipped down, Sam went up. The result was something like a seesaw.

Candace noticed his frustration and started to laugh. "You're trying too hard!"

"No, no," Sam said conscious of his reddening face. "I'm just getting warmed up."

"Sureeee you are," she said smiling. "Alright then, let's see some moves."

"I…well…okay…" Sam mumbled, racking his brain for a way out of the situation. "Let me see…" He was just about to turn and run from the cafeteria when the song faded out.

"You're lucky," Candace said, still smiling. "I need to take a break." She and Ali turned to leave just as Josh Basserman's voice boomed across the cafeteria from the DJ stand.

"Ladies and Gentlemen," he announced, "I have a special request." Sam looked towards the DJ booth. Max stood beside Josh, smiling. "I have just been informed by my friend Max here that a few sixth graders would like to demonstrate some dance moves for the crowd. Where are they, Max? Let's make sure we can all see them."

Max raised his arm and pointed to where Sam, Henry and Milo stood near the center of the cafeteria. There was a murmur from the crowd as eyes began to lock on the trio.

"So you really *were* just warming up?" Candace asked in astonishment. She backed away with the rest of the crowd, giving the boys room to move. Sam's heart began to thunder. The blood drained from his face.

"No… I don't… I didn't ask…uh, Henry?" Sam spun around.

Henry's face was white. "We've got to get out of here," he whispered. But it was too late, a new song had started.

"Show us something boys," Josh boomed from the front of the room.

Sam stood stuck in place. Hundreds of eyes stared at them from the edge of the circle that had miraculously formed. The music got louder, the beat faster.

"Come on," someone yelled from the shadows. "What are you waiting for?"

"What are we going to do?" Sam asked his friends. Laughter started to drift up from the crowd. Cell phone cameras were coming out.

"Nothing," Henry said. "We're doomed. This is how it ends for us."

"Hey," another voice called out. "Aren't those the kids from the bus video?"

"Yeah, I think you're right," another answered.

"Losers!"

The crowd burst into laughter. Cell phones cameras flashed around the circle.

"This video is going to be even better!" a girl shrieked.

Sam started to sweat. Someone spoke nearby. "Get behind Henry."

"Huh?" Sam spun around.

"Get behind Henry and crouch down." It was Milo.

"Like hide?" He was utterly confused.

"Just do it."

Seeing no other option, Sam moved back and crouched down behind his taller friend. This new position sent the crowd into an even greater frenzy. Sam caught sight of Max laughing uncontrollably from the stage. Henry remained rooted in place, dazed. The music began to rise.

"Don't move," Milo commanded.

"What the heck…?"

Milo backed to the edge of the circle. The music continued to climb. Sweat dripped down Sam's forehead as he crouched in place, at the mercy of the crowd. "Milo?!" he yelled. There was no answer. His chest heaved in and out.

Just as he was about to collapse, the beat dropped with a deafening roar, and Sam felt the thud of something slam into his lower back, then his shoulder. He looked up just in time to see Milo spring off him and sail into the air above Henry.

The crowd was instantly silenced.

All eyes watched as the tiny boy hung there for a moment, in the swirling strands of light, before falling, head first, toward the ground.

Sam thought Milo was going to smash into the cement, but at the last moment, he caught himself and froze in a half handstand. No one spoke. Milo slowly twisted his legs together, then suddenly dropped, unwound like a top and spun across the floor on his head.

The crowd gasped. Sam glanced at Henry whose mouth hung open in disbelief.

Milo effortlessly rolled onto his back, then up onto his hands. He split his legs apart and began to swing them back and forth, like a gymnast on a pommel horse, in perfect rhythm with the music.

Milo flipped over backward, caught himself upside

down, and froze on one hand. There he remained, legs outstretched like the arms of a slingshot, until the music finally stopped.

The crowd was silent. A full second passed.

And then the cafeteria exploded in applause.

Milo dropped down to his feet and walked over to his friends. "I love that song."

When the applause finally died down, the boys followed Milo back to the table. "Who are you?" Sam asked. "And where did you learn to dance like that?"

"Yeah," Henry added. "That was incredible,"

"Oh," Milo said, nonchalantly. "I just kind of taught myself."

"Right, of course," Henry replied sarcastically. "Just went ahead and taught yourself to break dance one Thursday evening. Who hasn't done that?"

"You saved us," Sam said patting Milo on the back. "We owe you."

"No," said Milo. "You don't owe me anything."

Even though Sam and Henry had done nothing but stand in the middle of the circle, they too became instant celebrities. Kids pointed in their direction for the rest of the evening.

"Did you see those three dance?" one asked.

"Yeah. That was sick," another replied.

"This has turned into quite an evening," Henry said, as they sat at the table enjoying their new status. "I'll have to thank Max."

The others laughed. "I think he left," Sam said. "I haven't seen him in a while."

"Oh well," Henry shrugged, "I guess our friendship will have to wait. Hey," he added, "look who's coming."

Sam turned around and felt his heart rate quicken.

Candace and Ali were approaching the table.

"Hi," Candace said in a cheerful voice.

Sam wasn't sure how to respond. He decided to play it very safe. "Hi."

"Where have you guys been?" Ali asked. "We haven't seen you on the dance floor since your big show."

The question had been directed at Henry. "Err…" He stuttered, "We were just taking a breather."

"There are only a few songs left," she said. "How about you three forget the breather and come dance."

Sam, Henry and Milo exchanged glances. Henry shrugged. "Why not?" With that, they followed the two girls back into the crowd, amazed at their good fortune.

27

The following Monday was unseasonably warm, even for early June. It had taken nine months, but Sam was actually excited about school.

"Milo," he whispered, as they walked down a corridor off the lobby, "look around. Kids are still pointing at us."

"It was quite a display," Henry said, "not soon to be forgotten."

A murmur of hushed voices followed the boys wherever they went. It had been the same in the days following the bus video's release. This time smiles and thumbs-up accompanied the whispers.

Juniper's treasure had not been forgotten, but there was still the problem of Margot and Missy. The pair had been relentless in their surveillance. Every afternoon they followed Sam and Henry to the buses and made sure they boarded.

The boys found themselves with just two weeks left in the year, still unable to shake the girls. Searching the gym during the summer would be impossible.

It was Milo who came up with a solution.

"They really like your teacher right?" he asked at lunch.

"They sure do," Sam said.

"Milo, they would die for her. And she's not someone who should be died for."

"Alright, well here's the plan. It came to me last night. We make up a flyer that says there's a big meeting right after school tomorrow. Something really important. We'll put your teacher's name on it, maybe say not to be late." Sam and Henry nodded. "I'll sneak down before the end of the day and hang it in the lobby. If Missy and Margot see it, I bet they'll be so worried about missing the meeting, they'll forget about following you."

"That is a brilliant idea," Henry said.

"Yeah," Sam said. "That's great…but…"

"But what?"

"It's just, there aren't really any flyers anymore. Everything's on the portal. Do you think they'll believe it?"

"You have a point," Henry conceded. "But I think we can work around that. We don't need them to believe it entirely, just enough to leave us alone for a few minutes while they double check."

"You may be right," Sam said. "It's worth a try."

"Leave the flyer to me boys," Henry said. "But give me a few days. I'll have to convince my mom to get some pink paper, and then I'll have to secretly print it. It seems a long way off, but I think we should wait until Friday."

"Friday?!" Sam exclaimed.

"Better to wait and do it right. Don't you think, Milo?"

"I guess," Milo replied. "Oh! By the way, something weird happened in my classroom today."

"Really?" Sam asked. "What?"

"This morning my class had gym, so we were out of

the room for an hour or so. When we came back, our backpacks were open. All of them. And everything was moved around, like someone was looking for something. Even Mr. Dean was worried about it. He wanted to know if anyone's bag had been broken into before."

"Wow," Henry said. "Weird. Did you tell him you thought someone had gone into yours?"

Milo shook his head. "I didn't feel like it. I've been using the new backpack you gave me and it's empty. There's nothing in it for them to mess up this time."

"Someone after more cell phones?" Henry suggested. "Whoever it is, they must really need money."

"Yeah," Sam agreed. "But why would they search Milo's classroom again? They already went through those bags."

Henry and Milo only shrugged.

The week that followed felt like the longest of the school year. Tuesday, Wednesday, Thursday. Each day crawled by at a snail's pace. The waiting was torture. But finally, at long last, Friday arrived.

"We might really find something this time," Henry said excitedly as they walked into the building. "As long as we can shake those two imbeciles."

"Did you make the flyer?" Sam asked.

Henry removed a bright pink sign from his bag and held it up for Sam.

NOTICE: EMERGENCY COMMUNITY MEETING
TO DISCUSS ONGOING THEFTS
TO BE LED BY MS. SNELL
THIS AFTERNOON IN THE CAFETERIA
MEETING BEGINS PROMPTLY AFTER SCHOOL
DO NOT BE LATE

"That's perfect," Sam said. "I just hope they believe it."

"They're not very bright," Henry said. "So they should."

All morning, Sam's eyes drifted to the clock. He couldn't concentrate on anything. His leg twitched anxiously and he kept clicking the wrong tabs on the student portal. Finally, it was time for lunch. He rushed to the cafeteria with Henry. They were so engrossed in conversation about the afternoon ahead, they walked right into Miss Partridge. A huge stack of cards she'd been carrying fluttered to the ground.

"Oh boys," she said with a sigh. "You'll be the death of me."

"Err…sorry about that," Sam said. "We weren't really paying attention."

"I guess not," she said, "and I was just on my way to get an elastic so that wouldn't happen. Second time today. Mr. Dean knocked them off my desk when he came into the office this morning. Never even told me what he wanted."

Sam and Henry bent down to help pick up the cards.

"No, no," she said. "It's alright. Didn't I tell you they'd take me all year, Sam? I'm just getting them over to Mr. Throxon now."

Sam remembered his trip to see the vice principal on the first day of school. Miss Partridge had been working on the student identification cards when they first met.

"I guess I really should have entered them online," she continued. "At this point in the year, what good are names and birthdays? Now off you go to lunch."

Apologizing again, the boys took off for the lunchroom.

Milo was waiting for them. "Do you have it?"

Henry slipped the flyer out of his pocket and passed it to Milo under the table.

"Thanks," he said. "I'll put it up after Industrial Arts. Come on, let's head there now."

"Good idea," Henry said. "I don't feel like eating."

Mr. Arthur was happy to see them when they arrived at the shop class.

"Perfect," he said. "It's time to start organizing things, and we need all the time we can get. I want Milo and Henry to make sure all the tools are put away, and Sam, I need you to shred some paper. We still get a good amount this time of year, even with everything moving online. After that, I need you to help me find the generator from the dance…not sure where I left it."

"Could I help Milo and Henry?" Sam asked. "I think the tools are pretty bad."

The shop teacher raised an eyebrow. "Either that or you three just want to keep talking."

Sam smiled. "We can do the paper as soon as the tools are all set. I bet it'll go pretty fast with three people."

"Fine. Fine," the old man said. "Suit yourselves. Keep an eye out for that generator… and those shovels. I know you brought them back but I can't seem to find them."

Final preparations for the afternoon were made over a pile of tangled wrenches, each with a thick *Y* branded into the handle.

"Just make sure you put it in an obvious spot," Sam said. "If they don't see it, we're back to square one."

"It'll be hard to miss," Henry said. "But we won't have much time to escape to the library before they realize they've been tricked."

When the school day ended, Sam and Henry left room 220C at their usual pace. Margot and Missy followed.

Sam spotted the pink flyer hanging near the front door when they entered the lobby. He approached it casually.

"Hold on, Henry," he said, stopping in front of the flyer. "I just need to tie my shoe." Sam knelt down and fumbled with his already tied shoelace. Henry leaned against the wall, his head inches from the flyer.

Margot and Missy watched from a few feet away.

"Did they see it?" Sam whispered through clenched teeth.

"Hard to say." Henry stretched out his arms in a yawn, trying to draw the girls' attention to the flyer.

Missy suddenly elbowed Margot and nodded to the sign. Margot squinted to read the words. Her expression quickly turned to shock. They turned and rushed out of the lobby, leaving Sam and Henry alone.

Sam sprang to his feet. "Quick, let's get to the library before they realize what happened." They rushed down a nearby hallway towards the back of the school.

"Thank goodness," Milo said, when they clambered into the library.

"Don't worry," Sam said. "It worked perfectly."

"So now what do we do?" Milo asked. "There are still lots of people in the school."

"Now," Henry whispered. "We wait."

Tucked in the back corner of the library, behind a wall of dusty books, they sat together in silence. Ever so slowly, the shadows on the floor lengthened, until finally, the sun dipped from view.

"What time is it?" Milo asked. Henry looked at his watch.

"Seven thirty. This is the latest we've ever been here."

"The school must be empty," Sam said. He reached under the table and took the bronze key from his bag. For a moment he stared at the words inscribed at either end. *Choose. Wisely.* He shivered, slid the key into his pocket and turned to his friends. "Let's go."

They slipped out of the library and snuck down the vacant halls toward the gym. At every corner, they stopped and listened for approaching footsteps. The only sound was silence.

When they reached the gym, Henry opened one of the double doors and waved the boys in.

"Spread out and start searching," Sam said. "Check everywhere."

Milo headed to the lockers, Henry to the trophy case and Sam to the equipment closet. After an hour, they switched. They looked under the bleachers and beneath the pile of gymnastics mats. Nothing turned up.

"We've searched everywhere," Henry said when they met in the circle that marked the center of the gym. "Every possible hiding spot."

He was right. It was large room, but there wasn't much to it. Just one big open space.

Sam sighed. He had been so hopeful that the mystery would finally be solved. He looked up in frustration.

High in the rafters he could just barely make out the bronze bell from the great rope race. It seemed like a long time ago. Sam thought of Roger reaching out to grab the Y-shaped gong.

The Y-shaped gong….

Sam squinted at the bell. There it was, just visible in the shadows.

"Guys…I…I…"

"What is it?" Henry asked.

"I figured it out."

"Huh?"

He pointed at the bell. Henry and Milo looked.

"The gong," Sam stammered. "The ringer, it's an

upside down…

"SLINGSHOT!" Henry screamed. "YES! How are we going to get up there?"

"We climb," Sam said. He walked over to the far side of the room where two cranks stuck out of the stone wall. Sam took one in his hand and began to turn it. Milo did the same. A loud clinking echoed through the gym as the two thick ropes slid down towards the painted circle at the center of the wooden floor. When the ropes touched the ground, Sam and Milo let go of the cranks and silence fell once more.

"Well," Henry said quietly, "let's go."

Taking hold of the nearest rope, Sam climbed into the air. Henry started up opposite him. Milo followed.

When they got to the rafters, the three boys hung there, staring at the bell. The gong had been cast, unmistakably, in the shape of the Juniper *Y*. It looked identical to the slingshot.

"I can't believe I didn't notice it," Sam murmured.

"None of us did," Henry replied.

Sam reached out and took hold of one arm, half expecting an alarm to go off. He moved it back and forth under the umbrella of the bell.

Nothing happened.

"What do we do with it?" Sam asked.

"I don't know," Henry said.

The bell itself was secured to the ceiling by a heavy chain. They tried pulling on the chain. They tried twisting it. They rang the bell repeatedly. Nothing worked.

"I don't get it," Henry said.

"Let's climb down and think it over," Milo suggested.

"Good idea," Henry said. "My arms are getting tired."

When they were back on the floor of the gym, Milo started walking around the circle where the ropes dangled.

"It couldn't be something as simple as ringing the bell," he said, "or twisting it. Juniper wouldn't have wanted someone to unlock his secret accidentally. Kids have been using that bell for a long time." He scratched his head.

"Yes," Henry said. "You're right."

"Think about the key," Sam said after a moment.

"What about it?" Henry asked.

"Well, you could only find it if you were sitting in the tree," Sam noted, "in the exact spot Juniper used to sit."

"Go on," Henry prompted.

"I don't know," Sam continued. "It's as if he wanted someone like him to find it. Someone who figured out a way to get to his tree, then spent enough time there to notice something in the water."

Milo nodded in agreement.

"So you think we need to hang from those ropes until we notice something?" Henry asked.

"I doubt it," Sam said looking around the gymnasium. "I think there's something else."

His eyes fell on the two cranks protruding from the wall. He walked over to them. Henry and Milo followed.

Like the bell, the cranks were cast from solid bronze, the same metal used to make the key. They were roughly two feet in length, had identical handles and both disappeared into the stone wall.

"Have you ever seen anything like this?" Sam asked. "These are connected to the ropes somehow. But it's all behind the stone. There's no way to see the gears."

"Strange," Henry said. "How would you fix them if they ever broke?"

"You couldn't," Sam said, pressing a hand against the huge stone blocks. "You'd have to knock down the wall. Maybe Juniper didn't want anyone to see how these cranks work."

"Some kind of lock?" Henry asked.

"I don't know."

"But Sam, the gym teachers use these every year. Like Milo said, he wouldn't risk someone discovering his secret by accident."

"You're right," Sam agreed. "So what's the least likely way these cranks could ever be turned?" There was silence for a few seconds as they considered the puzzle. "It seems to me, the ropes would most likely be all the way up, or all the way down. They would never be left in the middle."

"And I bet it would be even less likely that one would be left just shy of the floor and another just shy of the ceiling," Milo added.

Sam nodded. "Yeah, yeah, you're right. But he wouldn't just make it random. There's got to be a certain number of turns."

"Right," Henry said, his voice rising, "like a combination. What do people use for combinations?"

"Birthdays!" Sam exclaimed. "Everyone uses birthdays for combinations!"

"That's what I use," Henry said. "I guess I should try something more original. What was Juniper's birthday? I think it was July 4th, right?"

Sam's eyes narrowed. "July is the seventh month. Seven spins and four spins? The ropes would be right next to each other both near the top. That can't be it."

Henry furrowed his brow. "You're right."

"Maybe his wife's birthday?" Milo suggested.

Sam suddenly remembered Milo's notes in the Juniper file. Next to Samantha Juniper's birthday he'd written, *Same birthday as me!*

"May twenty-ninth" he whispered. "Five, twenty-nine."

Without speaking, Henry began to rewind the ropes. They rose and retreated into the ceiling.

"Okay," he said, when both ropes had disappeared from view. "Here goes." With great care, he began to turn the first crank.

"One," Milo said. "Two."

The rope slithered out of the ceiling.

"Three."

It inched downward.

"Four."

"Five."

Henry stopped. No more than a foot of the first rope was visible.

He moved to the second crank.

The clicking of gears echoed through the empty gymnasium. Milo counted twenty-nine rotations. The second rope stopped three feet off the ground. Nothing happened. They walked over to the circle painted on the floor and stared up at the ropes.

"Well, that didn't work," Henry said after a moment.

"Hold on," Sam whispered. "Let's climb up to the bell."

One after another they worked their way up the second rope, until they were once more up near the bell.

"It looks the same," Henry said from below Sam.

He was right. Nothing had changed.

"Yeah," Sam muttered. "I guess that wasn't it."

"Wait," Milo said from below Henry. "The gong, it's not moving."

"Huh?" Sam said looking back at the bell.

The Y-shaped gong had been swaying the last time. Now, it remained unnaturally still. Sam reached out and tried to flick it. Something held the metal in place.

Gripping one arm of the *Y*, Sam tugged it forward.

But it didn't budge.

"It's stuck," he said.

Repositioning himself on the rope, he tugged the gong with all his might. There was a soft metallic click as whatever had been holding it gave way. The gong lurched forward, slamming into the bell. A clang echoed through the gymnasium and died away.

"I don't know what that was about. Let's climb dow—" Sam stopped.

There was a dull rumble. The boys looked down and gasped. The flooring inside the painted circle directly below them slid slowly away to reveal a gaping black hole. There was a momentary silence. Then, the clicking of gears drifted once more through the air.

As the boys held tight, the rope descended into the darkness.

28

"What's happening?!" Henry screamed.

"Should we try to jump off?" Milo cried.

"NO!" Sam shouted. "JUST HOLD ON! THIS IS IT!"

Milo had already disappeared into the abyss. A moment later Henry was gone too. As the clinking of gears continued, Sam watched his own feet disappear, then his knees and waist. A moment later his eyes were level with the gym floor, and then everything went dark.

"Are you guys okay?" he yelled.

"I think so," Henry called back, his voice shaky.

"Where's it taking us?" Milo asked.

"We're about to find out," Henry said.

The descent continued, the clicking from above becoming more and more distant. Down they went. Deeper and deeper. Stale, cold air filling the empty space.

Just as Sam began to wonder if the rope would ever stop, there was a thud below him and Henry cried out.

"Ouch. Milo. Look out Sam!" But it was too late Sam dropped onto his friends who were piled in a heap on a cold hard floor. He couldn't see a thing.

"You're on my face."

"Sorry Milo."

Sam rolled over. All the boys lay on the ground, breathing heavily.

"We made it," Henry whispered. "We made it."

"Why is the rope still uncoiling?" Milo asked.

Sam couldn't see anything, but the faint clicking of gears was still drifting down the shaft.

"I don't know. Is it piling up?" Sam felt for the rope. "Wait, where is it? It was just here." His heart started to race. "Where's the rope?!"

He jumped up and clawed through the darkness. Waving his arm high, he was just able to graze the retreating rope before it slipped away from his grasping hand.

"It's going back up!"

Henry and Milo were silent. Together they stared up the shaft as their only link to the surface clicked away. Moments later, a terrible groan rumbled down as the gym floor slid back into place, leaving them alone in total darkness.

Panic simultaneously gripped all three boys.

"We're trapped!" Sam shouted.

Milo began pounding on the wall.

"No…" Henry said. "No…no…no…"

Sam collapsed onto the floor, trembling. His friends sank down beside him.

"Wait a minute," Henry gasped. "We've got to get a hold of ourselves. Don't panic. Let's just take a few breaths. We're okay."

Sam inhaled slowly. Then exhaled. Then inhaled again. "Okay," he said. "Okay. That's better. Milo, you alright?"

"Yeah, I'm okay."

"We're fine," Sam said, regaining his composure. "Let's just think about this. Does anybody have a light? I can't see anything."

"Yeah, yeah. A light," Henry said. "I have my penlight! Hold on."

Henry turned on his flashlight and a beam of white cut through the blackness.

The shaft opened into a small square chamber composed entirely of heavy stone blocks. It was roughly twenty feet wide and ten feet high, without windows or doors. Henry moved his flashlight over the walls, the floor and the ceiling. He took a step forward and repeated the process.

"No…" he whispered. "Oh no. Please no."

It was unmistakable.

"NO!" Sam shouted. "NO!

The chamber was completely empty.

Milo rushed forward, his head moving rapidly from side to side. "There has to be something," he said. "There has to be."

But there wasn't. No treasure chest. No padlocks. Nowhere to put the key. No way out. Nothing but cold gray stone.

Sam sank to his knees. Despair washed over him. It was despair deeper and darker than the shaft itself. He'd been able to fight it off during the wasted summers of the past, throughout the agonizing days with Snell, on the day the video had been released, every other time the treasure had eluded them. For the first time, Sam lost faith.

"I'm sorry," he said softly. "I thought it was real…but I was wrong. We'll probably never get out of here, but if we do I'm all done. There's no gold. I was stupid to believe any of it." He took the bronze key from his pocket and turned it over in his hands. "It was all a trick."

A full minute passed in silence, until Henry cleared his throat. "There is a poem," he said, "by a writer named Stephen Crane. I can't remember the title. It's about a man who chases the horizon and the setting sun. Around and around he goes…never quite catching it…but never losing hope. And that's us, Sam, we're going to keep going. We're going to keep going after the horizon…"

Sam picked up his head, but didn't turn around. He couldn't yet face his friends. "Thanks," he said. "Really, it means a lot. But the guy in the poem was a fool and so are we, because sometimes you just have to know when it's time to give up."

With that, he stood, cocked his arm and hurled the key across the chamber and into the stone wall. Sam turned around and finally faced his friends.

Henry looked at him with concern, but Milo's eyes were fixed on something else. Without a word, he walked past Sam.

"What are you doing, Milo?" Henry asked. "Come on. We need to find a way out of here."

Milo ignored him. He picked up the key, looked at it for a moment, then tapped it against the wall.

"What?" Sam asked. "What is it?"

Milo didn't answer. He walked to one of the other walls and hit that one. The sound was different. "Let me see the light, Henry," he whispered.

Henry handed him the penlight. Milo began to move it over the stones at the back of the chamber. "This wall," he said. "I think it's hollow."

"What?" Sam said in astonishment. "How do you know?"

"When you threw the key, it just didn't sound right. I think something is hidden here." He gasped. "Look!"

Under the yellow beam of the flashlight, two narrow

slots appeared. Cut into the rock, each had a word written above it. Sam's heart began to race again.

"We didn't see it!" he shouted. "We didn't see it!"

"Can you make out the words?" Henry asked. "What do they say?"

Milo brought the flashlight closer.

"Not sure. I think this one says *A-D-V-* "

"*Adventure*!" Henry shouted. "It says *adventure*! Wait…what is that supposed to mean?"

Milo shook his head.

"What about this one?" Sam asked. Milo moved the beam to the right.

The word above the second hole was unmistakable. Sam read it and was unable to speak.

"*G-g-gold*," he stuttered. "It says… *Gold*."

They stepped away from the wall. Henry looked at Sam, Sam at Milo, Milo looked down at the key.

Choose. Wisely. The words appeared to shimmer in the dim light.

Sam's eyes moved back and forth across the key. "One end for *Adventure*, one end for *Gold*."

Henry nodded. "I think you're right."

"But what does *Adventure* mean?" Sam asked.

Milo shrugged.

"I can't imagine, and I don't want to find out. We've had enough adventures." Henry reached for the key. "Let's try for the gold."

"Wait!" Sam gasped. "Choose *wisely*, remember? I think we only get one chance."

Henry paused.

"He's right," Milo said. "We need to think about this."

"Alright," Henry said. "Let's think." He began to pace slowly around the chamber. "Juniper spends his life playing tricks on people, but he also loves the woods…"

"And fishing…" Milo added.

"And camping and slingshots and legends and riverboats," said Sam.

"He found the tree," Henry went on. "And he protected the forest from someone who was trying to destroy it out of greed."

"Yes," Sam said. "Then, before disappearing, he came back and planted the key in the river, where no one could find it."

"Well, not no one," Henry asserted. "We found it."

"Right," Sam said. "*We* found it. Three kids. We weren't looking for gold though."

"We were looking for…adventure," Milo said softly.

"The thing Juniper valued above all else," Henry added. "Except Samantha."

"Are you sure?" Sam asked. "We only get one shot."

Henry shook his head slowly. "I don't know."

Sam studied him, then looked back at the slots carved into the wall. "I do," he said. "I don't know what's behind that wall, but I know we're not supposed to choose the gold."

He took the key from Henry and held it up to the hole under the word *Adventure*. The rectangular wing with *Wisely* across its center aligned perfectly with the slot.

"Here goes nothing." Sam slid the key into the hole and turned it. For a second, nothing happened. Silence surrounded the boys.

"It didn't work—" Henry started to say.

"Look!" Milo gasped.

The bronze key began to tremble.

"It's vibrating," Sam whispered. "Something is happening!"

Slowly, the key began to turn, propelled by some unseen mechanism deep in the wall. One rotation. Two

Rotations. Three. It stopped. Then, slowly, the stone holding the key, slid back into the wall taking the key with it. A second stone slid into its place, this one with words carved across it.

You have chosen wisely.

A rumble filled the chamber. To their right, the unused keyhole, slid, like its brother, back into the wall and was replaced by a nearly identical stone. This one said: *You have chosen unwisely.*

The rumble intensified and to their astonishment, an entire section of wall next to the word *unwisely*, started to lower into the floor. Behind it, a rectangular space about the size of a refrigerator was revealed. It was empty.

There was another rumble.

Another span of stone next to the word *wisely* began to rumble and then, it too, began to lower into the floor.

Sam's mouth fell open. So did Henry's. Milo's lip trembled.

The second cutout was the same size as the first.

It was filled from top to bottom with gold.

Hundreds of nuggets, shining and shimmering in the glow of the light.

"AHHHH!" They all started screaming at once. "We did it! We did it! YES!"

Milo jumped into the air. Sam fell to his knees. Henry only stared. "Wow!" he said. "Look at it all. Can you believe it?! And there at the side, I bet that lowers the rope back!"

He was right. Behind the mountain of nuggets, a lever protruded from the wall. "Rope," was stenciled along the handle. They weren't going to die.

Together they walked forward and examined the pile. The nuggets were the size of golf balls, some bigger. Even in the darkness and dust, the shine of gold was unmistakable.

Henry picked one up. "Unbelievable," he said.

They picked up nugget after nugget, turning them over and over in their hands, unable to speak. The months of searching, the endless hours in the library, it had not been in vain.

Milo finally broke the silence.

"I'll bet if we had chosen the other slot, that's all we would've gotten." He pointed to the empty space that had appeared below the word *Gold*.

"You're right," Sam said, staring at the decoy. "And there's no lever to lower back the rope. If we'd chosen this side…well…."

Henry and Milo nodded gravely.

"I guess he only wanted to give his gold to someone willing to pass it up for adventure," Sam added.

They stayed in the chamber for several more minutes, examining the treasure and reveling in their triumph.

"We're going to have to leave most of this here," Sam said. "Don't you think?"

"I'm afraid so," Henry said. "No way of carrying it back up. Of course, the one day we don't have backpacks, we find a mountain of gold."

"That's okay," Milo said. "We can come back for it. Let's each take one nugget. I bet just one'll be worth a fortune."

This seemed like a good idea. They each found a large nugget, took one last look at the enormous mound of gold, and Henry pulled the lever. After another dull rumble, the rope snaked its way down from above, and they began the long journey back to the surface.

Milo climbed all the way to the rafters of the gymnasium. The gong on the bell was still rigid.

"Give it a tug!" Sam yelled. "That's what got it going."

Milo pulled on the gong and the rope resumed its slow withdrawal into the ceiling. When the floor slid back into place, they jumped to the ground and stood together at the center of the circle.

"Thank goodness it resealed," Sam said. "I get a feeling Mr. Montero would start asking questions if he came in on Monday and found a gaping hole in the floor."

"Come on," Henry said. "The hunt is finally over and it's time to celebrate…let's get out of here before somebody sees us.

"Let's celebrate with some food on the way home," Sam suggested. "I haven't eaten anything since yesterday. Get whatever you want." He took the gold nugget from his pocket and held it up to the boys. "I think we can afford it."

29

The last week of the school year dawned hot and humid. A light breeze drifted through the huge trees as Sam and Henry walked towards the building.

They had spent most of the weekend together, rehashing the exploits under the gym, speculating on the gold's value and wondering how Juniper had managed to build such an elaborate fortress.

Sam stopped in front of the statue.

"What a year," he thought gazing at Juniper's all-knowing expression. "What a fantastic year."

His thoughts were interrupted when a thin figure brushed past. Sam gulped. It was Mr. Dean. His pockmarked face looked even paler in the daylight. He wheezed heavily and seemed to be searching for something. Sam hurried after Henry.

"That guy is frightening," Henry whispered.

"I'm glad we're not wearing the same clothes as the night we copied Juniper's map," Sam said.

"That's for sure," Henry agreed. "Speaking of Juniper, when can we go back down there and try to bring up some more gold?"

"Maybe tonight," Sam answered, "if I can think of an excuse to tell my parents."

"It'll be tough on a school night though," Henry said.

"Well, it's the last week of school. I don't think they'll mind."

After a morning spent on the portal, the boys hurried down to the lunchroom to find Milo.

"I bet he'll want to go tonight too," Henry said as they walked through the double doors. "Wait, where is he?"

Milo wasn't at any of the tables. They sat down to wait for him.

"Bathroom maybe?" Sam suggested when ten minutes had passed.

"I don't know," Henry said. "He's always here first. Maybe he's sick."

Sam shrugged. "If he's sick then I guess we're not going back for more gold. We can't go without him."

"Weird," Henry said. "He seemed fine on Saturday."

A few tables away Ali ate alone.

"I wonder where Candace is?" Henry said.

"I don't know. Maybe we should ask her to join us," Sam replied. "She looks lonely."

"No." Henry shook his head. "Things went too well at the dance. I don't want to push my luck."

"So you're just going to go the rest of your life without talking to her?"

"That's the plan."

"Come on. Let's go say 'hi'."

As they approached the table, Ali looked up and smiled.

"Hi," Sam said. Henry smiled weakly behind him.

"Hey," she answered cheerfully.

"Eating alone?" Sam asked.

"Yeah. Not sure where Candace is. She was here this morning. Must be helping a teacher with something."

"Oh really?" Sam said. "Milo's not here either."

"WHAT A COINCIDENCE!" Henry blurted loudly.

Sam glared at him. Ali giggled.

"Anyway, do you want to come sit with us? You know, until your friend gets back?"

Ali nodded. "Sure."

Before she could stand, the bell rang signaling the end of lunch.

"Oh well," Sam murmured. "Maybe tomorrow."

"Yeah, tomorrow sounds good."

"See ya later," Sam said. He turned and walked away with Henry in tow.

"That actually went pretty well," Henry said. "We practically have a date set for tomorrow. I better wear my blue shirt."

"Your blue shirt?" Sam questioned.

"Yes. It's quite striking."

Sam rolled his eyes. "Strange that Candace was missing from lunch too, right?"

"I don't think so. Like Ali said, she's probably with a teacher, and Milo might have a cold or something."

An uneasy feeling was rising in Sam's stomach. He couldn't shake it. Milo had been fine on Saturday.

In Industrial Arts, Mr. Arthur set the boys to work shredding paper. There were huge plastic bins full of it.

"Where's your friend?" he asked.

"Not sure," Henry said. "Sick maybe."

"Sick?" Mr. Arthur asked. "In June?" He laughed. "That kid hasn't missed a day of class all year and decides to get sick right when I need his help. What a scam."

Henry laughed. Sam didn't

"Paper and shredder are over there," Mr. Arthur said.

"Don't lose a finger. The generator hasn't turned up, so keep an eye out for it. There are a couple of big pulleys missing too, and I can't find the shovels. Got a storage room for lawn equipment on the other side of the school. I'm going to check there. Show yourselves out when you finish the paper."

The boys headed to the industrial sized shredder, and Henry flipped it on. Together they began feeding page after page into the whirling teeth.

"Did you ever think," Henry asked, "in this day and age, that three kids could have so many adventures in just a few months?"

Sam smiled. "Nope. Not in a million years. I didn't think there were any adventures left."

They continued to stuff paper into the machine. There were unused worksheets, folders and cardboard boxes from every recycling bin in the school. One by one, they were sliced to pulp.

"I feel like we're destroying evidence the year even happened," Sam said.

"Someone's year," Henry said. "Not ours. I don't think we used a piece of paper all year. Wonder who used all this?"

"Yeah," Sam said. "Here's some junk mail. And this one looks like a bill for supplies." He tossed the papers into the machine and picked up another. "This one's all crumbled up. I wonder what the secret is—" Sam's words trailed off. He felt the pace of his heart quicken.

"What?" Henry said. "What is it?"

Sam didn't answer him.

The paper in his hands was a gray and white copy of the original. Across the top *Notes* was written in block letters. But it was the words below these that caused Sam to shudder.

Sophia Juniper born May 29th, 1845.

An arrow pointed to the last date, and next to this *Same birthday as me!* was written.

"This," Sam managed to whisper, "this is a copy of Milo's notes."

"Huh?" Henry was confused.

"This is a copy of the notes from the Juniper file. Milo's notes."

But it wasn't just a copy. *Same birthday as me!* had been circled in red pen and next to it, a question mark was drawn. Below this, several names had been written and then scribbled out.

Only two remained: *Candace Pierson* and *Milo Milner.*

30

"Where'd it come from?" Henry asked in astonishment.

Sam didn't answer. He was struggling to make sense of the discovery himself. "It was stolen," he said at last, "from Milo's bag."

"When?"

"A few weeks ago. Milo said he thought someone had gone through his backpack, but he wasn't sure because nothing had been taken."

"You mean someone took it out and made a copy?"

Sam nodded. "I think so."

"But who?" Henry demanded. "Who would do that?"

"I don't know," Sam said. "The folder did say *Treasure File-Top Secret.* They probably thought there was money or something. If they saw Milo's notes, they saw everything else, which means…."

"They know about Juniper," Henry finished his thought.

"Yeah. They know about Juniper. And I bet they've been looking for Milo."

"What do you mean looking for him?"

Sam pointed to the red question mark. "They didn't know whose stuff they had stolen. I bet they've been trying to figure it out."

"Why not just see which kid was wearing the backpack?" Henry asked.

"Because we gave him a new one. On his birthday. But it looks like they figured it out anyway."

"Why is Candace there?" Henry asked, his voice shaky. "Wait! She has the same birthday as Milo. She said so at the dance. Whoever stole the file knew its owner was born on May 29th!"

"I think," Sam said slowly, "someone else is after the treasure. And it's possible they have Milo and Candace."

"You may be right," Henry said gravely. "But let's not panic. He might just be sick."

"He's never sick…and what about Candace? Ali said she was here this morning."

"There could be a logical explanation. At the end of the day, we'll call his house. If he's not there, we'll have to call the police or something."

After school, they rushed out of room 220C and down to the lobby.

"Maybe he'll be down there," Sam said nervously.

"Let's hope."

The boys stopped in the doorway of the lobby and surveyed the crowd. There was no sign of Milo. A few feet away, Miss Partridge and a woman with straight red hair spoke near the office door.

"Who's that?" Henry asked. "It looks like something is wrong. Can you hear what they're saying?"

"I know you're upset, Mrs. Pierson," the secretary said. "I would be too. Can you tell me again what happened?"

The woman with red hair spoke at once. "I came home from work to a strange message on my answering machine. It said Candace and her classmates would be going on an overnight field trip. I never heard anything about a field trip! There was no permission slip! And now look—" She waved her arm at the passing students. "She's nowhere to be seen. Why wasn't I told about the field trip earlier?"

The secretary looked deeply concerned. "I was unaware of any field trip. Come into the office. We need to let Mr. Fiddlesbee know. He should be back shortly," she gestured to the nearby door. "Who was it you said left the message?"

"It was a man," the woman replied. "He said his name was Mr. Dean."

31

Sam and Henry left the lobby and retreated deep into the library. There, in the shadows, they tried to piece together what was going on.

"Dean," Sam said. "*He's* the one that's been stealing from the classrooms. *That's* why he was in Throxon's office. He was looking for things to steal. Now he's got Candace and Milo!'

"But why?"

"Why does anyone steal? He needs money for something. He must have gone through Milo's backpack looking for a cell phone and found the Juniper File instead. He made a copy of it. And if he's found the Juniper file, he must have seen the map and the newspaper clippings about the gold. From there, he put everything together."

"You're right," Henry conceded. "It's the only explanation."

"What do we do?" Sam asked. He was really worried now. If Dean had Milo, he could be in serious trouble.

"I don't know," Henry said. He looked scared.

"Maybe we should tell the police or something."

"We could try," Sam said. "But that will take time. Besides, Miss Partridge is probably calling them right now.

Henry flopped down on a nearby chair in frustration. "They could be anywhere."

"Wait a minute," Sam said. "We saw Dean this morning. Remember? By the statute. He's probably nearby."

Henry nodded slowly. "Yeah. Maybe he wanted to see what Juniper looked like. If he has the map, he thinks it leads to the gold. I bet he's already followed the *X* to…"

"The boulder graveyard!" Sam exclaimed. "Dean is digging in the cave! That must be where Mr. Arthur's shovels are! Maybe the generator too!"

"He's probably been digging for a while and when he couldn't find anything, he tried to figure out whose backpack the map had come from," Henry said.

"Dean must have looked for Milo's bag, but Milo had a new one. So, all he had to go by was the birthday, May 29th." Sam was pacing back and forth between the shelves.

"Why didn't he just look up the birthdays in the office?" Henry asked.

Sam considered this for a just a moment, before the answer came to him. "Miss Partridge was still working on the sixth grade files just a few days ago. Remember? When we bumped into her? As soon as she put them away, Dean must have looked through them, discovered Milo's birthday, and snatched him up."

"Candace too?" Henry asked.

Sam nodded.

Henry stood up. His eyes narrowed under the horn-rimmed glasses. "Well," he said, "there's no other option.

We have to go after them. We can't waste any more time. They may be in danger."

Sam looked down. His hands were trembling.

"Is the slingshot in your bag?" Henry asked.

Sam nodded.

"Bring it," Henry said.

"But it's still unstrung."

"Bring it anyway. I have a feeling. Come on. Let's go."

They left the library and hurried down to the first floor.

"We should go out through the Industrial Arts room," Henry said. "Not the lobby. Less chance of being seen."

"Right," Sam agreed. "If we get caught, there's no way we'll be able to go after Milo."

They were turning onto the Industrial Arts hallway, when a woman's voice caused them to stop dead

"Just where do you think you're going?" It was Ms. Snell. She marched over to the boys.

"I knew it," she said. "I just knew it." As usual, she wore a smile, but this one seemed genuine.

Henry tried to protest. "Ms. Snell, listen. This is an emergency. Our friend is in trouble. We need to go. We need to help him!"

"What was your plan?" Snell said quietly. "One last theft before the school year ends? Well, you're not getting away with it! Not this time. Hand over your bags."

Sam's heart pounded. The slingshot was in his backpack. If Ms. Snell saw it, there was no telling what she would do.

"Ms. Snell," Henry pleaded. "Our friend Milo is in trouble! Another student too! We didn't steal from the classrooms. It was Mr. D—"

"Henry," she interrupted, her voice dripping with glee. "You will hand over your bags and then accompany me to Mr. Throxon's office."

Sam could think of no way out of the situation. They were doomed.

"One…Two… Thr—"

"What seems to be the problem here?" Mr. Arthur had emerged from the shop room door, a cordial smile on his face. "How are you Bethany? It's been a long time."

"Never you mind how I am," she answered curtly. "These boys are—"

"These boys," the old man said, "are here to see *me*, and they're late."

Ms. Snell's face reddened.

"They are not allowed—"

"Not allowed in school unsupervised. I know. I must apologize. But here I am, and now they're supervised. Thanks for your help. Come along boys." He opened the shop door and Sam and Henry followed him in, leaving Snell fuming in the hallway.

When the door was shut, Mr. Arthur's smile disappeared. He turned to Sam and Henry with a grave expression. "What's going on?" he asked. "I overheard your conversation. Where's Milo?"

"We don't know for sure," Sam started. "But we think he may have been taken."

Mr. Arthur looked shocked. "Taken? Taken where?"

"It's a long story," Henry said. "We…well were looking for Juniper's gold…and now someone else is…and they have Milo…"

"They took him to this boulder graveyard on the grounds…" Sam said reluctantly, "into—"

"The cave," Mr. Arthur finished his sentence. Henry and Sam looked at him in astonishment.

"How do you know about—"

"Never mind that," he said. "Who took him?"

"We think it's Mr. Dean," Henry replied.

Mr. Arthur didn't question the response. He just nodded. "We need to call the police."

"We can't wait that long!" Sam cried. "They might not even believe us."

"We're going now," Henry stated firmly. "We have to."

"No," he said sternly. "It's too dangerous. I'll go to the principal and explain what's happening. We'll call the police. Wait here."

Mr. Arthur moved out the door as fast as they had ever seen him.

"We can't just wait here!" Sam cried.

"You're right," Henry said. "It may be dangerous, but we don't have a choice. Mr. Arthur would probably do the same thing. Let's go!"

They jumped up, ran across the shop, and out the side door. They darted across the lawn and into the woods. The path soon came into view.

"What are you looking for?" Sam asked. Henry appeared to be studying the ground

"A stick. Something I can use as a club. We're kind of going into this empty handed. We should have taken something from the shop."

Sam had the unstrung slingshot in his backpack, but he didn't see how that would help. Soon the embankment hiding the boulder graveyard came into view. The boys crept to the top.

"I don't see anyone," Sam whispered.

"Me neither," Henry replied. "Do you hear that?"

A dull hum came from somewhere below. Sam searched the boulders for its source.

"There," he said, pointing to the foot of an enormous rock. "Mr. Arthur's generator. I bet it's powering lights and stuff. Come on, let's go."

They slipped noiselessly down the hill and crouched behind a boulder. They crawled from one rock to the next, until the mouth of the cave came into view. It looked exactly as they'd left it, except for an orange power cord that snaked down into the darkness. Sam opened his backpack, took out the unstrung slingshot and tucked it into his belt.

"Last chance to turn back," Sam whispered. "No telling what we're going to find down there."

Henry slowly shook his head. "*The coward is the one who lets his fear overcome his sense of duty*," he declared shakily. "*Once more unto the breach dear friend.*"

A chill ran down Sam's spine as Henry stood up and approached the opening. "*Out of the blue*," he murmured, "*and into the black…*"

Sam stood and followed Henry into the cave.

The light from the surface disappeared quickly and the pair groped their way along the narrow passageway in darkness. Stumbling over rocks, they saw a faint glow up ahead. Sam realized it was the first in a long line of electric lanterns illuminating the steep corridor.

"No question about it," Henry said. "There's someone down there."

"I think the generator kind of gave that away."

"Right," Henry muttered.

They moved on slowly, trying not to make a sound. The mechanical humming had died away and the cave was quiet.

"Look," Sam said, "the lights get brighter up there."

"The first atrium," Henry whispered, "where you fell."

They crouched down and crawled towards the opening on hands and knees. Just before the chamber, a jagged rock shot out of the wall. Ever so slowly, they peeked around the edge. Sam's eyes widened at what he saw.

A few feet away, Candace sat against a massive boulder. She was covered in dirt and looked scared. Around the enormous rock, a thick chain was wrapped, secured in place by a heavy padlock. The chain was fastened to Candace's ankle.

"Holy…" Henry breathed. "Where's Milo?"

Sam's heart thundered in his chest. Milo was nowhere to be seen.

"I don't know."

"What do we do?" Henry asked.

Sam bent down and inched forward, being careful to stay out of the light.

"Psst…" he whispered. "Candace."

She didn't move.

"Candace," he whispered again. This time, she turned her head and squinted in Sam's direction.

"Candace," he said. "It's Sam."

"Sam?!" she questioned, apparently unable to see him. "What are you doing here?!"

"Never mind that. Where are the keys? Is the coast clear?"

Candace looked around the cavern. "I think so."

Sam stepped into the light, followed by Henry. "Are you okay?" he asked, kneeling beside Candace.

"I'm alright, been better, but I'm okay."

He looked at the shackle on her ankle. The chain had been fed through an eyelet at one end.

"If I can get the chain off the rock you'll be free."

"But it's locked," she said.

"Let me see what I can do." He turned and cut across the cavern to the rock that anchored the chain. The lock was a shining hunk of forged steel. Though he'd seen Milo do it several times, Sam had never picked anything himself. Frantically he scanned the area for anything he could slip into the keyhole.

"Henry," he said, "I need something to pick the lock! Do you have anything?" Henry felt his pockets.

"Here," he said. "I always keep one on hand for situations like this." He handed over a paper clip.

"How often do you find yourself in situations like this?"

"I'm kidding. It's from the paper we were shredding. Hurry!"

Sam rushed back to the rock and studied the lock carefully. He twisted the paper clip into an *L* shape and slipped one end into the keyhole. Turning it carefully back and forth, he felt for the cogs holding the lock in place. Milo had explained how the lock would only open when these were aligned. One by one he raised the cogs. Hearing a faint click, he pulled the base of the lock. To his amazement, it fell open in his hands.

"Wow," he thought, "that was lucky."

Both ends of the chain were now free. "I got the lock undone," he said in a hushed voice. "I'm going to the pull the chain out."

He lugged the heavy chain towards the rock. It passed through the ring on Candace's ankle and she was free.

"Thanks," she whispered.

"Where's Milo?" Henry asked.

"I don't know. He was tied up separately. He was here earlier, but then he was taken down there again." She waved towards the drop off.

"We're going after him. You better head for the surface. Try to get help."

"No way," she said. "I'm staying."

Sam opened his mouth to object, but it was clear from Candace's expression she wasn't going anywhere.

"Okay," he said. "Let's go."

"There's another chamber this way, and a huge hole."

"Yeah, we kn—" Henry started to say, but Sam jabbed him in the ribs and he fell silent.

"Here," she continued, "crouch down and follow me."

"Wait," Sam said. "We need a weapon or something. A club or a rock."

"What about that?" Candace whispered. She gestured towards Sam's pocket where the slingshot was showing.

"Oh, that's a slingshot. Unfortunately, I don't have a string for it."

Candace looked at the piece of wood.

"Give it to me."

"Huh? Why?"

"Just let me see it," she insisted.

Sam gave it to her.

"My grandfather had one that looked exactly like this. Did you look inside?"

"Inside?" Sam asked.

"Yeah," Candace said. "That's where he kept his string so it wouldn't get stretched out." She twisted the handle. To Sam's amazement it started to unscrew. He watched as she slipped off the base and reached a finger inside. She slowly withdrew a thin white cord.

"No way," Henry whispered. "It was right there the whole time."

The cord had a small braided loop at each end and these Candace slipped over the arms of the slingshot.

"Here," she said, handing it back. "And take this pebble too, for ammunition. Now follow me."

Dumbstruck, the two boys crawled after Candace.

When they neared the ledge that dropped into the second cavern, Sam noticed something metallic sticking up from the lower level. It was a ladder. He and Candace shimmied to one side of it, Henry on the other, and peered over the edge.

Far below, a single lantern illuminated the center of the lower chamber. The pit the boys had filled in was once more a gaping hole ten feet across. A pulley system had been rigged above it, apparently to lift dirt up from the depths. Shovels lined the far wall and between them, tied in a coil of thick rope, his mouth taped, was Milo.

Without a second thought, Sam and Henry sprang to their feet and started down the ladder. "Stay here!" Sam instructed Candace. "You may need to go for help."

"Don't!" Candace protested. "He might be down there!"

But the boys didn't hear her. They were halfway down the ladder, eager to free their friend. Sam lunged from the third rung and dashed over to Milo. Henry was right behind him. Together they began untying the knots. Milo began to wiggle like a madman. He was shaking his head from side to side, his muffled voice straining against the tape.

"It's nice to see you too, buddy," Henry said, working furiously on the long coiled of rope wrapped around Milo's legs and torso. "This would be a whole lot easier if you'd just stop moving."

Milo didn't stop.

"What?" Sam said, abandoning the cord around Milo's hands and reaching for the tape. "What is it?" It was as if Milo was trying to indicate something behind the boys.

Suddenly, a light appeared overheard. Sam looked back to see Candace racing down the ladder. There was a man right behind her, holding an electric lantern. As Candace jumped from the ladder, the second figure came into view. Skin waxy, the jagged scar glowing, it was Mr. Dean.

Without thinking, Sam reached into his pocket and withdrew the slingshot and pebble. He fit the stone into the elastic and pulled it back. Dean, seeing what he was doing, lunged forward. "Nooooo!" he yelled. But it was too late. The stone zipped forward and slammed into the teacher's skull right between his eyes. He slumped to the ground.

"Sam!" Candace screamed. "What are you doing?!"

"Saving your life," Henry retorted. "I knew it was him all along."

"Saving my life?! Are you crazy? That's a teacher. He just got here. Mr. Arthur saw him in the lobby and told him about the cave. He was trying to help!"

"Huh?" Sam muttered.

Milo wiggled free of the last ropes and tore the tape from his mouth.

"It's not Dean," he gasped. "It's—"

The light from the lantern was suddenly distorted as an enormous figure stepped from the shadows at the other end of the cavern.

"—Throxon."

Beads of sweat covered the vice principal's face. His black hair was stringy and tangled. There was barely a resemblance to the man who'd been pushing eBooks and apps the months before.

With one step, he reached Sam, seized his collar and lifted him into the air. Throxon ripped away the slingshot and tossed Sam like a rag doll.

Henry and Candace rushed forward and pelted the principal with blows. He grabbed Henry's shoulder and sent him reeling to the ground. He turned and shoved Candace away. As she fell back, she slammed into a nearby wall and crumpled to the floor, unconscious.

Throxon looked down at the slingshot.

"This," he said in a deep voice, "has been causing you trouble all year, hasn't it Sam?" He shook his head as if to indicate disappointment.

"Funny," he continued. "I've seen it before. When I moved into my office it was in the desk. Some men came to the school asking about it, but I told them I'd already thrown it away. How did *you* get it?"

He looked up at Sam.

"I found it," Sam growled. "Remember?"

His eyes narrowed. "Ah yes," he said quietly. "The story from the first day. You should have taken my advice, Sam. You should have forgotten about slingshots and concentrated on building a better digital self. You might not be here right now."

Sam opened his mouth to reply, but before he could, Henry spoke.

"Oh please," he said, rolling his eyes. "Will you stop with the 'building a better digital you' stuff? I read your book. What a bunch of nonsense. Two hundred and forty eight pages, if memory serves me, of pure dribble."

Throxon's face reddened. Sam shook his head, but Henry wasn't finished.

"Here's a newsflash, some of us live in the real world. And your book…well don't get me started on the writing itself. Your inability to craft even a basic sentence speaks volumes of the shortcomings in American education. And the app…I looked into that too. It caused my mom's computer to crash…you—"

"SHUT UP!" Throxon screamed. "SHUT UP!"

Henry stopped talking.

"My book…no, no, my eBook will change the world. And the app? It's even better! When the bugs are fixed it'll be on every device in the western hemisphere! I just need a little more money. And you're going to get it for me!"

Throxon's shirt was soaked with sweat. His face was purple with rage. It suddenly occurred to Sam that a man who chained kids up underground might be capable of much worse. Throxon bent down and angrily scooped up the pile of rope that had been holding Milo's legs. He moved across the chamber and tied one of the ends to Sam's ankle. He pulled the knot tight, causing Sam to wince, before dragging the other end to Henry.

"Stop!" Henry protested, as Throxon lashed the rope to this ankle. "What are you doing?!"

"I can't have one of you scampering away. Now stay still!" With Sam and Henry secured to one another, and Milo's hands still secured, he resumed his story.

"Money got tight. For a while the cell phones were enough, the computers, I pawned them all. But then that moron started asking questions and following me around. Apparently, he used to be a cop."

Throxon motioned to Mr. Dean's still unconscious body.

"I needed more money. My computer guy said just a few more tweaks and the app would be ready. And then, I stumbled upon your friend's backpack and the folder. I found out about the gold! The map, it was right in my office!" He was breathing heavily now and his whole body twitched.

Sam glanced at Henry. He looked terrified.

"Let's....Let's all just calm down," Mr. Throxon said, lowering his voice.

He wiped the sweat from his face, reached into a pocket and withdrew the two shining serenity spheres. He closed his eyes and spun them in one hand.

"Owwmmmm," he moaned quietly. "Owwmmmmm."

"That's better," he said opening his eyes, before

gesturing to Milo. "I knew this sorry excuse for a human being couldn't have been working alone. In fact, I've been attempting to…persuade him, to divulge his associates for the last few hours. Unfortunately, he's refused. No matter. I have you now. So we'll talk. There isn't much time."

He took a step toward Milo.

"It's very simple. I need you to tell me what you know about this Juniper man's gold, or your friend gets hurt."

At this, he grabbed Milo by the back of the shirt and lifted him effortlessly into the air. Milo kicked his legs wildly, without effect.

"The gold's not here," Throxon rumbled. "So where is it?"

Henry spoke. "You're right. It's not here. But we can show you. It's back on the surface."

He laughed. "You must think I'm a fool. I'm not letting you back to the surface until I have the gold. Now, WHERE IS IT?"

To Sam's horror, Throxon took one step back, extended his massive arm, and held Milo out over the pit.

"It's deep," he said. "I've been digging nonstop for weeks. Had to borrow these pulleys so I could get in and out."

"No really, it's up at the surface," Sam urged, getting to his feet. "We know where it is, and we can show you."

"TELL ME WHERE!"

"Okay…okay…" Sam stammered. "I'll tell you."

Out of the corner of his eye, Sam notice Henry slowly reach out and take hold of the discarded slingshot. His eyes scanned the ground for ammunition, but the floor around the hole was only dirt.

"NOW!" Mr. Throxon screamed.

"I…err…"

"My patience is wearing thin." The two spheres zipped around one hand, Milo wriggled in the other. Henry searched frantically for something to shoot. "You have three seconds," Throxon bellowed.

Sam's heart pounded in his chest.

"Three…two…o—"

Before he could finish, Milo let fly one final kick. "Henry! Catch!" His right foot sailed into Throxon's left hand sending the two spinning metal balls into the air. Henry dove forward and caught one. Throxon exploded in rage and let go of Milo, just as Henry fired.

The silver ball shot back towards Throxon, striking him squarely in the temple. The giant dropped to the ground like a felled tree. Milo hung in the air for an instant and then tumbled into the darkness of the pit.

Without thinking, Sam lunged forward and dove after his friend. For an instant, all was silent and black. Air whooshed past him. He reached a hand forward, grasping aimlessly. Nothing. He stretched further…

And then his fingers struck Milo's.

He grabbed his friend under the arms and prayed Throxon's knot would hold.

The rope went taut with a jolt. Milo was wrenched downward. Somehow, Sam held on.

Henry groaned from above, and Sam had a flashback to the last time they'd been hanging from a rope in the very same cave. Henry had managed to hold them, but only for a moment.

The rope started to slip and Henry screamed. "You're pulling me in! It's around my leg! I'm slipping."

Sam looked up and waited for Henry to tumble into the pit. A silhouette blocked the light at the top of the hole. Henry. The rope slid further. This was the end.

Sam glanced down. Milo looked back at him with

watery eyes. They'd survived some close calls, but finally luck had run out. Sam nodded at his friend and closed his eyes.

And then, the rope stopped moving.

"Huh?"

"What's happening?"

They dared a glance up.

The silhouette blocking the light wasn't Henry. It was Candace! She knelt at the mouth of the hole and was helping Henry pull them back towards the surface.

"YES!" they cried.

How they did it, Sam would never know. Maybe it was because Milo didn't weigh much. Maybe it was adrenaline. Maybe Henry and Candace had summoned some untapped strength reserved only for times of crisis. Whatever it was, they pulled their friends out of the pit and up to safety. Milo was last to emerge from the darkness of the hole. When he finally stood before Sam and Henry, all three boys had tears in their eyes.

Sam turned to Candace, wiping his face. "Uh…" he began awkwardly. "You…saved our lives…thanks."

She smiled at him. Her face and clothes were filthy, but her eyes were bright. "Don't mention it," she said. "I owed you." She reached in and hugged him. Sam's face went very red.

"Come on," Henry said. "Let's get out of here before Throxon comes around."

"What about Dean?" Sam asked. The teacher lay unconscious next to the ladder. Henry walked over to his body and picked something up from the ground.

"His wallet fell out." Henry opened it. "Silas Dean. Hey look, he was some kind of police officer." He flipped the wallet around and displayed an identification badge with Dean's face on it. "Detective-retired. Says it right here. Seems young to be retired."

"That's why he was in Throxon's office," Sam exclaimed.

"He suspected him the whole time," Milo said weakly. "What should we do with him? We can't leave him here."

Henry leaned down and slipped the wallet into Dean's pocket. "I have an idea. We have to act fast. They'll both be waking up soon."

They tied the rope around the teacher's chest. With Candace and Milo pulling, and Sam and Henry pushing, they managed to get him up the ladder and out of the lower chamber. Then, they pulled up the ladder, leaving Throxon alone by the pit.

Carefully, the group made its way out of the cave. When they got to the surface, the sound of sirens drifted back from the school.

"My parents must be worried sick," Candace said.

"They are," said Henry. "We saw your mom."

"I bet my dad is looking for me too," Milo said.

Sam turned. "Sorry it took so long for us to find you."

"Yeah," Henry added. "We thought you might be home sick."

Milo chuckled weakly. "That's okay. It was all worth it."

"Are you nuts?" Candace said indignantly. "We could have been killed."

Milo smiled. "It was an adventure," he replied. "And you should always, always choose adventure."

32

Sam Torwey sat on the front steps of his house, excited for the upcoming summer.

Mr. Throxon had been taken into custody. Mr. Dean, as it turned out, had suspected him for months. He had been in the office when Mr. Arthur came in and had quickly realized what was going on.

Sam and Henry told the authorities they had simply stumbled upon the cave while searching the woods for their friends. As for the rumor of buried gold, they denied any knowledge of it. All three were praised for their bravery. Ms. Snell was interviewed by the local newspaper and suggested it was her positive influence on Sam and Henry that guided them in the rescue.

Mr. Arthur had called to check on the boys. He spoke to their parents, but made no mention of Juniper, the gold or the cave. Whatever secrets he had, he was keeping to himself. He talked briefly to Sam and said, "You boys have fun in that tree house this summer. Be careful. Don't do anything I wouldn't do."

The last few days had been a blur of questions and interviews, but things had finally settled down. Henry and Milo were coming for a sleepover, and Sam was excited to see them.

Across the road, Roger's door opened and he stepped outside, cell phone in hand. He shuffled down the steps and crossed the street to Sam.

"Sup?" he said.

Sam nodded but remained seated.

"How's it going?"

"Pretty good," Sam said. "My friends will be here in a few…."

Roger cut him off. "I heard what happened down there, what you did." Roger stared at him curiously. "The news says Throxon was digging for gold or something. Did he find any? What are they talking about?"

Sam looked up.

"Well…?" Roger prodded, glancing down at his phone. He clearly wanted information to text all over town. Sam didn't feel like giving it to him and thought of the perfect response.

"Dude," he said, "don't even worry about it."

Just then, Henry and Milo arrived, and Roger trudged back across the street, his questions unanswered. The longest day of the year was approaching and though it was past seven, the sun was just beginning to sink in the sky.

Sam's mom made cheeseburgers and the boys ate them outside. They talked about the gold, the cave, and Milo's time in captivity. They laughed about Snell, Dean and Throxon and wondered what the next school year would bring.

"Who do you think was asking about the slingshot?"

Milo said between mouthfuls.

"What do you mean?"

"Throxon. He said some men came to his office and asked about the slingshot."

"Who knows?" Sam answered. "He's crazy."

"I want to know why the name of the school was changed," Henry said. "and why there's no record of Juniper anywhere."

"We can talk to Mr. Arthur about it. I get the impression he knows more about the whole situation than he's letting on," Sam replied. "And the rest of the gold? We need to get down there and get it."

"Not until September," Milo reminded them. "The school will be locked during the summer."

"That's okay," Henry said. "We can wait. For now, we can figure out exactly what to do with it. I mean, it is a bit suspicious for a kid to walk into a pawnshop with a lump of solid gold."

Sam laughed. "You're right about that. Well, it's not going anywhere, and we have plenty of time to figure everything out. Besides, we deserve a little vacation."

The shadows lengthened and the first of the summer fireflies crisscrossed overhead. Before long, it was dark and the boys headed inside.

With their departure, the neighborhood fell silent. Down the road, a car started and a pair of headlights flicked on. It idled by the curb before moving slowly up the street and past the Torwey house. Almost a year earlier, the very same car had followed a garbage truck, carrying a slingshot, down the very same street.

It was a black Mercedes with tinted windows.

ABOUT THE AUTHOR

Benjamin Conlon grew up in New England and spent much of his childhood exploring the woods surrounding his hometown. After college, he moved to Boston and began teaching elementary school. He wrote *The Slingshot's Secret* as a reminder that even in a world filled with technology, adventure abounds.